THE UNLIT FIRE

She had fulfilled herself as an actress but never as a woman. Flack was right, really, about her being too reserved, too shy. But under it all there was a fire which wanted to be lit. Trevor's kisses and caresses had fanned that fire a little before he left, but the big glorious flame of the ultimate passion had yet to burn for her. She knew that she wanted it – with him. To be his wife would mean everything now.

THE UNLIT FIRE

The Unlit Fire

by

Denise Robins

Magna Large Print Books
Long Preston, North Yorkshire,
BD23 4ND, England.

British Library Cataloguing in Publication Data.

Robins, Denise
    The unlit fire.

    A catalogue record of this book is
    available from the British Library

    ISBN   0-7505-2206-2

First published in Great Britain
by Hodder & Stoughton Ltd. 1960

Copyright © 1960 by Denise Robins

Cover illustration © Heslop by arrangement with Allied Artists

The moral right of the author has been asserted

Published in Large Print 2004 by arrangement with
Patricia Clark for executors of Denise Robins' Estate

Magna Large Print is an imprint of Library Magna Books Ltd.

Printed and bound in Great Britain by
T.J. (International) Ltd., Cornwall, PL28 8RW

The characters and situations in this book are entirely imaginary and bear no relation to any real person or actual happening

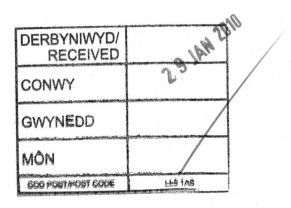

FOR MY GOOD FRIENDS
VERA AND FREY ASHTON

PART I

1

Flack Sankey, older of the famous Sankey Brothers – theatrical and film agents – was a man who prided himself that his large nose was designed for smelling out trouble.

He smelt it this morning. He positively sniffed the air as he walked into Andra Lee's flat. Rose Penham, secretary to Andra Lee, met him in the long low-ceilinged room of Miss Lee's beautiful penthouse which over-looked Hyde Park, and noted the expression on Flack's face. It was a big heavy face with two blue chins and heavily-lidded eyes and that distressing nose which never seemed to distress *him*. Poor old Flack was no thing of beauty, Rose thought, and, at forty, weighed eighteen stone. He breathed noisily. He reminded her of a porpoise – the way he swam doggedly through crowds, getting ahead of anyone else. Yet she liked him. Everybody liked Flack. He had a certain benevolence and charm which outweighed his lack of physical attraction. He even had a petite blonde wife who adored him. But London knew that Andra was the real love of his life, and his star client. Jay, Flack's wife, knew it too, but did not begrudge him Andra's friendship. She loved Andra too. And Rose, like all those who served Miss Lee, was her devoted slave.

Rose Penham, tall, thin, middle-aged, with silver-wings over both ears and a lot of nervous energy, eyed Flack with gloom. She knew exactly what was the matter with him. The same thing was the matter with her this morning; with everybody employed by Andra.

They were afraid she was about to ruin her life.

Flack came to the point bluntly. In his rich guttural Jewish voice which held all the sorrows and indignation of his persecuted race, he said:

'Ach! what a catastrophe! The girl is off her head.'

'We'll all be off our heads if you don't keep calm, Flack,' said Rose in her brittle, rather ill-tempered voice. She gave the impression that she was a sour woman, but she was really very kind and immensely efficient. She had done much to protect Andra Lee from the troubles and problems that beset a film star. Rose was Andra's bodyguard. It was she who answered the telephone and locked the doors to keep out unwanted photographers, reporters and fortune-hunters, or those who merely came whining, to beg for help.

12

Andra Lee was a new and sensational success. In her last film, *Poor Little Rich Girl,* she had captured the hearts of Britain's film-going public. Now Hollywood was rolling handsome offers to her across the Atlantic.

Andra was a success as an *actress,* not merely as a *body,* although beautiful she certainly was. But she appealed to a public with intellect, as well as to the masses. Flack, himself, who never paid fulsome compliments had declared after that film that Andra was the Ingrid Bergman of the future.

'Ach!' Flack repeated his anguished exclamation and held up podgy hands. On the little finger of the left hand there flashed a diamond. It seemed incongruous worn with linen slacks, blue shirt and no tie. It was a hot day in June. The warmest summer since 1947. London sweltered. But up here in the penthouse it was delicious with a special air cooling system. Striped blinds sheltered Andra's roof garden which was brilliant with flowers. A wicker *chaise-longue* piled with scarlet cushions, was there to tempt even a man like Flack, who liked to work eighteen hours out of twenty-four.

'Where is *she?*' he asked Miss Penham.

'Just had a shower and will be coming out to speak to you.'

Flack began to walk up and down the lounge. It was dimmed by the half-closed slats of the Venetian blinds on this roasting

13

morning. Moodily he looked at everything and thought to himself for the hundredth time since he had received Andra's letter, late last night, that it was tragic – even criminal – that a girl should write the word *Finis* to a brilliant career that had only just begun. With a stroke of her pen, he thought, she was signing a death warrant for herself as an actress, as well as for him as her agent.

Only twenty-four hours ago, Flack had offered her a contract big enough to make the head of any twenty-two-year-old girl swim. Even while he had prepared that contract, Flack had regretted the fact that he had not signed her up before; tied her down; *the little fool.* But they had waited to see how the world would receive *Poor Little Rich Girl.* Poor little rich girl, indeed, he thought furiously. She could hardly make a fortune out of one film and she was chucking away all her splendid chances to build one up for herself in the future.

And *why?*

Flack padded up and down the lounge, chewing off the end of a cigar. He really did look like a porpoise or a seal, Miss Penham thought, bending that oily black head of his as he surged forward. She sighed. She pitied him. She pitied herself, too. It looked like the end for her, after the happiest year of her life. It was hard work, being confidential secretary to a film star, but Rose enjoyed it.

She did so love Andra Lee. She was such a *darling*. So simple, so kind, so *unlike* a film star, really. She had the shyness and reticence of a Garbo. Perhaps that was it. Perhaps she would have become another Greta Garbo if she had gone on with her career. In her private life Andra tried to avoid too many bright lights, glittering suppers and hectic parties. She hadn't even wanted this expensive flat. It was Flack who made her come here. Andra had shied at moving into such a palatial home. She had been quite happy, so she said, in her little two-roomed flat in Chelsea. But Flack had talked her into moving after the rapturous reception the critics and the public gave her film. He intended to make her *the* great Andra Lee. She had only to put herself in his hands.

The trouble was, thought Rose Penham, that Andra in her quiet way was extraordinarily stubborn; not at all easy to control. Flack was here this morning to try and make her change her mind but Rose knew that he was wasting his time. Nothing would make Andra change it.

'Ach!' for the third time Flack almost shouted the exclamation, then sat down on a low satin-covered divan and grabbed a photograph which stood on the glass-topped table beside him. He stared at it while he puffed at his cigar, his breathing growing more and more noisy.

'You!' he said to the photograph, *'you* are responsible for this. If I could but assassinate you in my thoughts, you would lie at my feet – a fearful corpse. A *corpse,* do you hear?'

'Really, Mr Sankey,' protested Miss Penham.

Flack glowered at her.

'Do you not agree with me that it is better that he should be a corpse and Andra should continue her fine flight upward to stardom?'

'Yes, I think it's a pity, Mr Sankey, but Miss Lee happens to be in love.'

'Ach! In love with what? With this tailor's dummy – this hulk of handsome boyish smug stupidity? Or is it she is in love with love?'

'Oh, I think Mr Goodwin is quite fascinating,' said Rose Penham. 'And she adores him – truly she does. She write to him every day. *Every day.* And she has so often told me she would rather be just any housewife living with her husband than Andra Lee who has the world at her feet.'

Flack's small black eyes disappeared into the white folds of his eyelids. He set Trevor Goodwin's photograph down on to the table with a crash that threatened to smash it and which made Miss Penham jump. He growled:

'I tell you it is a terrible, a fantastic, a gargantuan mistake on her part. Mr Goodwin is an ordinary young man with a handsome face. There are thousands more in the world. She need not ruin herself, and all of us, just because she wants to go out to Cape Town and marry *this* one. If she waits she will find more men to choose from and possibly a better one. Most certainly. Who is Trevor Goodwin? *Who is he?*'

Miss Penham gave a somewhat hollow laugh.

'Just the man whom Andra Lee fancies, that's all.'

'I don't believe that she does,' said Flack. 'She has talked to me of this Trevor but I do not think he can be the love of her life. He is just a man to whom she engaged herself when she was twenty. And because she is a nice girl with nice ideas, she thinks that she must keep her promise.'

'Keeping one's promise is really quite a good idea,' remarked Rose dryly. 'I used to be engaged once – oh, a million years ago, when I was a young girl – and my charming fiancé broke *his* promise to me. I've never cared for anybody since. I wouldn't like that to happen to Miss Lee's boy-friend, though he means nothing to me.'

Flack puffed cigar smoke somewhat vindictively in the direction of Miss Penham.

'So Andra does not mind turning me into a nervous wreck and herself into an imbecile who surrenders her fortune and slides into a marriage which will make her nothing but a nonentity. In Cape Town she will become one of a million other wives with little to offer the world and to whom the world offers nothing in return.'

'Oh, dear, Mr Sankey, you *have* worked yourself up this morning,' said Miss Penham shaking her head.

Flack spread his hands out in a gesture that was meant to be appealing. In Miss Penham's rich imagination, it was the porpoise begging for a fish.

'Can you not reason with her? Make her see sense. Send for her parents, her lawyer, her bank manager – anybody to whom she might listen.'

Came a voice from the doorway – that low and singularly sweet voice that could charm the hearts of cinema audiences in their thousands.

'Flack dear, it's much too hot this morning to get yourself into such a tizzy. Do calm down, and please don't bother to send for any of these people. My mind is quite definitely made up.'

'But *why?*' Flack Sankey lumbered on to his feet and perspiring profusely, began to mop his face and neck with a large silk handkerchief. 'Why are you doing this, Andra? My darling, you are insane! When I received your note it stunned me. I nearly cut my throat.'

Andra Lee smiled as she moved towards her manager. That smile was full of natural charm. Miss Penham regarded her with dog-like devotion. Flack Sankey looked at her with the tragic realisation that here was a glorious actress for whom the world had waited. He was so genuinely moved to grief by the decision Andra had made, that he would willingly have forfeited his own commission in order to keep her at the top of the ladder.

It had been a rush upwards, he thought – no ordinary climb. Perhaps that was the trouble. Fame had come too quickly to Andra – she hadn't had time to grasp it or to realise what she was doing by throwing it all up.

'Do sit down, Flack, and relax,' Andra said kindly.

He returned to his yellow satin sofa. Rose retired discreetly. Andra's Austrian maid came in with the iced coffee which Flack adored. He took a gulp from the tall frosted goblet, then opened his eyes to their fullest in order to examine Andra; as though he wanted to make sure that she was the Andra he knew, rather than a lunatic-stranger.

She looked heavenly, he thought, with deepening gloom, in a white bath robe with a wide sash around the incredibly small waist. Her long reddish hair had been piled up on top of her head with combs. Soft pinkish tendrils, still wet from the shower, clung to her rounded forehead and the nape of the long slender neck. She had that very white skin which goes with auburn hair – pure and unblemished. The oval face had a certain child-like gravity and the long-shaped eyes, darkly grey, with very long lashes, were full of sweetness. There was no voluptuousness in that face, yet a trace of passion in the finely-cut lips. But Andra's beauty in Flack Sankey's opinion – and the opinion of many others who were her friends and critics – would improve, like her acting, after she had had one or two love affairs, and suffered.

The expression in those lovely eyes was almost innocent now. Andra, as Flack had said to Rose, was a nice girl, born of nice, ordinary people. The film that had made her name had required her kind of grave, even angelic sweetness. But she still lacked the measure of the deep feeling that a truly great actress needs. The potentialities were there, of course. In the last scene with her lover, they had been so very evident.

Flack groaned and put his hands up to his head, moving it from side to side.

'Oh, my darling! Why, *why*, must you do this thing?' he cried aloud.

Andra leaned back against the cushions of the chair in which she had seated herself. Between her long slender fingers she held a box of cigarettes and a lighter. She did not open the box. Her eyes had closed. Her face had that shut-in look which Flack recognised. It was the look he had grown to dread during the past year as her manager, for whenever he had wanted her to do something that he had thought good for her and to which she had objected, those shutters came down across that small face and seemed to bar her completely from him. Oh, she was stubborn all right, and amazingly self-contained for one so young. Who was to know what she was thinking? She never seemed able to give of her full self until she was on the stage, participating in the dream world of the film studios.

'Andra, I am your true friend as well as your manager,' Flack began in a voice of real tragedy. 'Please, my dear, *dear* little Andra, speak to me and tell me why you have made this terrible decision? You have the world...'

'At my feet,' broke in Andra, opening her eyes and smiling at him. 'I know. I know all the things that you are going to say. I'm sorry only because I've disappointed you and let down all those who believe in me.'

'But you are letting down yourself, too,' Flack protested, waving his cigar in the air. 'Look at your notices. Look at all this–' he waved a podgy hand around the lounge which was full of expensive flowers, boxes of chocolates still tied up in their cellophane wrappers with gay satin ribbons, and the basket of fan mail which Rose always brought in from the study for Miss Lee to read, quietly, after her bath.

'I tried to explain myself in the letter I sent you, Flack,' Andra sighed.

'It was no explanation. It only gave me your cr-r-r-azy decision to get out of films and go to South Africa to be married.'

'Is it so crazy?'

'Madness. Who and what is this man, Trevor? What can he offer you?'

'Very little if it's only money and position that count in life, Flack.'

'You know that they count. Gone is this old-fashioned nonsense that love comes first. Young people of today realise that bread and cheese and kisses do not work.'

Andra's grey, lovely eyes now crinkled into laughter.

'I think Trevor can offer me a little more than bread and cheese. I am sure there will be butter and even the odd spot of caviare and the occasional glass of champagne. After all, Trevor is manager of a huge business in Cape Town.'

'But what of *you* and of *your* life? You have a great future before you. Glamour, money and fame for the asking. Trevor Goodwin will make of you a housewife whose spare time will be spent drinking in clubs, or playing tennis or golf or bridge.'

'Or having children,' added Andra gently.

'Ach, very well. Have your children and become fat and frumpish.'

'Now *you* are out of date, Flack. Modern mothers preserve their figures. Even Marlene Dietrich is a grandmother.'

'But she didn't become one until her name was made and her position secure. Why can *you* not wait and marry your boy-friend once you have established yourself as Andra Lee? One successful film has put you on the top but it won't keep you there. You must go on or ... you will be like a meteor...' Flack wheezed asthmatically, 'which soars into the heavens, then crashes into the earth and is seen no more.'

'Flack, I don't think I want to be a great star and stay in the firmament as one.'

'Then why did you ever begin? Why did you work so hard for these last two years of your life and reach this pinnacle if it was only to throw it all up?' Flack demanded angrily.

Silence for a moment. Andra bit at her lower lip and then slowly drew a cigarette from the box and flicked on her lighter.

'That's the way it's worked out,' she said. 'I didn't anticipate my success. In my wildest dreams I never thought I'd do what I've done in so short a space of time. What you don't realise, Flack, is that I belong to Trevor and that I've been waiting for him to send for me. I always intended to go out and marry him as soon as that day arrived.'

'And do you not think he is an egotist? A ... a *supreme* egotist?' flashed the man on the sofa. 'To know that you are a star and yet be willing to throw you back into the sea to swim with all the other fish, just in order to run his house in Cape Town and sleep in his bed and bear his children. Is that not abominably selfish?'

Andra rose to her feet.

'You go too far, Flack. Besides, Trevor knows how I feel. He is not demanding anything I do not wish to give.'

Flack too, rose, wiping his wet face and neck. He had lost his temper. He did not care what he said now.

'You object to the mention of the word *bed.* Is Andra Lee such a Victorian Miss that she cannot allow the world to think of her in the arms of a lover or a husband? Always you shrink from the word *sex,* yet in your film you managed to convey it so beautifully that every audience that sees your film goes home intoxicated with passion. They have watched you in your moment of surrender and you have given them the thrill they need. The passion is yours but you deny it.'

Andra was pale now and trembling very slightly. She said:

'This is absurd. You and I have never agreed on the subject of sex, Flack. I'm not

24

a fool and I'm not a prude, but I've never wanted to be a sex-kitten or any pin-up girl. Sex is not my line. Anyhow the whole thing is ridiculous, because if you analyse it, my decision to go to South Africa and marry my fiancé, cannot be sexless, can it? It means I want a husband.'

Flack stared at her hopelessly, his fat face creasing as though he wanted to cry.

'Oh, my darling, do not let us hate each other. I adore you. I have wept for joy over your notices. There has been nothing greater in my life than you. You can remain the most intellectual actress in the world so far as I am concerned. I know you are innocent and that there has been nobody in your life except this Trevor, but I hoped you would take a lover and learn the meaning of passion, of woman's fulfilment ... not become a house-wife and a mother ... not yet. Oh, my darling, *not yet!*'

Andra's eyes which could be so cool, even stern, softened now. She came up and put her hands on her manager's shoulders and touched one of his cheeks with her fresh lips.

'Forgive me, Flack. I know I've disappointed you. But I've got to lead my life as I think it should be led. I gave Trevor a solemn promise before he left me two years ago. I wear his ring. He has been working to make a home for me. I must go to him now.'

'But why can you not do so – get married

– but fly back to make your next film?'

'Because that's the one way to ruin a marriage. You know yourself that in the film world there are endless divorces and separations. I want my marriage to be a success – to give everything to Trevor.'

Flack groaned.

'And he is quite willing, this young man, to accept such a sacrifice?'

'I don't think he *thinks* that it's going to be a sacrifice. After all he has got quite a lot to offer me and I think it's rather insulting to him to suggest that I'm making a sacrifice by becoming his wife. Out there in Cape Town perhaps, he hasn't realised all the fuss that has been made of me here in London. I've sent him a few notices, but all that he has said about them when he has written, is that they are most exciting but that he needs me, and wants me to give up filming and marry him.'

'He is mad – and *you* are quite, quite mad,' said Flack in a suffocated voice.

Andra turned. She walked to one of the tall windows, pulled up the Venetian blind and looked out at her roof garden and the glare of the sky over London. Soon she thought, she would be looking at a bluer sky, and the hot African sun. Her home would be the white house in Cape Town which Trevor had bought, and so often described and photographed for her. She would exchange life

26

here in London for that other, quieter life as Mrs Trevor Goodwin. She would never now go to Hollywood. She would never again hear the whirl of the cameras, feel the heat of the lamps, hear the sweet music of the producer's praise.

Would she miss it?

No, she decided, funnily enough she could give it all up without a pang.

She had fulfilled herself as an actress but never as a woman. Flack was right, really, about her being too reserved, too shy. But under it all there was a fire which wanted to be lit. Trevor's kisses and caresses had fanned that fire a little before he left, but the big glorious flame of the ultimate passion had yet to burn for her. She knew that she wanted it – with him. To be his wife would mean everything now.

There was one thing that she conceded to Flack. She had made a mistake by ever starting out on this career. But it was all so different from what she had imagined or planned.

She stood staring out at the roof garden, smoking a trifle nervously, letting her thoughts trail backwards into the past.

2

Andra – christened Alexandra because she had been born on the same day as the Duchess of Kent's daughter – was the only child of Geoffrey Lee, a civil servant who had spent most of his life in the Ministry of Civil Aviation. Dorothy, Andra's mother, had been a clergyman's daughter. Andra often told herself with a touch of humour that it was because she had the blood of a parson in her veins that she was more prude than sensualist. But on Daddy's side there was the stage. His aunt had been quite a well-known actress of the 1900s.

Andra had received a mediocre education in a small convent on the South Coast (not that her parents were Catholics but they believed in a convent education for girls) and on leaving at the age of sixteen-and-a-half, she had first of all studied dancing with a view to teaching, and then feeling the call of the stage, went to R.A.D.A.

At the age of sixty her father retired and they were all living in a small house in Godalming when the first note of Andra's fame was struck.

Flack Sankey picked her out, in her

drama-school play, as a young actress of potentialities. He then found her her first real part in a repertory company but after only a few months there came an opening in a film, and Flack got her into it. From then onward, a spectacular and rapid rise led her to the title *rôle* in *Poor Little Rich Girl*.

But unfortunately for Flack, while Andra was still in 'rep' up in the Midlands, she met Trevor at a weekend house-party. He was on holiday from South Africa. His extraordinary good looks and charm captivated Andra from the start. He had a dignity of manner too – a cool assurance which she found intriguing. Six foot two of masculine magnificence, his head covered with short dark curls, a sun-tanned face, and a slow, slightly superior smile. Andra immediately christened him 'The Roman Emperor' and told him how wonderful he would look in a toga. She had also remembered that it had always been her wish to marry a serious-minded man. Trevor seemed more thoughtful and sincere than many of the men she had met. She felt secure with him. For her it was a brief period between learning to admire Trevor and to fall madly in love with him.

After he first told her that he was as much in love with her as she was with him, they spent every possible hour together before he returned to South Africa. Then they began to write to each other regularly. Twelve months later he flew back to tell her he was in a position to ask her to become officially engaged to him. He was now assistant manager of the firm of Cape Town importers for whom he worked, which was known as Felders (Pty.) Ltd. They imported almost everything. It was a flourishing concern – and the new job for Trevor carried with it a salary of eighteen hundred pounds a year.

They should have got married that first Christmas after their engagement but fate had stepped in with a hold-up on both sides. Trevor received a cable ordering him to go on a round-the-world business trip which might last a year, before settling down to his new job, and Andra was offered her momentous part in that big film.

So the engagement had lasted for two years. By that time Andra had grown to love Trevor deeply, and with the confidence that he loved her, too. But he was less impulsive. Gently, firmly, he pointed out to her the wisdom of their waiting a little longer until he returned from his world-tour to Cape Town.

She had been loth to part from him but agreed that his was a sensible decision. She remembered saying to him:

'I'm terrified you'll meet a much more wonderful girl and throw me over.'

Then he had kissed her with passion and answered:

'You are the only girl I've ever wanted to

marry, Andra. I'll never change.'

She believed him. And he became the great, the only thing in her life, too. They exchanged endless love letters and snap-shots and kept the tender passion between them fresh and exciting.

A few days ago Trevor's excited air-mail letter arrived from Cape Town to tell her that he was back for good; was further promoted to general manager of the whole company, which carried a salary of four thousand a year, and now wanted her to go out to South Africa immediately and marry him.

She did not hesitate. Her answer was 'Yes'.

Did she truly realise what she was giving up? She asked herself the question and turned and looked around the beautiful lounge, and at Flack's despairing face. She sighed a little. Not with regret for herself, but for him, because he had helped her to get all these things and she felt that she was being ungrateful.

Flack's dark Jewish eyes met hers. He said:

'Do you know that you *really* love this man? You've seen so little of him. It may just be an infatuation. You may wake up and find you have made a terrible mistake.'

'I don't think so, Flack.'

'Suppose you do?'

She pulled another cigarette from the box.

'I repeat – I don't think I will.'

'You may be exaggerating his attractions

in your own mind.'

She smiled wryly.

'Is anybody as wonderful as one thinks? One must give and take. But I'm not an infatuated schoolgirl, I assure you. And Trevor and I have been writing to each other for a long time. We seem to have much in common.'

He sighed and held out a hand to her.

'Will you swear to come back to us and carry on with your career if you ever *do* find you have made a mistake, Andra?'

She took a breath of her cigarette. Now for the first time she felt the tiniest thrill of fear. Flack's words opened up such a disagreeable vista. It would be more than tragic if she were to throw up fame and fortune only to find that her idol had feet of clay and that she was bored and miserable as his wife. *Could* such a thing be possible?

She thought hard about Trevor. She could see him plainly standing here before her. Her tall sun-tanned lover. She could see the way he struck a match and cupped it between his big brown hands before he lit his cigarette. The sort of sidelong glance he used to throw her in a crowded room; the look that said *'I love you'*. The way he had of taking the combs from her hair, watching it ripple down her back, then making two long strands, he would pull it gently until her face was against his.

'You heavenly girl!' he used to whisper.

She remembered, too, a meeting she had had with the middle-aged woman who was his stepsister and his only living relative. Both Trevor's parents were dead. His father had been an osteopath in Cape Town and his mother an English girl who had gone out there to get married, just as Andra was doing. Grace, Mr Goodwin's daughter by his first marriage, was unmarried, and now headmistress of a girls' school in Bexhill. The only resemblance she bore to her handsome stepbrother was that they were both tall and dark. Grace was, on Trevor's own admission, 'a bit of a bore'. He took Andra down to Bexhill to meet Grace when they first became engaged. They had had what Trevor called a 'sticky' lunch together. Andra, however, got on quite well with the big commanding woman and Grace took her up to her bedroom after lunch and showed her one or two early photos of Trevor.

'He was always a handsome little boy,' she had said. 'My parents spoilt him and, of course, so did I.'

'I'm not surprised,' Andra laughed.

Grace had looked at the girl with something approaching sympathy.

'You'll have your work cut out with him,' she had said.

When Andra had asked why, Grace had answered that men who had been spoiled by their parents were never easy to live with, whereupon Andra, full of self-confidence, laughed again and said that she thought she could 'tackle Trevor'.

Now, standing before Flack in her penthouse, Andra remembered the last thing that Grace Goodwin had said before they rejoined Trevor.

'Trevor is an egotist. Don't you let him walk over you. You're such a nice child…'

After they left Grace, a tiny gnat of doubt hummed around in Andra's mind, nagging a little.

There had been a certain paragraph in the letter received from Trevor this morning, which she could not quite forget. He had first of all told her more about *La Poinsetta,* his house.

She would have four servants and she would be waited on hand and foot. She would suffer none of the paltry domestic worries of the average married woman at home in England. They would have a good time socially because Trevor knew all 'the right people' in Cape Town. Anybody who was 'anybody' was already waiting to throw a party for the bride.

Then came the words that had made Andra a little uneasy.

…You seem to have done amazingly well in this film, darling, but I prefer to think of you as the

34

future Mrs Goodwin, and not the film star, Miss Lee. From the moment that you set foot on this soil, Miss Lee will be no more. We will be married the next day and you will become just Andra Goodwin – MY WIFE.

Grace would call that selfish and self-important. Perhaps Andra, when she had first read it had wished a little that he had expressed some regret, for her sake, that she was giving up so much to marry him. But she tried to understand and forgive him – it was, after all, noble of him not to want to benefit by her success, or the money she earned as a film-star. He just wanted her for his wife.

Once more she set to work this morning to try and convince Flack that her true happiness lay with Trevor. At last Flack accepted what she said.

'I only pray you will be happy, my angel,' he said with a deep sigh.

'I shall write you long happy letters from *La Poinsetta,*' she laughed.

He shrugged.

'And when do you fly?'

'At the end of the month,' she said. 'That will give me time to order some clothes.'

Flack grunted.

Rose Penham came quietly into the room.

'Miss Lee, you are wanted on the phone. It's an urgent call.'

'I'll take it in my bedroom, then I must get dressed,' said Andra.

For Andra, the day had started. Flack left, as frustrated as when he had first arrived.

This afternoon, as promised, Andra drove down to Godalming to see her parents.

Tea with them usually left Andra feeling 'deflated'. Mrs Lee, certainly, had the power of making her feel that she was nothing and nobody: still a schoolgirl who needed advice and even occasionally a 'ticking off'.

The Lees were a middle-aged colourless couple, like a million others. They were living on a pension. Geoffrey Lee played a little golf and devoted most of his time to his garden. His wife, Dorothy, liked sewing and shopping, and spent her spare time in good works; (she was secretary to a Blind Children's Home). She was also a great supporter of the Parish Church and all its activities.

The Lees had felt at first astonished and later a little uneasy because of their daughter's startling rise to fame. After attending the première of her big film, they were tremendously proud but they could not grow accustomed to having a daughter whose photograph was always in the newspapers and who looked as though she was going to hit the jackpot twice over. Dorothy Lee, in her heart, did not approve; never had wanted Andra to train for the stage – (remembering her own youth in the parsonage and her

36

strict upbringing). Neither of the Lees had kept pace with the times. Mrs Lee certainly failed to understand the surging thirst of excitement and adventure in the heart of the young. She was quite relieved to hear that Andra intended to give this all up and go out to her fiancé.

She approved of Trevor. She preferred the idea of Andra settling down to a nice marriage and producing nice grandchildren whom Andra could bring back to stay in Godalming. It was all so much more *secure* that way. As Mrs Lee often said to her husband:

'One never knows *what* is going to happen to a film star!'

Not that either of her parents could complain of Andra's treatment of them since she started to earn big money. She visited them regularly. They had seen all the best shows, in the best seats. She had given them expensive presents. But Mrs Lee, at heart, remained astonishingly unimpressed.

Today over tea she told Andra that she would go to South Africa with her parents' blessing, and that it was the best thing she could do.

'But we shall miss you,' Mr Lee put in sadly.

He was fonder and prouder of his pretty successful daughter than he dared let his wife know. Dorothy was so jealous – which was curiously unchristian of her – but it was Mr Lee's private opinion that the more a woman indulged in good works, the less amiable and tolerant she appeared to become in her own home.

'I shall miss you, Daddy,' said Andra, 'and Mummy, too.'

'Never mind, dear, I always say that what is to be, is to be,' announced Mrs Lee wondering how much her daughter's perfectly tailored linen suit had cost, and thinking how much better that the money should have been spent on the poor. 'And it's God's will that you should have made this decision to give everything up and marry dear Trevor. He wrote us such a *nice* letter this week.'

'What did he say?' asked Andra vaguely.

She didn't feel very well. It might be imagination, but she fancied she had a little fever; her head ached violently and there had been a niggling pain in her right side all day.

'Dear Trevor said that under no circumstances would he ever allow you to go on acting,' continued Mrs Lee with a note of victory in her voice. 'He has waited for you long enough, he said, and what he wants is his wife, *not* a film star.'

Once more – perversely – Andra resented this thought. She pouted.

'I don't understand Trevor over my career,'

she said. 'Most men would be thrilled to see my name in every paper or in neon lights over the cinemas.'

'I always found Trevor very serious-minded,' said her mother, 'I'm sure he thinks, as your father and I do, dear, that earthly glories and successes are transient and it is the Hereafter that really counts.'

Andra examined the red varnished toe-nails visible through her gossamer stockings. She thought with a grimace:

'How like old times. Mummy does so love to preach, and Daddy daren't disagree with her.'

She was fond of her mother. Nobody could deny that Mrs Lee had been an excellent mother, in her way, and quite affectionate. Daddy's affection went deeper, only he was too repressed to show his feelings.

Andra lit a cigarette. There came the expected rebuke from Mrs Lee.

'I wish you wouldn't smoke so much. It isn't good for you, Andra.'

'It's my nerves,' laughed Andra.

'That's what I say,' Mrs Lee nodded her head, 'the life you are leading is most unhealthy and I shall be thankful once you are on that plane, flying out to Trevor.'

Andra got up, feeling unaccountably irritable. As a rule she smiled at her mother's clichés and lectures. Yes, she had better go home, she thought. She really didn't feel well and the tremendous elation which had rushed over her like a torrent at the idea of her marriage after the long waiting, suddenly fell flat. She was almost frightened. She resented her parents' attitude to life, the dreariness of her old home, and even Trevor's all-embracing love. It *could* be a selfish love. Grace *might* be right.

Anxiously Mrs Lee looked at Andra; her anxiety being not so much for her lovely slender daughter as for the fact that she was leaning against the mantelpiece.

'*Do* mind, Andra, you'll knock that *Famille Rose* cup and saucer off, dear.'

Now Andra burst out laughing. This *was* back to the old home with a vengeance. There had always been such a 'carry-on' about the *Famille Rose* in case it got broken. Years ago the warnings about that one good piece of china which Mrs Lee possessed had discoloured the little Andra's life whenever she was in this room. I *must* go, Andra thought, or in another moment I shall have to listen to the deadly dull story of how Grannie had brought the cup and saucer in a sale and how Mummy remembered it when she was young.

'I'll come and see you before I fly, darlings,' she said, and the visit was over. Rose drove her back to town.

That same night, soon after the Lees had retired, they received a phone call from

40

Miss Penham.

'I'm sorry to have to tell you,' she said, 'that Miss Lee has just been taken to the London Clinic. She felt very ill by the time we got back from Godalming and the doctor diagnosed acute appendicitis. They're afraid of perforation as she is being operated on immediately. I'll keep in touch with you, of course, and tell you the result but she asks me to say that she does not want you to come up to town as there is nothing you can do until she is able to have visitors.'

Mr Lee who had taken this call, broke the news to his wife. Dorothy put down the report she had been reading on one of her Charity Homes, and clicked her tongue against her teeth.

'Oh, dear! Now she won't be able to get out to Trevor – I *thought* she looked very seedy. Poor child! What a worry!'

'I suppose Miss Penham has cabled Trevor,' said Mr Lee anxiously.

'I'm quite sure she has, and I wouldn't be surprised if Trevor doesn't get leave and fly home, he'll be so worried,' said Mrs Lee.

And that was precisely what Trevor Goodwin decided to do. Twenty-four hours later after the doctor and newspapers reported that a successful operation had been performed on Miss Lee, a cable arrived from South Africa.

Expect me end of week very anxious best love stop
  Trevor.

3

By the end of that week, Andra was not as well as her doctors expected her to be. There was no cause for alarm, as Miss Lee's physician, Dr Havant, told Mr Goodwin on the day he arrived at the Clinic, but Andra was a delicately made girl without a great deal of resistance. She had had a good deal of pain and slight complications, but both Dr Havant and the surgeon, Mr Green-Maitland, were confident that Miss Lee would make a complete recovery and be on her feet after a couple of weeks. They then advised after that a long period of convalescence. Certainly no more work in the studios.

'Don't worry. There will be none,' Trevor Goodwin told Dr Havant. 'She will be out in Cape Town under my care.'

Dr Havant, who had attended the famous Miss Lee since she had moved upward into the limelight and who was one of her fans as well as her medical adviser, sighed.

'It seems a pity that the world has got to lose such a brilliant actress.'

'On the contrary, I think a film star's life the worst possible thing for Andra. She's been a bundle of nerves ever since she went into films. It'll do her a lot of good to settle down in my country,' said Trevor stiffly.

'Of course, of course,' murmured Dr Havant.

He eyed Miss Lee's fiancé out of the corners of his eyes. He was not particularly impressed. Too much of a 'gorgeous specimen' for the doctor's liking, and too damned superior. Queer, the men women fall for! Too often they were blinded by excessive good looks. After only twenty minutes' conversation with Trevor Goodwin, Dr Havant wondered if there was much in the upper storey there beyond a very good opinion of Trevor himself.

Why on earth did that lovely little thing want to shed her glamour and go out to Cape Town to live with *him?*

But Andra did not ask herself that question when at length Trevor sat beside her holding both her hands and looking down at her with those exceedingly handsome eyes which fascinated her. She was immensely pleased to see him again. He seemed strong and masculine and *safe to be with.* A man with all the answers; the supreme confidence that Andra felt that she personally lacked at times.

She still felt very ill. She had never known before what it was to suffer.

One of the nurses had put her in a pale

blue chiffon nightgown, with a little pleated cape tied by a big satin bow. Her hair hung in two red-gold plaits over her delicately rounded bosom. Her hands in Trevor's big brown fingers looked very white and exquisite.

He felt a real tenderness for her. Her beauty was breathtaking. He would be proud, for instance, to introduce her to his friends in Cape Town. She would take them by storm. There wasn't a woman out there to touch her. She would get strong and well. She would ride and dance with him. He would teach her to play bridge (which he adored), and to manage a coloured staff. They would give big parties which would further his career.

He stayed with Andra for an hour longer than advised, aided and abetted by the young nurses who threw him sidelong glances, and in the corridor whispered to each other that Miss Lee's fiancé was 'smashing'.

Trevor gave Andra long descriptions of life in Cape Town and the beauties of *La Poinsetta* – their future home. He boasted of his triumphs in the firm and his big position in Cape Town, ending with:

'And I'm damned glad I have got all this to offer you when we are married.'

Andra lay still, watching him with a rather touching devotion in her grey misty eyes, never mentioning her own career or ability to give herself so much more than Trevor could ever buy. She knew that he didn't like her to be independent and she thought it rather sweet of him to want to do all the giving.

He began to walk around the room, looking a trifle disagreeably at the huge bouquets. Andra's flowers from her friends and fans not only made an exotic garden of this big corner bedroom, but were in bowls and vases stretching down the length of the corridor. He sniffed.

'I should think you must get fed up with all this–' he waved a hand around the room. 'When a person has so much, they can't appreciate anything.'

'No, darling,' said Andra humbly.

'It makes my little offering look very small,' went on Trevor, indicating the cellophane-covered dozen red roses which he had bought on his way from the airport.

'But they're the only flowers that mean anything to me,' said Andra hastily, 'and if you like I'll tell nurse to take every other flower out of my room except yours.'

He gave her a benevolent smile, glancing at himself in a mirror, and smoothing back his dark curly hair.

'You needn't be quite so drastic, my sweet. I only meant that my little bunch of roses comes from a sincere heart and more than half these vast expensive bouquets are just formal gestures.'

'Of course, darling,' said Andra in the same meek little voice. She felt meek and weak. She gave herself up completely to Trevor, letting his robust personality engulf her. The big bronzed man seemed to glow in her bedroom and to infuse her pain-racked body with the strength she needed. She clung to one of his hands.

'Oh, Trevor, I can't wait to come out to you.'

'No, it's time our marriage took place – we've waited too long,' he said.

'I really had a fantastic success with my film–' she began, but he held up a warning hand.

'No talk about films. That life is finished and all behind you. It's damned lucky that the contract you signed was only for the one film.'

Now Andra's lips twisted a little.

'Flack doesn't think it's lucky.'

'That corpulent fellow! I can't stand him.'

'Oh, Flack's really a darling and he'll always be my friend even when he stops being my agent.'

'He'll be no friend of mine. For heaven's sake don't ask him to visit us in South Africa. He wouldn't go down at all well with our friends out there.'

Suddenly that little flame of independence

– what her parents called her 'stubborn streak' – asserted itself and burned up in Andra. Her white face grew pink and hot.

'Well, I've already asked Flack to visit us because he's flying out to South Africa to see about a film-set for next winter.'

'You can find some excuse not to see him. You know I can't stand his type.'

Shocked, Andra stared up at her fiancé. Where was her adoring lover? Her charming Trevor? Surely the fact that he had become the manager of an important company had not robbed him of all humour and turned him into a pompous bore?

She gave a little gasp. Then she said:

'But Flack is a *friend* of mine. He's done a tremendous lot for me and I've just dealt him a mortal blow in refusing to sign up for him, yet he's still sweet to me.'

'Sweet,' sneered Trevor, 'because he hopes to sign you up again, no doubt. But if he tries to sign up my wife once she's living with me, he'll get the rough edge of my tongue. Please *don't* encourage him to visit our home, darling.'

The 'darling' did little to sweeten this speech for Andra. She lay there on her pillow, the colour fading from her cheeks, her heart pounding from weakness and distress. So Trevor really did mean that he didn't want Flack to be numbered among her friends. A few moments ago she had been filled with joy because Trevor had flown all this way home to visit her. She knew what an expensive flight it must have been and how Trevor, who was mad about his job, must have disliked absenting himself from the Company even for a few days. She had felt warm and flattered by his action in coming. But now suddenly she was cold and horribly afraid that she had built up an ideal which did not exist, and that this tall wonderful-looking man was by no means a hero. He was just an ordinary man with such a conceit of himself that he was thoroughly satisfied she should throw up her friends as well as her profession. Neither interested him.

'Oh, God!' she thought.

So complete was her silence that Trevor, thick-skinned though he was, realised suddenly that he had gone rather too far.

He was as much in love with Andra as he could be, or ever had been with any other woman in his life. And a great many had fallen for Trevor's extreme good looks and charm.

He rarely managed to sleep on an air-trip, and he was over-tired, he thought, otherwise he would not have been so tactless with Andra. Poor little thing, when she was ill, of course she must be humoured. Later on, he could direct her likes and dislikes – later, when she was his wife.

49

He fell on his knees beside the bed and laid one warm glowing cheek against Andra's.

'My little love, do forgive me. I'm just a brute. What the hell do my opinions matter? You've been so angelic giving so much up for me and of course if you want old Fat-Tummy Flack to call on us he shall, and I'll give him a cigar and a nice bit of ham. Jews like ham, don't they?' ... he laughed at his own joke. 'But honestly, sweetie, I want you to do exactly what *you* want and I was just being silly and behaving like a spoiled child. I *am* spoiled out in Cape Town, you know. It's time I had a wife to take me in hand.'

Swift to respond, Andra's black thoughts vanished. She pressed her cheek against Trevor's and stroked his hair.

'Darling, darling, we were almost quarrelling.'

'We never will again, darling.'

'I love you. I've been thinking of nothing else except getting out to you. My success hasn't meant anything apart from you.'

'Neither has mine without you, insignificant though my career may seem to my little "star".'

'But it isn't insignificant.' She made haste to say. 'It's *wonderful*, the way you've got to the top in your job.'

'We're both at the top,' he said grandly, then added with a laugh, 'but you are going to *top* the top in Cape Town with me and everybody.'

'Hold me fast,' she whispered, hungry for his love, and desperately eager to be reassured.

So he held and comforted and kissed her with all his old guile. Soon she was happy again and he, in turn, became once more the smiling confident Trevor.

He did not notice until a nurse came in and sent him out of the room, that Andra had had far too much excitement, and was on the verge of fainting.

Pleased with life and satisfied now that he had seen Andra and made sure that she was not dying, he left the Clinic and installed himself in her flat, as arranged. Miss Penham had fixed dinner and a show for him. He would spend all tomorrow and the next day with Andra, and perhaps nip down to Bexhill to see poor old Grace. Then back to Cape Town and work.

Suddenly he had a brilliant idea – so brilliant that he telephoned through to the Clinic and handed it to Andra before he went out that evening.

'Why the devil don't I get a special licence and we'll get married before I leave?' he suggested eagerly. 'When you arrive in Cape Town it will be as my wife and we can go straight to our own home.'

Perhaps the turning point in Andra's

whole life had its roots in those few seconds, when she failed to come back with the answer 'yes'. She felt speechless. His voice came again, anxiously:

'Andra, are you there? Andra–'

Then her reply tumbled out in a rather weak voice:

'I – Trevor, darling, I can't really give you an answer without thinking it over. It's ... it's so frightfully serious ... I mean ... I don't know that I want a ... death-bed marriage.'

'Whoever suggested such a thing as a *death*-bed?' he asked shocked.

She gave a feeble giggle.

'Sick-bed, I meant. I .. I think I'd hate a mumbled sort of wedding at my bedside, even if it could be arranged. After all I've never been married before...' another giggle ... 'I want to be a white bride out in Cape Town and have a proper wedding.'

Trevor interrupted.

'You disappoint me terribly, darling,' he said in rather a stiff voice.

There followed an argument. But the stubborn Andra was uppermost that night and Trevor was forced to put down the telephone receiver fully aware that he had been temporarily mastered. He didn't like it. Andra was just not going to be coerced into a bedside wedding before he left England. When he had accused her of not

52

loving him, she had assured him that she did, but that she had no wish to alter their original plans. Besides, she added, she was not well enough for a wedding now, and why shouldn't a girl thoroughly enjoy her 'one and only'? No – she was going to travel out to him by boat instead of air and get thoroughly well during the voyage. Then they could have a glorious sensational wedding in Cape Town – a ceremony to remember all their lives.

When Trevor said that he couldn't understand this and was afraid she must be doubtful about wanting to marry him at all, she had burst into tears and sobbed:

'I'm terribly sorry, darling, but I'm just not fit enough for this sort of discussion. I *do* love you and I *am* going to marry you but please don't rush me.'

'Rush you – after all this time–' he had begun indignantly, then a cool brisk professional voice had interrupted in place of Andra's:

'Forgive me for butting in, Mr Goodwin, but my patient isn't fit to talk any more. Her pulse is not satisfactory. I'm just going to call Doctor...'

Of course after that Trevor was all apologies. In a contrite spirit he rushed around to the Clinic with an armful of flowers. He was not allowed to see his fiancée but he sent a note with the bouquet saying that he adored her and he would do exactly as she wished and that it was just because he loved her so much that he was anxious to make her his wife at once. The note ended:

...But of course I won't mention this again, darling angel, when I see you tomorrow. The last thing I want to do is to harass you, and for God's sake get better soon as I shall not really live until you are safely in Cape Town, living in 'La Poinsetta' with
Your utterly devoted,
Trevor.

When Andra recovered sufficiently to read this, she felt comforted and even remorseful because she had disappointed Trevor. She was still in love with him and she still believed that her fate lay with him out there in South Africa. But she remained slightly shocked and upset by her primary reactions to his shotgun proposal. Why hadn't she answered *'yes'?* Why hadn't the idea appealed to her, since she had so long held him in her heart as her *beau idéal? What had held her back?* She did not really know. Certainly tonight she wasn't strong enough to start analysing the situation too closely. Her present emotions were largely governed by pain and her extreme physical weakness.

A doctor gave her tablets to steady her

pulse and make her sleep. Before she drifted into that blissful state of unconsciousness, sorry though she was for hurting Trevor, she told herself that she had done the right thing. She needed that sea voyage – time in which to settle her business at home and prepare herself for her new existence. *It was the right thing,* she kept thinking, but just how right, she was not to find out for many weeks to come.

4

Trevor had gone again.

Certainly he departed in what might be called a blaze of glory. Andra believed that he was reinstated in her heart and that her mind was cleared once more of all doubts. Like any illogical female, she told Rose Penham, she even regretted turning down his offer of a bedside wedding.

Trevor had been magnificent during those few days he remained in town. He rarely left her bedside. He stopped being the rather pompous egotist who had disturbed her when they first met again. He was gentle, considerate and entirely sweet to her. All the nurses were in love with him (so they told Miss Lee). Photographs of him sitting at Andra's bedside appeared in the newspapers. Fans wrote in their hundreds to congratulate Andra on her glamorous boyfriend. And even Rose Penham, who had never quite favoured Miss Lee throwing up her career for life with Trevor Goodwin, was wooed round to the idea.

'I've really been seduced by Mr Goodwin, Miss Lee, if you know what I mean,' she declared, laughing.

Andra, at this time sitting up and feeling miles better, and looking it, gave that infectious laugh which Rose was delighted to hear again. It had been missing lately.

'Hi there, if anybody's going to be seduced by Trevor, it's got to be *me!*'

Rose Penham laughed again.

'But seriously speaking, he was so very kind to me, Miss Lee; taking me out when he wasn't allowed to be with you, and in this heat I so appreciated that drive into the country on Sunday while your parents were with you. He's a huge man, yet there's something of the little boy about him, isn't there? It's rather sweet – he is so ingenuous at times.'

'I know what you mean,' said Andra nodding at her secretary. 'For all his good business brain and his capability, he's sort of dependent. I never realised until I saw him again this time, how dependent he is on *me.*'

'Oh, he just worships you, Miss Lee. We all know that, and you make a *wonderful* couple.'

After that Andra was left to herself and she thought tenderly of Trevor. Her room was full of his presents. He had insisted on having a little gold bracelet made for her. On it were engraved the words: *'With more than my love, T.'*

He had a colour-camera. Photography was

a hobby of his and he had spent hours taking photographs of her, with her bed drawn up to the window and the sun lighting her frail beauty.

She thought a trifle wryly that she had been overwhelmed, almost anaesthetised by his constant flattery and adoration. She told Rose to book her passage to Cape Town definitely now.

Rose Penham came back from the shipping company to tell Miss Lee that she had, on the strength of her name as a 'star', been lucky enough to get a cancellation on board a liner which was to leave Southampton in the middle of July. That would give her a further fortnight in London to get strong, and then a busy week for shopping.

Some of her dresses had already been ordered. She had a 'stand-in' at the studio who was delighted to earn some extra money and go to all the fittings for her.

The first night she left the Clinic, and was back in her flat, she had a terrifying nightmare.

She dreamed that she was driving with Trevor along a narrow road which was near the edge of a cliff, in a big white open car. He drove at great speed. Andra was nervous in a car at all times and this particular drive petrified her. She could feel the sweat pouring down her body and the nails of her fingers digging into her palms as the speedometer leapt up. She begged him to stop and he snapped at her:

'I'm in a hurry and I like driving fast, anyhow.'

She could feel in her dream how her heart pounded. Her throat closed with fear.

'I'm frightened, Trevor,' she screamed at him. *'Stop! Stop! Please.* We're too near the edge of the cliff.'

She put a hand on one of his, gripping the steering wheel. He shook her off and turning, she saw the gleam of his white even teeth, and a smile that became a hideous snarl.

'*My* wishes count – not yours, so shut up,' he shouted.

She remembered the shock and disillusionment she had experienced as she heard those words and saw that look on his handsome face. Her subconscious pain culminated in blinding terror as the big white car suddenly swerved to the cliff edge and pitched over the side. She heard herself screaming as she fell out. She felt, too, a rush of wind against her face as she hurtled into space. Then, fantastically, she was caught and suspended in mid-air by a man's strong arms. She could not see his face but she heard his voice. Nobody that she knew spoke quite like he did. His was a very low, rather husky voice. He said:

'Steady, steady, Andra darling. I've got you …

you're safe now.'

She woke up and switched on her lamp with trembling fingers, the tears pouring down her cheeks. She saw her Austrian maid standing in the doorway in her dressing gown looking scared.

'You are ill, plees? I hear you cry out,' the girl said, goggling at Andra.

By this time Andra was smiling. She found a handkerchief and blew her nose, looking at Mitzi rather sheepishly.

'It was just a bad dream. I'm all right now. Go back to bed and I'm so sorry I woke you, poor Mitzi.'

'If there is anything I can do for you–' the girl began, adoringly. Andra was always so good to her, she felt privileged to serve such a glamorous English lady.

But Andra sent her away. She lay back on her pillows and smoked a cigarette to calm her nerves. She tried to laugh at herself and the dream. So ridiculous to be upset, but that accident and the awful look on Trevor's face had been so vivid, it had terrified her.

Then she fell to wondering about the unknown man who had caught her and comforted her. If only she could have seen his face. *Who was he?* How intriguing it was!

By the time she had finished her cigarette, she was feeling sorry for Trevor. She really couldn't blame *him* for her dream. Besides – he certainly would never behave as the man in the nightmare had done.

She fell asleep making light of the whole incident. By morning she had almost forgotten it.

During that week she received two loving and eager cables from Trevor and an air-letter full of tenderness and longing which put her on top of the world again. She felt she had been mean ever to doubt Trevor's love, or her response to it.

The day on which she sailed to South Africa was one of excitement and some sadness.

Her parents had wanted to go down to Southampton to see her off. She had pre-vented it knowing it meant a long tiring journey for them. The last conversation she had with her father upset her. He sounded tired, and despite her efforts to cheer him up she knew that he was deeply saddened by this parting. Her mother, of course, was different, and sounded delighted when Andra spoke to her – because her daughter was actually going out to be married to Trevor at last. That was Mummy all over, thought Andra; practical and unimaginative.

It was a day of gloom for Flack Sankey and for Rose Penham, both of whom went down to Southampton with Andra to see her off. The usual crowd of photographers, anxious to get some good shots of Miss Lee for the evening papers, had arrived. Rose

Penham said that she had a fair notion what those headlines would be like.

Beautiful Film Star Forsakes Screen
For Matrimony...

(and so on)...

'I'll post the cuttings to you, Miss Lee,' she sighed.

'Cuttings...' mumbled Flack. 'Ach ... Andra is just cutting her own throat ... chucking her golden chances away ... crazy girl!'

Andra felt happy and excited. The sea looked calm and inviting. The sky was a clear pale blue, and she had never seen a lovelier ship than the new *Outspan Queen* with its lemon coloured hull and deep blue and yellow funnel. The new slim streamline product of a modern age.

Andra walked up the gang-plank, her arms full of roses; Flack behind her carrying more flowers and parcels; Rose Penham bringing up the rear, clutching Miss Lee's white hide jewel-case and beauty box. The quay surged with people. Passengers and their friends. The decks of the *Outspan Queen* were already crowded. Stewards and porters, laden with luggage, swarmed over the ship. Here and there a solitary officer in smart blue and white uniform, and peaked cap, mingled with the rest.

In another half hour, the splendid new ship would start on her second voyage to Cape Town. It was a stirring sight, and appealed vastly to Andra's dramatic, emotional nature.

'Oh, I'm so glad I chose to take this trip instead of flying. Flying is so cold and impersonal!' she exclaimed to her companions.

Miss Penham agreed. Flack Sankey grunted. They found a steward and asked for Miss Lee's state cabin. Here a nice-looking stewardess was struggling with so many bouquets that she could not cope, and thankfully handed the job over to Miss Lee's secretary. There were a pile of telegrams waiting for Miss Lee on the table; a huge gilt basket of fruit that had been sent by Flack; and the one cable that really mattered to Andra. From *him*.

Bon voyage, my darling stop thank God every mile you cover brings you nearer me stop
  Trevor.

'Isn't he sweet?' she asked her cheeks pink, her eyes shining as she read this cable aloud.

'*Sweet!*' echoed Flack and grimaced.

Andra patted his shoulder.

'Don't be so miserable, Flack, darling, just try to understand and forgive me – and think nicely of the man I love.'

He took her hand and put it to his lips, his big flabby face working.

'I think only of you and the wish that you should be happy,' he said.

'Oh, Miss Lee, I don't know how I am going to do without you,' said Rose Penham, and she sat down and groped blindly in her bag for a handkerchief.

Then it was Andra's turn to cry. After which they left the beautiful cabin and retired to the bar – Flack exclaiming that he needed a strong drink. There, of course, there were more fans and photographers. There was little time left. The last glasses of champagne were drunk. The last toasts were made. The die was cast. Andra was cutting adrift from England. She was on her way to Cape Town. It was only when she was back in her cabin after another emotional half hour of standing at the rails and waving at Flack and Rose Penham until they were out of sight, that she began to feel depressed.

She really wasn't very well yet, she thought. It took time to recover wholly from any operation, and this *was* a big step; the turning point in her life; no denying it. Besides, all those goodbyes and cheers and the noise and hooting from the sirens from the docks, as the *Outspan Queen* sailed gracefully out of Southampton Water, were emotional enough to upset anybody.

Andra felt suddenly very much alone.

The penthouse had been *home*. This was strange – this cabin, and quite impersonal. Luxurious; spacious and attractive with its gleaming panelled walls and soft modern lighting, its polished wood furniture, and the charming blue satin curtains and covers. Andra began to examine the cards on the bouquets. All her friends had remembered her and dozens of people whom she didn't know but who admired her work, had sent flowers.

Rose had unpacked for her. Already Trevor's photo stood on the bedside table. It comforted her to look at the familiar face. She was going to *him*. She could and would trust him to give her a new and wonderful life – far better, far more worth-while than the old.

Someone knocked at the door. The head steward came in. He looked with respectful admiration at the beautiful girl surrounded by flowers. He had seen Miss Lee's film and thought her wonderful. He offered his services and begged her to call on him at all times if there was anything she needed. He handed her a card with the times of meals, and suggested that she might like to go and see the purser now and hand over her valuables. He added:

'The Staff Captain would like you to sit at his table, Miss Lee.'

Andra listened with that earnest and interested look which she gave anybody who was with her, whether they were important or not. The look that so endeared her to strangers.

'The Staff Captain – who is that?'

'Well, Miss, it's quite a new innovation…' the steward mouthed this word, as though proud of his vocabulary… 'The Union Castle have only just started it and the Outspan Company are carrying it on. He is what you might call a *social* Captain, Miss.'

'I've never heard of such an officer before,' said Andra intrigued.

'Captain Rowland has been a great success so far, Miss Lee. He was very popular on our last voyage back from Cape Town, when he started with us. He's an English gentleman – not a South African.'

'Tell me about this social gentleman. He sounds like the ship's chief entertainer.'

'Not exactly, Miss Lee, although he does arrange a lot of such things as tombolas and dances, etc., but he's also second-in-command to Captain Stevens who commands the ship.'

'Oh, yes, I think I saw *the* Captain up on the bridge when I came aboard. He has a grey beard. What does Captain Rowland look like?'

'A very fine looking gentleman, with a splendid record.'

'Beard?'

'No beard, Miss,' smiled the steward, 'and youngish for a Captain. Not yet thirty-five.'

'I suppose that is young,' said Andra with the attitude of one still in her early twenties.

'Anyhow, Miss, I think you'll like Captain Frey Rowland – everyone does.'

'Fray!' repeated Andra. 'Is that his Christian name? How do you spell it?'

'Spelt with an "e", Miss, FREY, I've never heard it before.'

And Gregson, the steward, thus encouraged by Miss Lee's interest in the staff, now gave her a further resumé of the other officers. No. 1, Mr Arkland. No. 2, Mr Fuller, not forgetting the Chief Engineer, known as 'Chief' and one of the most important men on board.

But it was plain to Andra that the Staff Captain, Frey Rowland, was a bit of a hero to underlings like Gregson. He was a fine sportsman and had won a tennis championship in South Africa last year. On leave in East Africa two years ago, he had taken some of the finest colour photographs of wild animal life that had ever been seen. They would be shown on this voyage, Gregson informed Andra, then made his exit.

Andra found it cooler on board than ashore. A strong breeze blew from the sea through the open porthole. Andra sniffed it appreciatively; found a cardigan and went up on deck to view the coastline. The *Outspan Queen* was moving steadily down the Channel towards Selsey Bill.

As she stood looking out to sea, a page came up to her, and held out a salver.

'A cable for you, please, Miss Lee.'

'Never-ending,' sighed Andra, but when she opened it, tender laughing lines almost closed her eyes.

You are on your way stop I love you stop
Trevor.

Two cables within an hour. How silly and extravagant and delightful. How could she help being in love with such a man! The impatience of a woman passionately in love, caught at her heart.

She walked along the shining decks to the wireless room – followed by the admiring gaze of several young men, and sent a cable back to her fiancé.

Can't get to you fast enough stop I love you stop
Andra.

The Staff Captain did not appear for lunch. Somebody told Andra that he never did when the ship was still being drawn out to sea by the tugs. He stayed on the bridge with Captain Stevens. So Andra did not meet the man with the intriguing name during that first meal on board.

It passed pleasantly enough. There were seven of them at this important table, with the empty chair at the top waiting for the Captain. Andra was numbered among other 'important' passengers who had been picked out for this privilege. There was a director of the Outspan Shipping Company – Sir Ashton Bolliver, and his wife; grey-haired, charming people who appealed to Andra's sense of humour. They admitted that they had never heard of her but told her apologetically that they never went to the films. But they had been 'briefed' that Miss Lee was a 'star'. Whereupon she quickly told them that she had just stopped being a 'star' and was going to Cape Town to be married and become an ordinary housewife.

While Andra's attention was engaged elsewhere, Sir Ashton murmured to his wife:

'You'd better hold on to me, Mavis. Did you ever see such eyelashes?'

Lady Bolliver whispered back:

'Behave yourself, Ashton, and just remember that you're growing bald and that you've got gout.' But she agreed that Miss Lee was devastatingly pretty.

Andra liked most of the party at her table with the exception of a South African lady named Oppendorf. It was whispered to her by the doctor who sat on her right, that Mr

Oppendorf was one of the richest of the diamond tycoons in Johannesburg, and that they might expect to see some outsize 'rocks' on the stout bosom of Mrs Oppendorf when she came down to dinner in full regalia.

Then there was a bachelor who introduced himself to Andra as Benedict Lane (call me Ben). He was a well-known London journalist. A tall lanky young man in his middle twenties with a mass of curly fair hair. He wore horn-rimmed spectacles. A snub nose and a huge mouth spoiled his looks, but he had an engaging smile and a wealthy fund of racy stories, and Fleet Street gossip. He couldn't take his eyes off Andra. He threatened to 'write her up' in no small way. She thereupon warned him that if he didn't tell the truth, she would sue his paper.

'And the truth is–?' he grinned at her questioningly.

'That Miss Lee, once she becomes Mrs Trevor Goodwin, will never, *never* return to the films.'

Here the South African lady pricked up her ears, and turned panting to Andra. She panted perpetually, Andra discovered, mainly because she was so fat and because it was hot. Mischievous rumours aboard were circulating that she wore a wig and that under it her head was as bald as a coot's. It was a flaxen and rather obvious wig, and she used too much rouge, but she had a kindly face. Andra felt sorry for her. How foolish it was, she thought, for a woman with all that money to let herself go so completely. Edna Oppendorf couldn't be more than fifty and yet looked an elderly, unattractive woman, despite her jewels and her expensive clothes. Andra vowed to herself:

'I shall always diet and do exercises and keep my figure for Trevor – no matter how old I am.'

Said Mrs Oppendorf:

'Did I hear the name of Trevor Goodwin?'

'Yes, he is my fiancé. I am going out to marry him,' said Andra.

'Some chaps have all the luck,' said Sir Ashton gallantly.

'*And* how,' murmured Benedict Lane.

Mrs Oppendorf panted:

'How *amazing!* Trevor Goodwin is quite a friend of Simon, my husband, and myself. He often comes to Johannesburg on business and we've met him at several "do's". Now I remember it, he did say his future wife was shortly going out to Cape Town to marry him. He's *so* handsome. Quite one of South Africa's heart-throbs. You'll have to watch out, Miss Lee.'

'I'll watch,' laughed Andra.

'I reckon it will be Mr Goodwin who will have to do some watching,' said Ben Lane with one of his sidelong glances at Andra.

Andra looked at Mrs Oppendorf.

'Do tell me more about Trevor – I'm so glad you know him.'

Mrs Oppendorf launched into a graphic description of the last ball in Johannesburg at which she had met Trevor and danced with him. She was full of his praises.

It was a light-hearted conversation and a friendly meal which did much to cheer Andra up. By the time it was over and she went down to her cabin to rest, she felt altogether better than when she had waved her last farewells at Southampton.

Later she sipped China-tea in the big glass-covered loggia on the top deck where several people recognised her and came up to speak; to ask for her autograph – which included all the children who were on board.

After that Ben Lane found Andra and walked her round the ship. Andra heard more about the Press and any ship's gossip Ben had already gathered. Then it was time to have a bath and tidy up for dinner.

Nobody changed into evening dress on a first night out at sea, but as it was distinctly cooler by seven o'clock, with a fresh breeze blowing, Andra found a warmer dress – heavy dark grey silk which made her look very elegant. She brushed her reddish hair back from her forehead, twisted it at the nape of her neck and smoothed on a touch of eye-shadow which made her eyes look more green than grey.

She was a little late in taking her bath, so it was some time after the gong had sounded for dinner that she walked into the dining salon. She liked the dining salon. It was a delightful room with frescoes painted by a contemporary artist, white chairs with scarlet cushions, scarlet and white curtains looped at the portholes, and electric candles with scarlet shades on the tables.

A small orchestra played soothing background music. The atmosphere was glamorous.

When Andra walked to the Staff Captain's table, the head waiter darted forward to hold the back of her chair. Benedict Lee half rose.

But now for the first time Andra came face to face with the Staff Captain himself. He was already in his place this evening. He stood up and bowed to her.

'Good evening, Miss Lee...'

'Good evening, I'm afraid I'm a little late,' she replied, smiling.

'I don't think we expect our lady guests to be punctual,' he smiled back.

'I am as a rule – very punctual.'

'Then you must be an unusual woman,' put in the Harley Street specialist who was one of the party and gave a significant look at his wife who tossed her head.

Andra sat down and tried to concentrate

on the menu which the waiter put in her hand. But she was conscious only of Captain Frey Rowland's presence; still more so of his voice. She remembered at once where she had heard it before. It was the husky voice of the man in her dream – that awful nightmare in which Trevor had driven her over the cliff. Then, the face of her rescuer had been obscured from her. Now it was as though she saw it for the first time – in Frey Rowland's.

She was at once aware of his vitality. He was not as tall as Trevor, but taller than the average man, with powerful shoulders. He wore the white uniform into which the ship's officers generally changed when they reached the tropics. But they were all using it now because it had been such a hot summer over here.

The short monkey-jacket and tight white linen trousers, suited Frey Rowland extra-ordinarily well. He had long slim legs. Against the stiff white collar, his skin looked darkly brown. His hair was short and thick and Andra was surprised to see that it was already flecked with grey, young though he was. But that greyness was attractive, with the colour of his eyes which were a quite startling blue.

It was a strong face. The eyes were watchful – half-closed. He had the typical look of a sea-going man.

Gregson, the steward, had called him 'a

clever gentleman'. That, too, was obvious to Andra. He had a fine, intelligent forehead. She could believe that nothing escaped Frey Rowland. He was looking at her intently now with his penetrating gaze.

'It's a great thrill for us to have you on our ship,' he said. 'Unfortunately I missed *Poor Little Rich Girl* when it was on in Southampton – which is my home town – but I've seen plenty of photos of you, Miss Lee.'

She stammered:

'Oh – have you?'

'And how do you like our beautiful *Outspan Queen?*' went on Frey Rowland, a trifle too brightly she thought, as though he felt as nervous as she did.

'I think she's a marvellous ship and you must be very proud of her,' she said.

'I certainly am,' said Frey Rowland, 'and so is our commander, I assure you.'

'And aren't we lucky to have someone like Captain Rowland to keep us all happy,' put in Mrs Oppendorf who was, as expected, glittering with diamonds, although nobody else had 'dressed up' tonight.

'Oh, frightfully lucky,' said Andra, feeling slightly brittle and unsure of herself.

'You won't think so once you discover what a horrid organising sort of fellow I am. I shall make you do the things that you probably don't want to do,' smiled Frey Rowland.

Andra tried to study the menu, aware that the steward was still patiently waiting for her order. Instead she felt compelled to look up again into the Staff Captain's blue, half-closed eyes.

Time seemed to stand still for her. It was as though she hung suspended between two worlds – the one in which she was living – the other unreal – unexplored.

But for Frey Rowland she was just another VIP, whom he had to entertain.

Frey was utterly bored by the flow of important personages constantly moving through the ships in which he had served. Invariably there was some unattached girl who tried to attach herself to him. But he was adept at being awfully nice without getting himself involved. He had done *that* once – but never again!

His interest in Andra was faint. Film stars – actresses in general – model girls or glamorous society women were all the same to Frey Rowland. Attractive cargo being shipped from one port to another, and who must be taken care of en route. That was his job.

'Keep 'em happy, but try not to let your personal feelings come into it,' had been the advice given him when he was first placed in this new capacity.

Frey liked it that way, but he often wondered if he hadn't been a fool to get himself tied up to the Outspan Company in a job which meant almost entirely a social round, and where very little seamanship was necessary. After all, he held a Master's Certificate. He felt this 'palaver' as he called it, to be a waste of his time.

At thirty-five Frey was one of the youngest men in the service to hold that certificate, and he had always wanted to command his own ship. He fully intended to do so before another year ended. Luckily for him the new policy of the Outspan Shipping Company was to give command of their liners to the younger men. Fifty-five-year-olds like Stevens were retiring. This was probably the last time the Captain of the *Outspan Queen* would be making the round trip. It had been hinted to Frey that the time was not far ahead when the Company would give him a full command, but first he must do a year as a Staff Captain, and work directly under Stevens; or take control if necessary. When Frey had growled that he didn't think he could face long hours entertaining the passengers and attending endless parties, they had laughed at him.

'You're a good looking chap, Frey, and everyone appreciates you as a fine sportsman – you can get away with it,' they had said.

Well, he had done so and with singular success on the *Outspan Queen's* maiden voyage and back home again. But already he was feeling certain that he was not cut out for this job because he had what he privately termed a 'split' personality (in harmless fashion of course). He could be gay and amusing; sympathetic with the troubles of people who didn't really interest him. He danced well. He was a graceful gracious host. He could *make* himself popular. But there was that other Frey whom nobody knew. The deep thinker; the serious-minded Frey interested in philosophy and metaphysics – and serious music. When he was ashore Frey always took himself off to an opera or concert. He had a gramophone in his cabin with a supply of Bach and Beethoven records which might have astonished some of the frivolous girls on board who revelled in hot jazz or incidental music from films, and who believed that Captain Rowland revelled with them, because he could sit down at the piano in the smoke-room and play all the tunes from memory.

There were the two Freys; at times a conflict between them which disturbed him considerably. Yet somehow when the gay sportsman and socialite seemed to be winning, it was always that other Frey with the searching mind and intellect who came up on top. Then he felt curiously ashamed of himself.

5

Frey Rowland had been born thirty-four and a half years ago in Christchurch, Hampshire, in a small stone house with an incomparable view of the forest. It had belonged to his grandparents on the maternal side.

His father, who was in the Mercantile Marine Service, unfortunately died at sea after an emergency operation, when Frey was still an infant. His young mother was lucky enough to have parents to help her bring up her boy, because she had little beyond her pension. But her father was a retired country doctor with some money of his own; enough to guarantee a good education for young Frey who had been thus christened after his father. Nobody knew where that strange Christian name originated except that all the Rowlands had christened their sons 'Frey' during the last three generations. Frey's great-great-grandfather who had French blood in him had spelt his name FRÉ, but that Continental spelling had been abandoned by the succeeding generation. That particular Fré had been a professional pianist and played in concerts all over the Continent. No doubt it was from him that the present Frey had inherited his musical ability.

Frey's childhood had not been an unhappy one and although he missed not having a father, Penelope Rowland, his mother, was a girl with sound common sense, determined not to let her son grow up tied to his mother's apron strings or lack masculine control. The sea was in Frey's blood and in deference to his father's memory, she was determined he should follow those footsteps. So Frey was trained with a nautical career in view.

After the death of her parents, Penelope Rowland moved to the outskirts of Southampton. Frey's early recollections – at least from the age of five – were of the sea and of ships. The great liners gliding into the harbour and gliding out again. The dry docks and the workshops. The tall cranes. The tugs and the hawsers, the ferries, the cargo boats; the endless stream of shipping. Fascinating for a small boy with a sea-faring man's blood in his veins. If there was ever an injustice done to Frey by the sensible and kindly mother who adored him, but never let him see the fact, it was only her aversion to the musical side of his nature. She was and always had been a practical person with a predilection towards games. A sporting friend of her late husband was godfather to young Frey. This man had also discouraged Frey's fondness for music and except that they allowed him to take pianoforte lessons at his day school, they trod remorselessly upon all his real efforts to take special choral instruction, or follow in the footsteps of his great-great-grandfather. No, his mother said, a mariner and a sportsman young Frey must be.

He grew up with a fine physique and soon laid aside his artistic desires, and came out of the Nautical Training College where he was finally educated, with all the sportsman's honours that his mother could desire. Then Mrs Rowland married again. Frey was eighteen at the time. His stepfather was a retired sea-captain and, for a couple of years, a considerable help to the handsome boy who looked like fulfilling all his mother's hopes. Frey passed his exams and went to sea as a junior officer, engaged by the Outspan Shipping Company. They had known his father. It was not difficult for Frey to make the grade. The Outspan was a fine Anglo-South African company rapidly falling into line with bigger and better known ones like the Union Castle. Frey was well-established.

During his early twenties, he enjoyed his life at sea although, unlike most of his colleagues, he was always a little bit less at home afloat than ashore. Shore leave never meant to Frey what it did to them – endless parties, girls and leg-shows. It meant glorious days when he could hear the good music that was denied to him, a passion for which still crept up in him at intervals like a nostalgia – a wistful echo of his heredity. The serious books which he kept in his cabin for reading were a continual source of wonder and amusement to his brother officers whose taste in literature lay chiefly in 'whodunits'.

He was a queer chap, this Frey Rowland, they thought, but he never let that inner 'different' man betray him so badly that he appeared lofty or out of gear with the rest. If there was a party on board, or at any of the ports at which they touched, Frey could be as wild as any of them.

There was no particular girl in his life until he became third officer on one of the oldest of the Outspan liners on the South African run. So far it had been just girls to dance with – girls to kiss lightly at the end of a party – but nobody who mattered.

Then he met Leonore. Leonore was an American, twice married and divorced. (Frey had never really found out if it was she who had done the divorcing or the reverse.) But she was a type that had never come across his path before, and he was dazzled. She was sophisticated, extremely amusing, and beautiful enough to make all the men on board competitive.

When Frey very occasionally allowed himself to remember Leonore, he saw her as she had been that first evening when he found her seated next to him in the dining salon.

He had thought her the most attractive female he had ever seen; dressed with the chic that the American woman seems to be able to attain without effort. It had been a winter trip. Leonore was all in white – some sort of thick white woollen material with which she wore a heavy twisted turquoise choker and turquoise bracelets. Her hair was thick and dark and cut crisply short. He hadn't the least idea how old she was, and for a long time imagined she must be about his own age, twenty-six or so. He only found out afterwards that she was ten years older but had preserved her figure miraculously. She was as slight as a girl.

Her skin was not particularly good and her nose was blunt, but she had strikingly beautiful green eyes, with straight black brows; and a huge laughing mouth. Her voice held the sharp rather rasping note of the New Yorker which he found displeasing at first but later found irresistible. So many witticisms tumbled from those red laughing lips. Endless 'gags' and 'wisecracks'. The sort of laughter-making lines which he grew to associate only with her. *'Boy oh boy,'* she had grinned at him when he sat down at her side. *'Do you guys look swell in your uniforms? Now that little Lennie knows that she is going to sit right alongside a big beautiful boy like you, she's glad she is never seasick and will be right down here three times a day for the hot groceries.'*

Hot groceries! That had made him laugh at the time – like the other things she said that always seemed to hit the target. It wasn't long before 'little Lennie' as everybody called her, spent a lot of time in young Frey's cabin, listening to his records and discussing everything with him from ancient Greek to modern Subud.

She put over the intellectual stuff well and that, plus her strong sensual attraction, got Frey Rowland into a state he had never imagined possible. He fell madly in love with her. He didn't mind how many husbands she had had. He didn't mind if she wanted him to be the third. He expected to marry her. She seemed to return his love, and that short voyage to Cape Town became a series of ecstatic days and nights for Frey – most of the nights spent holding a responsive Leonore in his arms.

Nowadays when he looked back on that voyage he was amazed to think how simple he had been; how easily gulled. He had thought her a goddess and been amazed that she, with all her wit and experience of marriage, could care so deeply for a penniless ship's officer.

Came the day of awakening. Leonore was

supposed to be going to Johannesburg to stay with her brother. Frey suggested that they should go together and that he should buy a ring and marry her as soon as possible. Long afterwards he recalled the odd look she had given him when he had made this suggestion and how she had patted his cheek (her small hands had pointed nails varnished blood-red). She murmured:

'You're a sweetie-pie, lover-boy.'

But she had made no comment about marriage.

She had promised to come to his cabin after the other passengers retired. It was strictly forbidden of course, but Frey was beyond caring and little Lennie didn't seem to mind breaking rules. Then a steward brought him a note from her saying that she was not well and would he excuse her, but that she would see him in the morning before they docked.

Rare for Frey, he developed a blinding headache and having no aspirin went along to the cabin of the ship's doctor to fetch some tablets.

The ship's doctor was a good-looking young medical man not many years older than Frey – a South African in fact – quite a good friend of Frey's. When Frey knocked on the cabin door and heard no answer, he turned the handle and glanced in. In one staggering moment he saw Leonore there

85

wearing white silk pyjamas and looking particularly attractive. She was lying on the doctor's bunk. He, too, was in pyjamas, sitting beside her. Her dressing gown was flung over a chair. There was an open bottle of champagne and two empty glasses on the bedside table. There was little doubt as to the intimacy of it all.

The lovers stared at Frey. Frey stared back, white as death. Then he clenched his hands and spoke one word softly to Leonore which made her flinch. Only momentarily did she lose 'face', then she turned to the doctor and said with a laugh:

'You'd better give him a sedative, honey. The poor lamb looks as though he might get violent. Say, what kind of a fool were *you* not to lock your door?'

The doctor started to mumble some kind of apology. Frey did not wait to listen. He closed the cabin door with a crash, went back to his own room, and flung himself face downwards on his bunk. His world was shattered. He knew now exactly what sort of woman Leonore was and how many kinds of a fool he had been.

She didn't even try to see him again. She sent one of her famous notes on which was scrawled the words:

Sorry I disappointed you, lover-boy, but you must grow up some time. Don't be angry with little Lennie if she just helped you grow. Wasn't it a bit old-fashioned of you to think that our affair had to end in marriage? It was all very sweet but I didn't take it as seriously as you and if you want the truth I haven't got a brother in Jo'burg. I'm going out to marry a nice fat millionaire who'll give me diamonds as big as plums. Thanks for the memory. I wish you had a few diamonds.

Little Lennie.

Sickened, Frey had torn that note into pieces and let them flutter overboard in a strong breeze. With them flew away his last illusions about women. He forgave the doctor. The men even reached a pitch when they could both talk about Leonore (rather unpleasantly). The doctor echoed Leonore's counsel to Frey to 'grow up'.

'And steer clear of lone women on board ship. There are thousands of Leonores in this world, you chump, and the sooner you learn it, the better. Of course, there *are* some nice girls but you've got to learn to discriminate. Lennie was a bit of a snake – mind you. A very pretty one. But definitely reptilian.'

Thereafter Frey mentally associated Leonore in his mind with a sort of black mamba that kills with a bite. He felt that he had received the kiss of death from her lips.

He was a more cautious and sensible man

on the next run and, in the years that followed, nothing persuaded him to fall even
lightly in love. He tried to induce himself to
believe that he would never now marry.

Women were not to be trusted. It gave him
some sort of bitter satisfaction to know that
he was attractive to them and that he had
only to lift a little finger; but he would never
again lift it. He became the Frey of today
with that façade of charm and those half-
closed disbelieving eyes that could make a
would-be flirtatious or possessive woman
feel decidedly uncomfortable. But because
he was handsome and had so much charm,
he was always in demand.

This was the Frey who tonight met the ex-
film star Andra Lee. He put himself out to
be helpful and courteous to her and to the
others at his table, even when he longed to
yawn.

Lady Bolliver and Mrs Oppendorf held
most of the conversation. Frey did, at least,
note that Miss Lee was not a noisy or pushing type. In fact she was extraordinarily quiet
and self-effacing for a film star, he thought.
When he questioned her politely about her
career, she told him that it was ended.

He smiled at her over the rim of the glass
he had just lifted to his lips.

'Has the Poor Little Rich Girl become so
rich that she is able to retire in her extreme
youth?'

She echoed his laugh. He thought for a second time that she seemed nervous and distrait. Then he remembered that when he had discussed the VIP list with Jim Wilson, the purser, Jim had said that he'd seen in the papers that Miss Lee had just had an operation for appendicitis. The poor girl did look a bit fragile, Frey decided.

'I'm a poor little *poor* girl, I assure you,' she said, 'but I have decided that it's wasting my time hanging around studios waiting for the next "take". The life doesn't really suit my temperament.'

'Do tell me, what does suit it?' Frey said with one of those quick bullets of charm that he was always ready to shoot out of the machine-gun mentality he had developed for this social circle.

'I'm going out to Cape Town to be married,' Andra said quite simply.

That surprised Frey but immediately made him feel more friendly towards Miss Lee.

'*Are* you now?' he said. 'You see how ignorant I am about the private lives of the stars. But don't tell them that at headquarters or I'll be asked to abandon ship.'

'I really don't see why a ship's officer should know about the private lives of film stars,' said Andra, 'and anyway I don't want to be thought of as a star any more. Trevor doesn't want it either.'

'Trevor?' repeated the Staff Captain. 'Your

fiancé, I presume?' and as Andra nodded, he went on, 'So you're going out to Cape Town to marry this lucky fellow.'

Before Andra could say yes, Mrs Oppendorf intervened.

'Yes, isn't it thrilling, Captain? And I know Trevor Goodwin. They'll make the most handsome and gorgeous couple.'

'I'm sure they will,' said Frey. And as it was the end of the meal, he drew out his cigarette case and handed it to Andra, who took a cigarette with some relief. She had felt extraordinarily nervy all through dinner and had never wanted to smoke more. As the Staff Captain lit the cigarette for her, she caught again the full glance of his compelling eyes. They gave away nothing, yet seemed to probe into her own heart. She shivered suddenly, wondering whether she liked Captain Rowland, after all. He had a sombre look at the back of those eyes. Yet whenever he spoke, she was forced to remember that other voice in her dreams, and she was knocked off her equilibrium again. She felt she was being ridiculous, but could not entirely steady her emotions.

Frey noticed the engagement ring on Miss Lee's slim finger. He rose from his seat at the end of dinner. As Andra got up from her own chair, she dropped her bag. Frey picked it up and handed it to her.

'Thank you,' she said.

He could see now how exquisitely graceful she was. The wide belt of her dress confined a tiny waist. She looked as though she might snap in half, he thought. She certainly needed to put on weight. Rather fetching that glorious reddish-coloured hair, tightly drawn back from her forehead, showing the fine bones of her face. And *what* eyes!

'Love lies in her eyes,' he quoted to himself, 'and lies, and lies and *lies!* I'm rather sorry for the chap she'd going out to marry. How long will she be content with that before she leaves him lamenting and returns to the screen? Well, it's *his* funeral – not mine.'

And with this cynical thought, he asked Miss Lee if she drank coffee, for if so, they generally had it in the glass-covered verandah on the top deck where the orchestra would soon be playing.

'Thank you, yes, I love coffee, and it never keeps me awake,' she said.

'That's the thing,' said Frey, 'not to let anything keep you awake. Oh, sleep, blessed sleep. *It is a gentle thing.*''

'*"Beloved from pole to pole,"'* Andra finished the quotation.

Frey's eyebrows went up. He followed Andra out of the dining salon, noting how many heads turned to gaze at her with recognition. So she knew her Coleridge! He found himself continuing to quote as he walked upstairs by her side.

'Like one that on a lonesome road
Doth walk in fear and dread,
And having once turned round walks on,
And turns no more his head;
Because he knows a frightful fiend
Doth close behind him tread.'

Now Andra looked over her shoulder and her long lashes blinked at him.

'Gracious, Captain Rowland, what sinister verses to remember! I always think Coleridge produced a depressing poem in the *Ancient Mariner.'*

'I rather like it,' said Frey, 'knowing that one day I shall become an ancient mariner, myself.'

Now Andra, feeling more at ease, was impelled by a sudden imp of mischief, to say:

'Don't tell me that you are going to be *"like one that hath been stunned and is of sense forlorn; a sadder and a wiser man he rose the morrow morn..."'*

Frey opened his eyes as wide as he ever did and whistled under his breath:

'M'm ... bravo! I salute you,' and he put a hand smartly to his forehead. 'You're the first girl I've ever met who really *does* remember her *Ancient Mariner.'*

'Somehow it used to appeal to me when I

was at school. But I did think it was depressing,' she sighed. '"*Alone, alone, all, all alone, alone on a wide, wide sea.*"'

Frey nodded.

'That's why he found that sleep was such a gentle thing. He could then forget all his despair.'

I might have added, Frey thought wryly, *that once I had wanted to forget my despairs at sea.*

That time when he had been stunned by a woman's treachery and the bitterness of knowing that the luscious apple handed to him by Eve held a maggot at the core.

'So few people like poetry,' said Andra. 'Do you read it often?'

'Not these days. But I went through a stage when I found it fascinating.'

'Me, too,' she said with a disregard for grammar. 'What do you like reading nowadays?'

'Nothing that would amuse you, I am sure, Miss Lee. People who see my small library generally fall back three paces and think me a bore.'

'You could hardly be called that.'

'You little know,' he smiled.

'Well, I'd like to see your books and form my own opinion.'

'I shall shortly be holding a little cocktail party in my cabin. Captain Stevens and I generally have a competition during the run, as to who makes the best gimlets – if you like gimlets.'

'I don't really drink at all,' she said. 'Alcohol doesn't suit me.'

That surprised him. He imagined that film stars drank their quota. But he was to find out quite a lot of things about Andra Lee during the next few days which both surprised and convinced him that she was utterly unlike the sort of person he expected a film star to be.

He continued to talk to her lightly and politely while they sipped coffee in the attractive verandah. It was full of cream-coloured basket chairs with pale blue cushions, and little glass-topped tables firmly attached to the floor in case the ship started to roll.

She told him more about Trevor. Frey listened in his usual charming way, pretending to be intensely interested although Andra's stories about her handsome boyfriend, he found frankly boring. However, by the time he left her side to attend to other matters, he had at least decided that Miss Lee was quite sweet with none of the conceit he might have expected in her.

Later when he returned to the lounge, his gaze travelled through the crowd of passengers but Andra was no longer there. Mrs Oppendorf rushed to his side and informed him that Miss Lee had felt tired and gone to her cabin.

Andra lay in bed smoking a last cigarette. When it was finished, she kissed her fingertips, then laid them on the lips of the man in the photograph on her bedside cabinet. She whispered, as she had done every night since she became engaged to Trevor:

'Good night, my love.'

The *Outspan Queen* moved steadily on her way over the dark waters which were diamonded by the reflection of the summer stars. It was going to be a good voyage, Andra thought dreamily. She would be revitalised and quite well by the time she reached Cape Town. At the moment she felt languid and a little sad. She tried to concentrate on the happy prospect of her wedding.

'Until death us do part', she said the words aloud, as she lay in the darkness with her hands folded behind her head, thinking.

But 'gentle sleep' eluded her tonight. Perhaps she was over-excited. The strong sea air should have made her sleepy, but didn't. In a vague way she supposed she was almost afraid to go to sleep these nights. Ever since she had had that awful nightmare, she had felt uneasy.

It was terrible even to remember the malevolence of Trevor's face in that dream. Of course, she knew he could never look like that in real life, but it remained an unattractive memory. Then there was that voice that had comforted her – the voice of the unknown man who had caught her and held her close to him.

Andra stirred uneasily, switched on her lamp and looked around her cabin at all her flowers, blinking at them like a nervous child. She just mustn't be so ridiculous, and certainly she must not let the thought of the Staff Captain come into the picture because *his* voice was so fantastically like the one in that dream.

But try as she would, the memory of Frey Rowland kept returning to her consciousness.

6

Came the day when the *Outspan Queen* docked at Las Palmas – the only stop she was making between Southampton and Cape Town.

Andra got up early on that particular morning. It was fine and warm. A pale gold mist shimmered over the beautiful island and the sight of the picturesque port – the rich green of the palm trees – the limpid blue water in the harbour – filled her with intense pleasure. It was her first glimpse of a place with a sub-tropical climate and it gave her the sensation that she was much nearer Trevor and her future home. She would soon be used to heat, to colourful scenery and all the luxuriant beauty of South Africa; of course it would be winter now in Cape Town – not as hot, perhaps, as here in Las Palmas today. Trevor said they would need log-fires at night once the summer had gone. And it could be very cold up in the mountains.

Andra was one of the first up and out on deck – leaning over the rails, with her cine-camera, taking shots of the natives coming out in their small boats to welcome the big white- and lemon-coloured liner.

One lanky youth on board who had dogged the lovely film star's footsteps since they set sail, appeared with his own camera and tried to attach himself to her. But Andra, who couldn't bear him, escaped, and by the only means possible – up a steep ladder with brass rails marked *No Admittance*. She realised, guiltily, that she was on the bridge. She turned to descend the ladder again when the shadow of a white-uniformed figure fell between her and the bright sunlight. She was too late. It was the Staff Captain. He saluted her but looked reproachful.

'Good morning, Miss Lee. Sorry – no passengers allowed up here.'

She grimaced.

'Will Captain Stevens put me in chains in the hold if I refuse to go?'

'I'm sure he wouldn't be so ungallant to the charming Miss Lee – but he'd escort you downstairs again – as I must do,' Frey smiled dryly.

Andra felt curiously annoyed.

'Don't bother, Captain Rowland. I can take myself below. I actually came up here because I was making a getaway.'

'That sounds intriguing. From one of your ardent fans?'

'Don't always throw it down my throat that I am an actress with "fans". I prefer to be plain Miss Lee – the Mrs Goodwin of the future.'

'Sorry,' said Frey. 'I find it difficult to turn you into a commonplace Cape Town housewife. It doesn't seem to suit you–'

'What would, may I ask?'

He regarded her dubiously. He wasn't going to tell her so, but to him she appeared incredibly attractive even at this early hour when so many women looked their worst. The three days' rest at sea had already worked wonders with Andra. Her eyes were clear; her skin exquisite; a deeper gold than when she had left England. She had been sun-bathing and swimming every day. Frey had often watched and admired that glorious young body in the sky-blue bikini. She was a pale gold statue, he had thought; a perfect figure without an ounce of superfluous fat. She wore her thick waving hair tied back with a blue bow which made her look like a teenager. She positively glowed. She had lost that nervousness he had noticed at their first meeting. The tight green jeans and check cotton shirt she wore this morning suited her.

He said:

'I associate you, of course, with that photo of you that was splashed all over my daily papers. You know, the popular one of the posters – you, dancing on the marble floor of a *palazzo* in Venice, wasn't it? In a *bouffante* dress and you wore flowers behind one ear. Ravishing!'

'Oh, that!' she said with sarcasm. 'That wasn't me. That was my producer's idea of the ME the public wanted.'

Frey bowed.

'I am one of your admiring public, of course.'

Now she felt really cross. She was beginning to know the Staff Captain and discredit his flattery.

'You are the most insincere man I've ever met!' she claimed. 'I don't believe a word you ever utter.'

'Oh, I *say!*' he exclaimed with mock dismay and his very blue eyes narrowed to laughing slits. 'What a reputation! You depress me.'

'Don't be depressed by anything *I* say. Lady Bolliver and Mrs Oppendorf and all the pretty girls on board think you're God's gift to women. You're quite the pin-up boy of the ship. I now understand why they invented this social staff captain job – it must have been expressly for you.'

For an instant, Frey was furious. It was rarely he met with sarcasm, and lack of admiration from the opposite sex. What Andra had said, had rubbed him on the raw. He snapped:

'Fine! We ought to understand each other – a couple of unwilling pin-ups, so it would seem.'

She was in mischievous mood and ready to bait him.

'Oh, Captain Rowland, you're not unwilling, *surely*. You just lap up all the sugar and cream.'

His face burned. His sense of humour almost deserted him now.

'You are not particularly observant, are you? I must lend you one of my books on psychology.'

Andra suppressed a giggle.

'Yes, do that thing. It would be thrilling if by the time we reached Cape Town, I could have you taped as surely as any professional psychiatrist would do.'

He was about to make a snap answer but seemed to change his mind. He took off his peaked cap, wiped the perspiration from his forehead and replaced the cap. She could see that she had annoyed him. She wasn't concerned. Ever since she had come in contact with Frey she had been aware of the curious effect he had on her. She had also, in her hypersensitive way, reacted to every one of the barbs he had thrown at her. He couldn't fool her. She was certain that his flattering remarks and attentions had been studied from the start and that underneath, for some unknown reason, he despised her – more perhaps than the other girls. She had noticed a genuine warmth in him only when he was dealing with a certain elderly passenger who had been crippled by arthritis, and whom he often helped along to a deck chair or escorted to and from her table. To her, he was as tender and sincerely attentive as Andra had ever seen a man. He was the same with two small children whose mother was ill, and who stayed in her cabin. The children seemed lonely and needed amusing. Frey took them in hand and was wonderful with them. Andra had to admit that he had fine qualities. But on the whole, she mistrusted his facile charm, and she was upset because she secretly found him disturbing to her peace of mind.

She saw him mainly at meals. They talked a lot and had touched on most subjects. They found quite a few of mutual interest. He had seemed astonished that she could discuss classical music intelligently, and he learned that many of the records he most treasured, Andra herself possessed.

'Is your future husband musical?' once he had asked her.

She had found it rather annoying to have to tell him that Trevor was not at all musical.

Frey had commented on this.

'Ah! Great mistake. Cable him that you're breaking off diplomatic relations. Really musical people should never marry the unmusical. It inevitably causes a rift.'

'Might I ask if you have been married and are a judge?' she had enquired sarcastically.

Whereupon he had laughed and replied:

'Oh, all my wives worship the three B's who are my gods – Beethoven, Bach and Brahms.'

(Brahms. How she adored Brahms!) She found herself asking Frey if he had a recording of her favourite Brandenburg Concerto. He said 'yes' and asked her to go to his cabin and hear it one afternoon. So far she had not taken advantage of the invitation.

She had a chat with the purser, Mr Wilson, one morning and the name of the Staff Captain had been mentioned. Wilson told her that Frey was not married, and counted himself a confirmed bachelor. The purser had added warmly that Frey was one of the finest chaps in the ship's company.

'Under his frivolous exterior there lies real sincerity and a kind and generous heart, Miss Lee...'

Andra had wondered if she, personally, would ever get through the Staff Captain's crust of honeyed charm and exaggerated courtesy.

Last night the passengers had danced on deck. It was just before they reached Las Palmas. A clear moonlit evening.

Andra was sitting next to the bearded Commander, Captain Stevens, when Frey came up and politely asked her to dance. She had noticed that he left her almost to the last on his list. She felt strangely piqued and held on to Captain Stevens' arm.

'I'd rather talk to Captain Stevens, thanks all the same.'

The older man twinkled at his staff officer.

'My head'll be turned if I listen to Miss Lee much longer. But if you want a dance, Frey...'

'I do,' Frey cut in. He was determined not to be snubbed. He pulled Andra on to her feet.

She was forced to admit that he danced well. The band was playing a *cha-cha* – which Andra adored. (Trevor could never make it.) She found herself moving to the subtle rhythm with Frey as though they were one person.

They did not speak during that dance, or the encore. Andra dared not look up into Frey's strange eyes. She only hoped he wouldn't spoil that marvellous dance by being as flippant or cynical as usual. He seemed to sense what she felt. He, too, was absorbed in the dance. His arm held her close his fingers twined around hers. They were silent. But the silence was strangely eloquent. When the music stopped, Andra gave a long sigh. Frey wanted to dance again, but she shook her head and walked away from him. She did not come up on deck again. And that night she had hardly slept at all.

Hour after hour, she tried to concentrate on Trevor. But it was always Frey Rowland's face and voice that haunted her, and that silent, almost sensual dance. At last she switched on her lamp and sat up and smoked one cigarette after another.

Why, she asked herself, must she feel so *aware* of this man, Frey? It was disloyal to Trevor. But she knew how close she had grown to him. Their friendship had developed with frightening rapidity.

Their discussions were often combative. Yet even the battles of words had become strangely exciting. Andra had found out even within so short a space of time, that behind Frey's laughing cavalier manner, *another* Frey existed. A man who knew about history, archaeology and antiques. He was a connoisseur of the kind of paintings Andra had always longed to collect. He went regularly to Art Galleries all over the world.

'I'm sorry I'm not rich and in a shore job only because as a sailor I can never afford to buy or house things,' Frey told her.

'I want to try to start collecting lovely things once I'm married,' she had confessed in turn. 'Until now I've been too busy in the film world trying to build up a career I really didn't want. It's all been a waste of time and energy.'

'Which is one of the major crimes of the present generation – everyone wastes too much time and energy on the wrong things,' was his comment.

She thought frequently over such discussions. Her peace of mind, in consequence, was jarred and spoiled by the existing truth. She was going out to marry Trevor who had scant artistic knowledge; few intellectual pursuits. Why, then, had she waited so long and patiently for him? Why had she flouted all Flack Sankey's efforts to stop her from taking this crucial step?

In the early hours, this morning – still sleepless – Andra found herself sitting up in bed, staring blindly at Trevor's photograph, struggling bitterly to feel the old wild thrill and glamour; and failing. Her thoughts turned repeatedly to Frey.

It was madness to doubt her love for Trevor ... within a week of reaching Cape Town. But once the doubt crept into her mind, it stayed there, mischievously tormenting and harassing her.

Face to face with Frey this morning, she became once more intensely aware of him and conscious that Trevor's charm for her was fast fading.

She turned from Frey and began to step down the ladder leading from the bridge. Frey bent over the rails, his eyes twinkling at her.

'Mind how you go – those steps can be slippery.'

'I'm all right,' she snapped.

But her foot slipped on the last rung of the ladder. She collapsed in an undignified heap on the polished deck. Frey was down there in a moment to pick her up.

For a second she leaned against him. She felt the strength of his arms. She looked rather too deeply into his eyes. It was an electrifying moment. It frightened her. Then almost rudely she pushed him away and stooped down to rub her ankle.

'Thanks, I'm all right now,' she muttered. 'No bones broken. Just hurt my ankle a bit.'

A half-amused tenderness crossed Frey's face as he looked down at her. The sunlight was turning the auburn head to fiery gold.

'You have gorgeous hair,' he said, without inhibition.

The odd timing of this remark, made her look up sharply. She was prepared to snub him, then she burst out laughing.

'Thanks,' she said.

'You remind me of Rita Hayworth.'

'Friend of yours?' she asked, sarcastically.

He crossed his arms over his chest and grinned.

'Wish she were. I always think she is more attractive than any of your new starlets.'

'Including Miss Lee,' said Andra on the same sarcastic note, and bent to rub her foot again.

Frey looked thoughtfully down at the

pretty arched foot and slender ankle. He noted the rose-tinted nails visible between the strap of her white sandal. He did not rise to her joke, but said:

'Can you walk or shall I carry you to your cabin?'

'Certainly I can walk,' she said indignantly, 'and don't be afraid that I shall sneak up to the bridge again.'

'I'm sure Captain Stevens will invite you to see his quarters before the end of the voyage.'

'Thanks. Goodbye.'

She turned and began to walk away, trying to look dignified but she was forced to limp a little. The ankle hurt. Frey called after her:

'Sure you're okay?'

'Absolutely fine,' she called back over her shoulder.

As she disappeared from sight, Frey took a look at the little boats that were bobbing on the blue water. For a moment he listened to the excited voices of the native boys pulling in beside the big ship, trying to attract the attention of the passengers who were now coming out on deck in their dozens to see the sights.

Experienced though Frey was with women – used though he was to feminine provocation – he could not now blind himself to the fact that he was still vulnerable. He remembered with sudden swift desire the slender figure of Andra Lee in his arms. Her 'gorgeous hair' as he had called it, had brushed against his cheek, bringing to his nostrils a subtle fragrance. He was partial to light delicate perfumes and disliked the strong, musky kind used by Mrs Oppendorf and her kind. He had to admit that Andra Lee and everything about her was extraordinarily attractive.

He began to feel new curiosity about Trevor Goodwin; what manner of man was he? *Would* the marriage of these two turn out to be a success?

Down in her cabin, Andra rubbed her bruised ankle vigorously with strong bath lotion, stood up again, and found that the pain was easier. She was, herself, in a state of agitation – unable to forget the lightning-like flash of unity which had passed between herself and Frey just now. How closely he had held her!

The dream again!

She shivered and sluiced her face in cold water.

This thing was developing into a pattern that she seemed to recognise, yet which was unfamiliar. A paradox which confused her. She tried to put it out of her mind and could not. As though to restore her mind's quiet and the balance of her emotions, she sat on the edge of her bed and wrote out a cable to Trevor. She was, she knew it, deliberately trying to contact him mentally – extract a sort of spiritual reassurance which her association with Frey Rowland was rapidly taking from her. The knowledge of this was like a mist moving uncertainly across the mirror of her consciousness. It clouded the old devoted attitude towards Trevor. She kept saying to herself:

'I love him. I've loved him for a long time.'

But it was no longer strictly true.

In a panic she wrote three cables and tore them up, then carried a further one to the wireless-operator.

Four days nearer you stop madly thrilled stop your Andra.

When she came out of the cabin her lips were pursed and her face almost defiant ... as though she were saying to herself:

'*There!*'

She did not see Frey again even at lunch-time. He appeared to be busy behind the scenes on this day of arrival at Las Palmas. To add further to her consternation, she missed the fact that he was not there and kept looking at his empty chair. She only half listened to Ben Lane's chatter and Mrs Oppendorf's gossip.

Later that afternoon she received a cable back from Trevor.

Nearer and dearer stop I too am madly thrilled stop your Trevor.

Those words boosted her morale and made her ashamed of her inexplicable confusion of mind and heart. She kept reading the wireless message aloud. She mesmerised herself into believing all over again that Trevor was her heart's love, and that *the dream* (and Frey Rowland) were nonsensical.

7

Another forty-eight hours and the *Outspan Queen* was midway between England and Cape Town. The days grew warmer. The younger women lived in swim-suits, bikinis or sun-dresses. The swimming pool was always full. Starlit nights followed the warm splendid days and there was always dancing on deck, and ample opportunity for the shipboard flirtations without which no voyage can be complete.

Andra could not complain of having time in which to be bored. There was no end to the activities. Film shows and concerts. Regular hours of bridge for elderly people like the Bollivers and Mrs Oppendorf, while the younger and stronger ones busied themselves with table-tennis, bucket quoits or shuffle-board. There were races and tugs-of-wars. A variety of entertainment arranged by a committee selected by Captain Rowland. He had politely invited Miss Lee to sit on this committee but she had rejected the offer, maintaining that she wanted to be quiet and alone. In fact, Andra escaped whenever she could from the crowds. She had tipped her deck-steward generously so that he should keep her chair in a quiet corner where she was likely to stay unseen and undisturbed. There she spent quite a few hours of each day, reading or resting in the sun, pleased with the fact that she was tanned, now, from head to foot. She was one of the lucky 'red-heads' with a very white skin who could tan without burning. She gained not only in health and strength but looks. Her mirror told her that she positively glowed after the five or six days of rest, sunlight and sea air.

But she still failed completely to find the mental relaxation for which she had hoped. No amount of self-hypnotism, no will-power could help her to close her mind to the fact that she found Frey Rowland dangerously attractive.

How he felt about her she did not know because, as she had learned for herself, the Staff Captain hid his real feelings behind a façade of gaiety and *politesse,* and the charm which he expended not only upon her but all the other women on board. In fact, during those meals sitting at his side he seemed to Andra to be a little less charming to her than he was to the rest. Now and again his caustic comments and slightly contemptuous attitude towards her sex made itself so evident that it annoyed her. At times she was resentful because she believed that he had no use for *her* at all.

He held a cocktail party in his cabin on the sixth night out. There were so many guests and it was such a crush that it reminded Andra of some of those over-crowded, 'deadly' parties at home. Frankly, she was bored. That was, until the host edged his way through the guests, came to her side and pressed a glass of champagne into her hand.

'You're not drinking. Take this.'

'Thanks, it doesn't suit me,' she said rather coldly.

'But your dress does, if I may be so bold!' Frey gave his half-amused, half-scornful smile which made her wonder why he bothered to flatter her.

She had put on a white shark-skin dress cut low at the back, showing the dark gold of her tan, and the perfection of her small waist. There were large imitation black pearls in her ears, and a rope of black pearls twisted two or three times round her neck. She wore no stockings, only black patent shoes with very high stiletto heels. Her eyes were green-shadowed; her lips the flame-colour of her hair. Frey Rowland, as his gaze travelled over her, had to admit he had never seen Andra appear more sophisticated – or alluring.

'You really do look a hundred per cent tonight,' he murmured.

'Thanks,' she said dryly, 'a pity I can't satisfy my curiosity to see your books and

114

records. Your guests hide everything.'

'Stay a moment after the others go,' he said suddenly under his breath, 'and let me show you round.'

She felt her cheeks go warm and her heart give the strangest flicker of excitement, as well as surprise.

'I hardly think–' she began.

He interrupted.

'Don't think – just stay. There are one or two books I *must* show you and one record which you must hear. It's a buffet meal in the dining salon tonight because there are so many parties; it won't matter what time we eat.'

And he moved away without waiting for her answer.

Between half-past eight and nine o'clock, when the crowd had thinned out, Andra stood chatting to some man whom she only knew by sight, but her attention was on the cabin rather than her companion. She really was interested to investigate Frey Rowland's ocean 'home'. She liked it. The Staff Captain's quarters were almost as special as the Commander's. Spacious, with varnished wood-panelled walls. The furniture was fitted – designed in order to take up the least possible space; curtains and covers were a cool grey linen. Now she could examine the books over his desk. (No photographs. That interested her. There could be no special woman in Frey Rowland's life.) Only one picture – the small oil-painting of a stone house flanked by green trees. His grandfather's house and his boyhood home, so she learned from him later on.

It was a typical, impersonal, undramatic bachelor apartment, kept in shining order by an excellent steward, who bore the unusual surname of 'Pink'. He was a pallid Cockney of a man who came from the East End of London. Pink had sailed in ships since he was a boy in his teens, and he was devoted to the Staff Captain.

'I lose everything. Pink finds and returns whatever I've lost,' Frey informed Andra.

He told her these things after the rest of the guests had departed, and at last she was alone with him. Pink had cleared away the glasses. Darkness was falling. Frey switched on a green-shaded lamp on his desk and turned off the ceiling light which flooded the room. They were neither of them drinking now, but they smoked, and enjoyed the sudden peace. The cold tang of sea air blew in through the open porthole.

Andra felt suddenly stimulated. Earlier, the noise and the heat of the crowd had almost suffocated her. She did not really know why she had accepted the Staff Captain's invitation to stay on for this tête-à-tête. She should have gone down to eat with the rest. But something within her had impelled her, against her will, to remain. It was this strange compulsion that drew her to Frey time and time again. Against it, the memory of Trevor was no talisman.

Trevor was far from her mind tonight. Alone with Frey in his softly-lit cabin in this friendly intimacy, he had become the man that she most wanted to be with. He was serious, thoughtful, showing none of his usual flippancy.

He sat in a chair opposite her, his face slightly in shadow, and talked about himself.

Andra asked a lot of questions. She wanted to know about his childhood, his gradual climb to the position in the Outspan Company which he held today. He confessed to being unsatisfied.

'I know I'm supposed to be on the young side for a command, but it's what I want,' he said. 'I'm not a born poodle-faker, whatever you might think. I want to be master of my own ship.'

'I've never really thought you a poodle-faker,' she said, 'although you do your P.R.O. job extraordinarily well. It isn't everyone who can manage people and win the social campaign as smoothly as yourself.'

'Thanks,' he said, with an odd laugh.

She added:

'I can well believe that you would rather be in Captain Stevens' shoes. It must be a great thrill to be master of a ship, despite its terrific responsibility.'

'Responsibility is a challenge and I like a challenge,' he said.

'The born sportsman – always out to win.'

'A form of conceit, maybe,' he smiled and flicked the ash from his cigarette with his small finger.

'I've been examining your books,' Andra said. 'They are certainly on the serious side.'

'Borrow any one you like.'

'I've never really gone in for metaphysics, but I think I could be interested.'

'Try my book on "Subud",' he said, and found and handed her a slim volume.

She took it, grimacing.

'This will be above my head, but I'll dip into it, certainly.' Then she added: 'What a strange man you are. I suppose you never read ordinary novels – even thrillers.'

'Occasionally.'

'Unromantic,' she smiled.

'Surely you don't like *romantic* men.'

'Not romantic in a sort of sickening way.'

'Surely all really romantic men *are* sickening?'

They laughed together.

'Perhaps women are perverse–' at length said Andra. 'I mean, they don't like what you call a "sickeningly romantic man", but they *do* like a man to be capable of romance.'

'You can number me among the incapables.'

Her eyes derided him.

'You must have been crossed in love to talk like that.'

His mind flashed to the memory of Leonore. His lips curled.

'Crossed is the right word. Twisted. Turned into a tough guy – an unbeliever. I certainly have no belief left in romantic love.'

'I wonder what happened to him,' thought Andra.

She said aloud:

'Then how do you expect the world to go on? Is there to be no family life because Captain Rowland no longer believes?'

'Far from it. Let those who believe carry on. Only Captain Rowland need turn his back on family life.'

'I think you'll regret that when you're older.'

'That's what is said to all misogynists. However, I fully intend to sink into a nice peaceful old age, unhampered by wives or children.'

'The supreme egotist.'

'That's me.'

His eyes laughed at her in that half-closed way that she found irresistible. She went on:

'And how you have the heart to say such things to a prospective bride, I don't know.'

For him, those words seemed to disturb the peace and quiet of this hour. He frowned uneasily and looked askance at the beautiful girl whose skin was so satin-smooth and brown against her white tailored dress. She was a girl whom any man might want to make love to, he thought, and count himself fortunate to become her lover. Why did he find the fact that she was travelling out to Cape Town to be married so difficult to credit?

Abruptly, he said:

'Take no notice of my cynicism. The things I say apply to me – not necessarily to anybody else. No doubt your future husband will offer all the beautiful romance *you* personally desire.'

Before she could reply he had stood up and opened a cabinet in which there was a record-player, and switched it on.

'You must hear my last purchase before leaving Southampton,' he added. 'I know you enjoy classical music.'

Hurriedly, Andra put away the thought of Trevor. There was absolutely no place in this cabin for thought or mention of him, and she knew it – to her supreme consternation.

'Yes, please play me your record,' she said.

It was *The Adagio for Strings* by Barber. A composer who was little known to Andra. She sat back in her chair with closed eyes, smoking and listening, ravished by the beautiful, intense music. When it was finished she opened her eyes again and saw Frey staring at her, although he at once looked away.

'That was played by the Philadelphia Orchestra,' he said.

'It was marvellous. Put me wise about Barber. He is quite unknown to me.'

He told her that Barber was an American composer who wrote this particular *Adagio* in 1936, and that it had been chosen by Toscanini for its first performance two years later.

'I must get it,' said Andra, 'and thank you for introducing me to it.'

'I wish I had time to play you some of my others, but you must come in again and hear some more before we land.'

'I'd like that very much.'

He lit another cigarette. He had watched her closely while that record was playing, marvelling, despite himself, at the poetic beauty of her face with the sealed lids and the long, thick lashes, curling so gently against the bloom of her cheeks. He had wondered at the slight sadness of her finely-cut lips. He had felt that he learned quite a lot about her as he watched. Learned, for instance, that Andra Lee did not lack sensuality, yet there was a strength, even a touch of austerity in her face which he found intriguing. The frankly physical woman bored him. But he could see, when the music reached a crescendo, how Andra – a rapt listener – responded to it. He had watched her fingers clench and unclench; the way she swallowed; the sudden knitting of her delicately-pencilled brows. He could see how pain or pleasure could move her. Her understanding, her sensitiveness and sympathy for music found an echo in the core of his own being.

After the frivolous chatter and laughter of his cocktail party, this was a strangely fascinating hour, alone with Andra, and the books and the music that he loved. Inevitably he kept having to remind himself that she was not like himself, a lone wolf; but a dedicated woman bound fast to some man in Cape Town to whom she was going to give all of herself one week from now. It was a solemn and even alarming thought to Frey.

'Why should I mind?' he kept asking himself.

But the fact was that he *did* mind ... he was even concerned as to what might happen in the future to Andra Lee.

He tried to laugh off this new consciousness with the joke reminiscent of *My Fair Lady*.

'*I've grown accustomed to her face...*'

That was only a comic song from a show. But it hit the mark. He had grown *accustomed* to seeing Andra Lee and it was a habit that was growing more and more fascinating to the man who had sworn that never again would he allow himself to be 'taken in' by any woman's charm.

Andra was not just 'any woman'. She was a phenomenon, Frey thought. She, positively, day after day, unfolded before him in beauty and wisdom and grace; like a flower in the sun. All he knew tonight was that he wanted to go on learning more about her. And more and *more*...

They sat there in the deserted cabin and gazed at each other in grave, eloquent silence; tense, and both a little wary; like combatants waiting for the first blow to be struck.

'Play me something more,' said Andra, breaking the silence. Thankfully, Frey rose and picked out *The Lover and the Nightingale* by Granados.

Vittoria de los Angeles was singing it. The lyric beauty of her voice and the sadness of the nightingale's plaint filled the cabin. Once again Andra's eyes closed. This time, an intense expression of pain knotted her brows. Frey, observing her, saw once more how her lips quivered and how the small even teeth bit upon the lower lip as though to repress her feelings. He felt the perspiration on his forehead and wiped it away. He was a damn fool, he told himself savagely, to let this girl affect him any more, for instance, than he had been affected by the last girl who sat here and smoked and talked to him on a previous voyage. *She* had been pretty, if in a very ordinary way, and unattached. One of the ones who followed him around whenever she had the chance, and pressed tightly to him when they danced, and rather crudely invited his attentions. He could see her now, wandering around this very room, examining his things – waving aside his books as 'impossible' – begging him to put on a record of *Gigi*. When he said he hadn't got one, she fetched it from her own cabin, saying that she was taking the disc out to a friend in Cape Town.

When that line *'And your warmth becomes desire'* was sung, she had gazed at him provocatively through her lashes. He had kissed her, without tenderness, then turned her out of his cabin.

But this was different. *Andra was different.* He thought he understood now why she had decided that the stage and film studios were not for her. Yet marriage ... complete union with this fellow in South Africa ... what would *that* be like for her?

Frey got up and began to pace up and down his little cabin as though he were in a cage. When the record came to an end he did not even wait for Andra's thanks of appreciation. He began to shoot questions at her, like bullets – each one hitting a bullseye.

'Tell me about this chap you're marrying.

Who and what is he?'

Andra told him.

'What, if I may be so inquisitive, was the reason for your long engagement?'

'Circumstances. Trevor had to travel for his firm and find his feet. He didn't want to marry me until he had made his way and could offer me a settled home-life.'

Frey gave a quick, hard laugh.

'Trustful fellow, wasn't he? I doubt if I'd let a girl who looked like you stay behind me with only an engagement ring on her finger.'

'That's absurd...' Andra's cheeks grew pink and warm, and her eyes suddenly resentful because of this probing into her private affairs. Yet she was compelled to answer Frey. Why, she wondered – when she could so easily have got up and walked out?

'Trustful,' repeated Frey. 'Utterly self-confident. I admire his vanity.'

He had hit the mark. Now Andra's cheeks burned a deeper red.

There had been too much talk lately about Trevor's egotism and conceit. She said:

'Why shouldn't he trust me? Oh, I do hate your cynicism.'

His lips smiled.

'I told you not to let it trouble you. It only concerns me.'

'No, you're spilling it in my direction. You want *me* to be cynical and to say that Trevor was a fool for trusting *me*.'

'That isn't strictly true. I'm quite sure you *are* to be trusted.'

Thought flashed through her mind:

'I wonder if I am!'

'What else do you want to know?' she demanded ironically.

'More about Trevor. When we first met, you told me how attractive he was, and Mrs Oppendorf seems quite infatuated. But does your Trevor like all the things that *you* like? Will you find him the perfect companion?'

'Yes, of course!' she exclaimed.

But she knew that it wasn't so, and now at last the appalling truth found its way into her consciousness – not like the small, threatening snake that had wriggled into her reflections from time to time, but like a strong tide that floods and drowns. It submerged all the things that were on her mind's surface. It was as though she saw all her hopes, her belief in an idyllic glorious future with Trevor receding far out of her reach for ever. She gasped; terrified.

She went so white that Frey noticed and moved to her side.

'What have I said? Have I upset you?'

She got out of her chair, breathing hard like a hunted creature.

'Yes, I find your probing into my affairs unnecessary and impertinent.'

He flushed scarlet.

'Andra–!'

It was the first time he had called her that. Up till now she had been 'Miss Lee'. But she turned on her heel and ran out of the cabin, closing the door behind her.

Frey stood where she had left him. He took one or two quick breaths of his cigarette, then stubbed it in an ash-tray. He could see his own hand shaking. Once again he had to wipe the sweat from his forehead. He tugged at his collar as though it choked him. His thoughts were chaotic. But he knew one thing now. He knew that Andra Lee was not altogether certain about that man in Cape Town; for if she had been, she wouldn't have taken offence at anything *he*, Frey, had said. She would have laughed at his cynicism – and his curiosity.

He remembered her expression while she listened to his records. If she could feel like that about music ... what could she not feel in the arms of a man whom she loved as passionately as he loved her? *What*, Frey asked himself, *would it be like to kiss Andra Lee?* To feel that enchanting mouth respond?

'I'm crazy. Absolutely round the bend,' Frey said the words aloud, and pulling down the polished wood lid of his washstand, bent over and sluiced his face with ice-cold water.

When he went down to the dining-room his gaze darted straight to Andra's chair but she was not there. Neither did he find her in the crowd gathered round the long buffet, for the 'Help Yourself' supper.

There was dancing on board that night. Frey decided first of all to avoid it and go and play a game of chess, which he particularly liked, with the purser. But half-way to Wilson's cabin he turned back and went into the smoking-room bar. Several people hailed him and tried to offer him a drink. The female section of the community, as usual, gathered eagerly around the handsome Staff Captain. Frey exchanged some light, frothy repartee while his eyes restlessly flicked from side to side looking for Andra Lee. She was not to be seen and nobody seemed to have seen her.

Andra did not appear on deck for the dancing. Frey could only presume that for some reason best known to herself, she was really upset and had gone to bed.

Frey took himself off to the purser's cabin and played chess. But the game, absorbing though it was, could not altogether drive the thought of Andra from his mind. He was shocked at himself. He had not felt so disturbed since that mistaken interlude with Leonore, and God knew, he thought, *she* was about as unlike Andra as an orchid in comparison with a white rose. Andra was a white rose of a girl – fantastically untouched by her success; with a virginal quality which

128

he had not met even in some of the teenage girls who came his way. She had an elusive, starlike quality. She was as unattainable as the stars and yet this man in Cape Town had managed to monopolise her and bind her to him with a few words and a ring.

'She doesn't love him. I swear she doesn't really love him,' Frey told himself in the middle of the game, and made a stupid move that allowed the purser to checkmate him.

'You're not in form tonight, Frey,' Jim Wilson remarked. 'Didn't you see my castle?'

'No, I'm afraid I didn't. I think I'll hit the hay. I've got a head,' muttered Frey.

He walked out of the cabin and went up on the bridge where it was quiet. He stood leaning over the rails, staring at the dark violet of the water, iridescent with moonlight. The ship ploughed its way towards the Cape; the waves creaming against the sides. Las Palmas was a long way behind now. They wouldn't see land again for quite a while.

'Five days more,' thought Frey. 'Only five. Then he'll be there, to meet her...'

He clenched his teeth and suddenly hurled the cheroot which Jim had given him, into the water. His mouth felt dry. He no longer had any fancy for strong smoking. He thought:

129

'I really am going round the bend. I'd better stop thinking about this girl.'

During the next forty-eight hours, Frey and Andra sat, as usual, beside each other in the dining-salon and inevitably came across each other in one place or another. But they both behaved as though that little session in the cabin, all that had been said between them, had never taken place. They discussed trivialities, shared gossip with Ben Lane and the others at the table, but by mutual consent seemed to avoid looking straight into each other's eyes for more than a fleeting second. The conversation never struck a personal note.

For most of the time Frey was kept busy by his arduous job and Andra avoided him, except to congratulate him politely on the beautiful colour-film he had taken in the Cape Game Preserve, and which was shown to the passengers soon after leaving Las Palmas.

He thought a lot about her, but never once after his cocktail party did he see her alone. He could not fail to notice that she treated him coolly and with an indifference that made him feel that friendship between them was really a casual thing, if it had ever existed at all.

What Frey did not know was that Andra, herself, lived through those two days and nights in a state of complete inner turmoil.

Nothing she could do – no amount of effort to force herself back to the old way of thinking – could restore her once firm belief that she was truly in love with Trevor.

She knew now that she was not in love with him any more. *She never had been.* It had been only an infatuation which had developed into an engagement. Wishful thinking on her part that marriage to him would be the right thing for her.

The constant thought of Frey – his touch, his eyes, his whole vivid personality – flayed her like a whip and left her raw; petrified of this, her heart's metamorphosis.

She was in love with Frey – desperately in love. That was the truth which she finally had to admit. How she was going to meet Trevor at Cape Town and go through with her marriage to him now, she dared not think.

8

Two days before the *Outspan Queen* docked at Cape Town, Captain Stevens gave a cocktail party for a smaller, more select crowd, perhaps, than the one which had poured into the Staff Captain's cabin. Andra went to the Commander's quarters without enthusiasm. As one of his 'star' guests, she could not refuse, but she was not in party mood.

It had been a sunless day and it was now a sultry evening with dark clouds billowing up on the horizon; the menace of thunder in the air. The sea was sullen – ominously smooth.

Andra wore one of the perfectly-cut 'little black dresses' made by a French *couturier*. When Frey Rowland, already by his Commander's side, saw her walk into the cabin, his heart stirred in a fantastic manner which thoroughly alarmed him. God! he thought, she was beautiful moulded into that black dress wearing no jewellery except her enormous round earrings which were of yellow diamond-like stones that sparkled as she moved her head; and her engagement ring. Tonight the sight of that ring annoyed him. Still more did it worry him to know that in forty-eight hours' time she would be going right out of his life.

He looked at her, across the crowd. The bearded genial Captain had gone forward to welcome Andra, and said something to make her laugh. Her gaze met Frey's. The smile faded. It was yet another instant of psychic recognition that alarmed Frey. She was pale and lacked her usual animation, he thought. How did she really feel about him? Now driven by a queer desire to get near her, he went over to her side.

'Let me tell the Tiger to give you some champagne.'

She smiled coolly.

'The Tiger?'

'That's what we call my steward,' put in Captain Stevens.

'What lovely names – *your* "Tiger", and Captain Rowland's *"Pink"!'* laughed Andra.

But to Frey her laughter held a false note. Now the host's attention was claimed by another guest. Frey took a glass from the Tiger's tray, and handed it to Andra.

'Talking to me tonight?' He grinned at her.

'I talk to you every night, don't I?'

'Not so you'd notice it.'

'Rubbish!' she said lightly.

'We're nearly at Cape Town.'

He could have sworn he saw a look of

133

apprehension come into those smoke-grey eyes.

'I know.'

'Such fun for you,' he said with a bantering voice. 'With your eager prospective bridegroom counting the hours and buying up all the flowers in Cape Town to greet you.'

'You make it sound very exciting.'

'Aren't you excited?'

Despite herself, Andra blushed crimson. Frey watched her long slender fingers twirl the half-empty champagne glass nervously even while she laughed.

'Of course.'

Then suddenly Frey said under his breath: *'I'm beginning to wonder if you are.'*

That shocked her to speechlessness but before she could utter a word of protest or denial, he left her, walked across the cabin and attached himself to the side of another guest who had just come in. He left Andra standing alone. Alone with some strangely unenviable thoughts. She saw Ben Lane making his way towards her and quickly, before he could reach her, set down her glass and walked out on to the deck. She couldn't for the moment face the journalist's Fleet Street chatter.

She found a dark secluded spot in another part of the deck, leaned over the rails, and looked blindly out at the stormy sky.

What had Frey Rowland meant?

What on earth had induced him to say such a thing; suggest that she was not excited by the thought of meeting Trevor? *How dared he?*

She cupped her hot cheeks with both hands and fought for the control which had deserted her.

'What am I going to do?' she whispered.

The same question that she had been asking herself for the last two days and nights.

She felt that it was impossible for her to eat dinner tonight, seated next to Frey, having to join in the general meaningless conversation that usually took place. Mrs Oppendorf had become more and more unpopular as time went on, continually discussing Trevor with Andra; making the most sickeningly sentimental allusions to their future.

'*Dear* Mr Goodwin must be too, *too* thrilled by the thought that he'll so soon be meeting his lovely bride,' she had said during lunch today.

Andra had not dared look in the Staff Captain's direction, but answered bluntly:

'Who knows, Mrs Oppendorf? Maybe my dear Trevor is having a jolly good time with the girls in Cape Town, before the nagging wife arrives.'

Everybody had laughed but Mrs Oppendorf had exclaimed:

'There'll be no nagging wife about *you*, my dear. You'll just make the sweetest pair...'

Then Andra had heard Frey's acid comment under his breath:

'That woman will drive me round the bend. I could gladly chew a couple of sea-sick pills.'

It had been at the end of the meal. As she rose, Andra had caught the slightly scornful look in the Staff Captain's eyes. She knew exactly how he felt. He loathed what he called 'sickening sentimentality'. She was personally disturbed at the realisation that only a week ago she would have taken Mrs Oppendorf's cloying romanticism in good part. But today she had resented it almost as much as Frey did.

She buried her face in her hands, glad that she was there alone in the darkness, right away from the party, from the sound of the ship's band; from everybody and everything. She needed to be alone in order to sort herself out. But although she stood there for a long time, trying to rationalise the whole affair, she failed. She couldn't think straight. She only knew that Frey was the man she loved and that she had made a ghastly mistake in ever thinking that Trevor was right for her.

She was still standing there, leaning her full weight against the rails, and with her forehead against her folded arms, when the storm broke over the ship. Even then she did not move. She let the rain drench her. A storm at sea could be frightening but she felt no fear of it. She welcomed it with a queer primeval excitement as she watched the lightning zig-zag across the sky and listened to the deafening crash of the thunder.

'I don't care if I'm struck,' she muttered stupidly, 'I don't care about anything. I'm in the most awful, *awful* mess!'

She did not hear Frey's light springy step as he walked along the deck behind her. But when he called her name she swung round to him. The rain drove like small, cold spears between their faces. He said:

'Andra! So here you are. You must be mad, staying out in this rain. I've been looking for you everywhere.'

'Why?' Her rather silly question was lost in another clap of thunder.

'For goodness sake, come under cover,' he said.

'I don't want to.'

'But you're soaked through!' he cried, and caught her by both bare arms and stared at her ruined dress, her wet hair, and the little drops of rain clinging to her cheeks and lashes. She looked extraordinarily young and defenceless like this – no longer the sophisticated Miss Lee – but just a panic-stricken young girl with fear in her eyes.

'Let me go,' she breathed.

'What's the matter with you? You must come in out of the storm.'

'Let me alone. I don't want to go in. I like the rain.'

Her excitement and her craziness became part of his own mad desire for her.

'You really are round the bend,' he shouted angrily.

'So are you, to have said what you did to me in the Captain's cabin about Trevor.'

'It was true, wasn't it?'

'You had no right to suggest such a thing.'

'But it's true, Andra. You *don't* want to get to Cape Town and you don't want to marry this man, *do you?*'

She tried to shake her wrists out of his strong, warm fingers.

'I won't let you say that again.'

'You've got to. I'm as mad as you are,' he said. 'I've been fighting myself ever since that other night. So have you, haven't you?'

'Don't *say* these things!' she repeated wildly.

'They're better said. It doesn't do any good if one feels them and represses them.'

'Frey – please–!'

She stopped as a blinding flash of lightning lit up her face. He saw it. Wild and white and beautiful, in that electrifying light, with an unearthly beauty which dazzled him. The alchemy between them was too strong now.

138

In this savage, elemental storm, Frey himself became uncivilised, admitting neither right nor wrong, only aware deeply of the strong and passionate desire that had been beating up in him for a long time for this unusual girl. There could be no more words between them; no more protests or playing about with half-truths. The whole truth had got to be told, he reflected, whether acceptable to her or not.

'I love you, Andra,' he said with his lips against her cold rain-wet cheeks. 'I'm madly and desperately in love with you, and I think you are with me – aren't you? I haven't made a mistake, have I?'

She tried to say 'Yes', but weakly held her peace. For her, as for him, this was the moment of revelation and of surrender. Her body seemed to flow towards his. Now they were one, heart beating against heart in the drenching rain, and with the storm beating its wings about them. His kiss silenced whatever lie she might have tried to tell, in order to preserve her integrity – her loyalty to Trevor.

She was all Frey's now. Her arms were about his neck and her lips moved under his. It was a long sustained kiss. Afterwards, she knew that nothing could ever be the same again. She said:

'No, you haven't made a mistake, Frey. I do love you. I fell in love with you long before we met – in a dream that I'll tell you about one day. I recognised you as soon as I saw you. It's a terrible thing because I am going out to Cape Town to marry Trevor. Frey, Frey, what *am* I going to do?'

Drunk with her lips and the sweetness of her total surrender, he held and kissed her again – her eyes, her cheeks, her hair; threading his fingers through the damp, red waves of it. Mad though it was, this love-making in the rain and the darkness, it had a desperate beauty and urgency which made him understand to the very fullest extent what love could be between a man and a woman. It was an absolute love which he, the cynic, had thought a myth. It had nothing to do with the hot boyish infatuation he had once felt for Leonore. This was a love that wanted to possess and yet also to worship. From this night on he must for ever adore Andra and he could not possibly let her go out of his life.

'Darling,' he said, 'Darling, darling, you must break your engagement. You'll just have to tell Trevor as soon as we land what has happened.'

She gasped, shut her eyes and hid them against Frey's shoulder.

'I can't. How can I? It would be a monstrous thing to do to him.'

'What about me? Wouldn't it be equally monstrous of you to leave me?'

'You'd get over it,' she began, stupidly.

'Shut up,' he said. 'You know that isn't true.'

She clung more tightly to him, half laughing and half weeping.

'I know it isn't, and I can't live without you, either.'

'That's all I want to know. You'll take this off...'

His fingers groped for her engagement ring and pulled it off. He put it into the palm of her hand and closed her fingers over it.

'You must give this back. You've got to tell Trevor how you feel. It won't be pleasant. I shan't feel too good about it myself, but, thank God, you're not married.'

'I nearly married Trevor in London, when I was so ill. Something held me back. Now I know what.'

'I can't say I think it's a very good show – for me to take another chap's fiancée, but I can't help myself, Andra. This is something stronger than ourselves. We've both got to face up to it.'

'Oh Frey,' she said, 'I've been facing up to it, with both eyes wide open, for the past forty-eight hours. Ever since you played your music to me and talked to me that night of your party.'

'I watched you that night listening to my music. I felt suddenly mad with love for you.

141

But I did try to control it. I didn't mean this to happen.'

She strained against him, cheek to cheek.

'We neither of us meant it.'

'Come in out of the rain, my dear darling love,' he said, 'you'll get pneumonia if you stay out in the storm any longer.'

She did not argue. There was no fight left in her. But she was shivering violently as he put an arm around her and led her through the rain into his cabin. Without realising it, she had been standing close to the very door of that cabin – standing there alone in her torment of indecision and misery. Now it was all over. She must face the awful business of trying to explain to Trevor. She just couldn't marry him – no matter what the world thought of her and no matter what she thought of herself. Her love for Frey was far too intense. It had gone really deep this time.

A moment later, Andra was sitting on the edge of Frey's bed in the warmth and shaded lights. She had slipped off her wet dress and put on his Paisley silk dressing gown. He had switched on a radiator and started to dry her sodden dress. Then he knelt down and peeled off her wet stockings and wiped her feet. He kissed them and looked up at her with a face that had grown extraordinarily young all of a sudden, she thought, with all cynicism wiped from it.

She had never imagined Frey could look like that – so extraordinarily happy, no longer burdened by the load of sardonic mistrust that he had carried so long.

'I don't think you have any idea how much I love you, Andra,' he said.

She bent down, picked up the towel, and began to rub his wet grey-flecked hair.

'You're my child,' she said. 'That's how I feel. You're my little boy.'

'I've never been anybody's child until now. But you are everything to me – mother, sister, lover and wife.'

The word 'wife' brought a shadow to her face.

'Frey, it's going to be hell telling Trevor.'

'I'm damned sorry for the fellow. I feel a criminal. I've stolen you from him. And yet in a curious way I don't feel I've committed a theft, but as though you've always belonged to me and that *he* made the mistake, borrowing you while I was out of your life.'

'That sounds awfully glib,' she said with a laugh, 'and I agree with it, but oh Frey, think of the day we land! It'll be hell let loose. It's a major catastrophe for poor Trevor. He's fixed everything. Bought the house, the licence, the ring.'

Frey got up from his knees, found a cigarette and lit it. Lit another and put it gently between Andra's lips.

'Feeling warmer, darling?'

She was touched by his tenderness. It was a quality which could not fail to move her as much if not more than his passion. Comparisons were odious, but if she could compare Frey with Trevor, it was plain to her now that Trevor's love had always been what he was, himself: egotistical. He had tried to become master of her mind, her thoughts, her actions, before he even became her husband. Frey would not try any of these things. He would be to her what she wanted him to be, *when* she wanted him to be it. Of that she was sure. Their feelings for each other were completely mutual.

'Darling,' he said, 'surely an engagement is meant to be a sort of trial, a finding out about one's self and the other person. To bust up a marriage is one thing, but breaking an engagement another, and not a crime – damn it! I don't want to hurt Trevor any more than you do. But in my opinion it *would* be a crime for you to sacrifice yourself to a ring and a promise. No one should deliberately go and marry a person they don't love. It doesn't make sense.'

She smoked in silence for a moment.

'If you look at things that way – I suppose you're right. I do know I'd hate to live with Trevor, feeling as I do now about you.'

'I'm deeply grateful to you,' said Frey quietly. 'If you'd insisted on marrying

144

Trevor, you'd have wrecked me. I want you now and for ever, Andra. I couldn't bear to lose you.'

She looked at him with infinite sweetness. He thought how youthful and desirable she was in the masculine dressing gown that was too big for her. The beautiful red hair streamed over her shoulders and curled damply about her forehead. He had a fierce longing to take her and make her his with absolute possession. But he felt that now was neither the time nor the place. She was going through a bad phase – struggling against the old loyalties and values. He respected the reluctance she felt to destroy Trevor's faith. It wouldn't be easy for her. She wasn't a sufficiently hard person.

'Darling Frey,' she said. 'This is a pretty marvellous thing that's happened to us, isn't it?'

'Quite terrific, my sweet. I swore I'd never marry, but believe me, if I can get the licence in time, I'll marry you as soon as you've told Trevor and we can find a parson and a ring!'

She was silent for a moment. She felt a little dazed by the prospect of a future as Frey Rowland's wife. *Frey's and not Trevor's.* How fantastic! What a complete reversion of all she had been thinking and planning for so long.

Said Frey:

'Of course I'm nuts – I've nothing to offer you except my pay in this company and a very small private income – and you're the famous Andra Lee!'

'You know that I hate being famous. I want to get away from publicity and settle down. The future to me means living with you.'

He took her by the hands and pulled her up into his arms.

'Oh, darling, it really is a kind of miracle,' he said softly, and closed her lips and her eyes with kisses. Then he pushed her gently back into the chair, walked to one of the portholes and looked out.

'Storm's over. There are stars in the sky.' He turned back. 'Your dress is dry. Get into it, sweet. I'm going to leave you and go down to dinner, or Pink'll come and hunt me out, and we don't want a scandal. Just dress and slip out. No one's around. Will you go down to your cabin, and shall I send you something to eat?'

She said breathlessly:

'I don't want anything. Just some coffee. I'll change and come up on deck again – I'll be where you found me just now. I must go on talking to you. We must make some plans. We must sort out some way of getting this problem solved so that it'll hurt Trevor as little as possible.'

'Darling,' said Frey, 'there is nothing you

can do but tell him the hard facts. It's bound to give the wretched man a crack over the head, but you must face up to it. So must I. And I refuse to feel too much of a cad. This is no shipboard flirtation. We both know that. We've been looking for each other for a long time.'

She ran into his arms and for a moment pressed her face against his shoulder.

'Yes, and I suppose I oughtn't to be happy, but I am. Terribly, terribly happy. Just as though there's a ghastly load off my mind. I didn't know how I was going to get through the day after tomorrow. It's so funny, Frey, but although I've been sending Trevor cables and whipping myself up into a state of joyful anticipation, I haven't really felt it. I've been miserable. Terribly confused. I didn't even know why until I started to fall in love with you.'

He bent over her head, kissing her hair, inhaling its fragrance, his eyes shut.

'Stay in love with me, my darling. Please stay in love, even if I don't deserve it.'

'Perhaps we neither of us deserve to be happy as we're being so unkind to Trevor.'

Frey drew back and looked at her, frowning.

'God! I've just thought of something. Supposing when you see the chap again you realise it's all right and that you've made a mistake about *me?*'

'Darling, *please!* I'm not such a turncoat as that! I've made one mistake but I'm not making another one now.'

'Sure?'

She nodded.

'Sure.'

'It won't be easy for you breaking with him. You're too kind-hearted.'

'I've got to harden my heart. I'd rather be cruel to Trevor than leave you.'

He said curtly:

'I'm taking all you give, with both hands, I've never wanted anything so much in the whole of my life as I want you.'

'Same here.'

He kissed her on the mouth. Passion flowed between them.

He whispered:

'I damn well daren't stay. I'm off, darling.'

Then he was gone, shutting the cabin door behind him.

She shut her eyes, feeling dizzy. She could not think straight. She picked up the dress that had been steaming over the radiator. It was dry now. She took off Frey's dressing gown and buried her face in it.

Of course she was mad. What would they all say at home about her breaking with Trevor at the last moment and running off with Frey Rowland. But she had absolutely no doubts in her mind whatsoever about Frey. She felt a sense of blinding relief that they had neither of them tried too hard to fight this thing and that she need not now spend the rest of her life with Trevor.

PART II

9

Cape Town. The *Outspan Queen* had dropped anchor in Table Bay at two in the morning. Now it was six o'clock. Leaning over the ship's rails, Andra saw the grandeur and beauty of Table Mountain with Cape Town spread out at its foot. It was cool, for it was winter now in South Africa and she wore a warm blue coat and had tied a scarf about her head. The Customs and Immigration Officers were just coming aboard. In a few moments all the passengers would be in the saloon, filling up necessary forms. At half-past eight friends and relations would be allowed aboard.

Andra felt wildly excited, and miserable, too. A perfectly horrible task awaited her. She had got to break to Trevor the unhappy news that she no longer meant to marry him. It was a far from pleasant prospect.

She hadn't slept much last night. She'd been too busy rehearsing what she was going to say to Trevor. Some of the things she prepared seemed too brutal – others too negative. When she and Frey had talked things over, Frey had been insistent that she should not beat about the bush. That would only hurt Trevor more, he said. She had got to let him know at once that she had changed her mind en route from England. Frey had wanted very much to be with her. When they had talked things over last night, he had said:

'This is all my fault and I ought to take the rap with you. If he turns nasty, for which I won't blame him, I ought to be at your side to hold your hand.'

Some latent loyalty to Trevor had made her answer:

'I'm sure he won't be nasty. If he really loves me he'll understand.'

'If it happened to me, I'd feel pretty sore,' Frey had added, 'but I certainly wouldn't want my girl-friend to marry me if she'd fallen for another fellow – that's dead certain.'

In the watches of the night, when Andra had tried to imagine what Trevor would think, say and do, she had reached no definite conclusions. It was all too harassing. What a little beast he would think her! Oh, poor dear Trevor! She could not just be too cruel, too ruthless, and without a tear or sigh just wipe him off the face of the earth because she had found her heart's desire in Frey. Yet the thing had to be done.

If only she had never cabled him from the

ship earlier on, making him feel right up to the end that she still loved him. That seemed one of the worst aspects. But she had sent those cables in good faith. It had all been her unconscious desire to remain loyal, and in love, even while the insidious truth crept into her mind.

She would certainly have an unpleasant hour with him. But on the other hand tremendous happiness awaited her – something so big that it overwhelmed her whenever she thought about it. Marriage with Frey.

Possibly she would never be able to make her parents understand. Mummy would certainly never approve, or excuse her. For one thing, it wouldn't be such a good marriage, in Mummy's opinion. A ship's officer had less of this world's goods than a rich Cape Town business man. Even when Frey got command of a ship, he would never be as much 'in the money' as Trevor. He had said, himself, last night, that he would never now lead a life at sea, apart from her. He intended to tell the Shipping Company that he wanted a shore job at home; something on the executive side in an office.

'But your whole life's ambition has been to command a ship and you're a sailor at heart – you'll hate a land job!' Andra had protested.

'I would have said that a week ago,' he had replied, 'but now only one thing matters to me. To live with you.'

Money and position didn't seem to matter to either of them. Frey was ready to leave the sea for her sake and she was more than willing to forget that she had ever been a film star, and live in obscurity with him. Dreamily and romantically they had gone so far as to discuss finding a little cottage on the coast in some remote English village where they could live away from the world. They would have a family because they agreed that no marriage could be complete without one. When Frey had grimaced and asked her where the money for the children's education would come from, she had answered that she didn't know. That had made them both laugh again. The sort of low, happy laughter that is followed by the inarticulate silence of love.

But now she was serious and nervous. She wouldn't see Frey again for several hours. He must be with Captain Stevens. Not until later this afternoon would he be able to leave the ship and meet Andra ashore. They had arranged to find each other in the lounge of the Mount Nelson Hotel. After she had talked to Trevor, of course, and cancelled the arrangements for tomorrow.

As she stared at the modern looking buildings and customs sheds on the docks, Andra began to feel more nervous than ever. She wished Frey was with her. She felt so dreadful about Trevor.

With all her heart she wished that she need not have to walk over *him* in order to reach Frey and happiness.

'I must keep remembering what Frey and I agreed upon,' she thought. 'It would be a graver injustice to Trevor if I married him feeling as I do about him now.'

Later on, all the formalities were over. She said goodbye to people like Sir Ashton and Lady Bolliver and Mrs Oppendorf. Benedict Lane kissed her hand gallantly and said:

'Lovely getting to know you, Andra. I'll look you up. I must "cover" the wedding for my paper.'

That had made her heart jerk guiltily but she couldn't say a word in denial. But she felt a trifle sick.

It was with this sick, sinking sensation that she searched the crowd on the dock for Trevor's tall figure. She had wondered why he hadn't come on board to find her. She could not see him even now. After another hour she began to feel uneasy. She would have thought he would have been one of the first to rush up the gang-plank to meet her.

Then her cabin steward elbowed a way through the crowd and spoke to her.

'A lady in the bar would like to speak to you please, Miss Lee.'

'Oh!' said Andra, and she turned and followed the steward. Who was the lady?

155

Where was Trevor? Surely he wasn't away on business on this 'day of days'.

Carrying her white bag and jewel-case in one hand, and her make-up case in the other, Andra left her steward to see to the rest of her luggage and walked down to the bar, which was empty now. It was shut, and almost everybody was up on deck, anxious to disembark.

Andra saw a tall, thin woman waiting, alone. She wore a camel-hair coat and had tightly-waved hair confined in a net. She looked unfashionable and had a brown, dried-up look, and a very harassed expression. As Andra approached her, her eyes lit up a little and she came forward.

'Miss Lee?'

'Yes.'

'Oh, how are you, Miss Lee? I'm Mrs Graeme. My husband is the Reverend Alistair Graeme. Your fiancé – Mr Goodwin – attends our church. I mean, he had arranged the ceremony there for tomorrow and you are coming to us for the night, if you remember.'

Andra gave her sweet, sudden smile, and putting down her cases, held out a hand.

'How do you do, Mrs Graeme. It's exceedingly kind of you to meet me. Of course I remember now that I'm supposed to stay with you and Mr Graeme. Trevor wrote and told me.'

Mrs Graeme looked very unhappy. She was a practical unsentimental woman, who had had a staunch Scottish upbringing. She and her husband had lived in South Africa for the last twenty years. They had had their fair share of good luck and of misfortune, insomuch as they had no family. They had lost three children at birth and now it seemed that the good Lord was denying them the privilege of ever rearing a family. Monica Graeme was passionately fond of young people and if there was one thing she enjoyed, it was a wedding.

She had thoroughly looked forward to tomorrow's wedding between Mr Goodwin and the English film star. And what a *pretty* girl Miss Lee was – an absolute winner – although of course, very made-up, Mrs Graeme decided. She didn't really like all that stuff girls put on their faces, but she knew it was considered 'the thing'. Her own pale mouth had never known the outline of a lipstick but she was tolerant of those who *liked* make-up and full of generous appreciation of the prospective bride's glamorous appearance. She only wished with all her heart that she had not got such terrible news for her.

Andra was still smiling.

'Has Trevor been sent away for the day on business? Is that why you've been so kind as to meet me?'

Mrs Graeme cleared her throat.

'Come and sit down on the sofa a moment, my dear. I'm afraid I've got bad news for you.'

Andra's pulses jerked uneasily.

'Bad news?' she repeated. 'Do you mean something has happened to Trevor?'

'I'm afraid so,' said the parson's wife. They sat down together in the cool, deserted bar, and Mrs Graeme put out her hand and took one of Andra's. She held it between her own, and gave herself up to her difficult task. 'Very cruel news, I fear, my poor child, which will distress you greatly. As, indeed, it has done all of us.'

Andra changed colour.

'Please tell me, Mrs Graeme.'

Monica Graeme told her story briefly but concisely, for she was a concise, methodical woman and she did not believe in beating around the bush. Andra sat in shocked silence listening to the very last news for which she was prepared. She had thought of every other kind of disastrous repercussion of what she, personally, had done, but never once had she anticipated *this*.

Forty-eight hours ago Trevor had been involved in an accident after flying from Rhodesia where he had just pulled off a big business deal for his firm. The last job he expected to do before his marriage and honeymoon.

It had been at the airport as they were landing; something to do with a faulty undercarriage, Mrs Graeme said. She could not give the technical explanation but the plane had crashed. Fortunately, only two of the passengers were killed – others had had a miraculous escape and crawled out of the wreckage with only minor injuries. But Trevor had had to be pulled out, both his legs badly crushed.

Here Andra broke in, her throat dry, her whole body shaking with shock and deep distress for Trevor.

'Is he *dead?*'

'No, no thank God in His infinite mercy. He is alive.'

'How badly is he hurt? Tell me please, Mrs Graeme, I want to know.'

'Very badly, although he is not critically ill. But his spine is affected. He is paralysed from the waist downwards and if I must break it to you, my poor girl, the truth is that the doctors doubt if he will ever walk again.'

Andra felt frozen. She said:

'I can't believe it.'

'I wish it were not true,' said Mrs Graeme unhappily.

'Why should he never walk again? Modern physicians and surgeons seem to work miracles.'

'It's his spine, my dear. I repeat, I wish it

weren't true, but they just don't think he *will* walk again.'

Andra, who had been tensed up to meet Trevor and tell him about Frey – and so full of her own emotions – collapsed a little, covered her face with her hands, and burst into tears.

'Oh, poor, poor Trevor – it's too horrible!' she kept sobbing.

Later, when she was calmer, she allowed the parson's wife to take charge of her. Without feeling that she any longer had a will of her own, she followed the kindly woman out of the bar and up on deck again. She did not even turn her head in the direction of the bridge or wonder where Frey might be. This was no time to break the news to *him*. She must go at once to Trevor.

Still in that frozen condition of body and mind she drove in Mrs Graeme's car away from the docks and into the centre of the town. She hardly saw the sunlight or the broad tree-lined streets nor was she at all interested in her first glimpse of Cape Town. She could think of nothing but Trevor and this appalling accident.

They drove through the city down a double-track road to Groot Schuur Hospital which stood in its own flower-filled grounds. Here there was cool green shade and coloured gardeners drenching the sun-baked earth with water-sprays. Mrs Graeme looked at the mask-like face of her passenger a trifle anxiously.

'Let me ask Sister to get you a cup of coffee before you go in to see Mr Goodwin.'

'No, thank you,' said Andra in a dull voice. 'I'd like to see him at once.'

Then she was in a small white room dimmed by green rush blinds and air-conditioned, to which a nurse led them.

She saw Trevor lying flat on his back in a narrow high bed. A Trevor whose appearance shocked her. His sun-burnt face was haggard and the eyes preternaturally big and sunken. It went to her heart to see the big, handsome, vital man reduced to this state. She gave a little murmur and moved to his side.

'Oh, Trevor – darling–'

His gaze turned to her. She saw relief and pleasure light up his miserable face.

'Andra!' he exclaimed.

Mrs Graeme tactfully withdrew followed by the nurse. The door closed behind them.

'Darling Andra, thank God you're here,' said the man in the bed.

She had no memory now of Frey. She *dared not remember.* She flung off coat and scarf, knelt down by the bed and laid her cheek against Trevor's.

'My poor darling. I'm so dreadfully, *dreadfully* sorry!'

His arms went round her. There was still strength in his fingers even though there was no movement in that taut, still body which looked so long under the white coverlet.

'Hell of a thing to happen on my wedding eve,' he added.

Andra began to weep again. Her tears were of deep, sincere compassion. If she was no longer in love with this man, she had been engaged to him for a long time and she could not so entirely disassociate herself from old affections, the old association.

Her tears were wet against his cheek and his hand.

'My poor darling...' she kept saying.

His fingers ruffled her hair. He began to grumble.

'I don't know why this should have happened to me. I don't know what I've done to deserve it. At first I thought I was lucky to have been dragged out alive. Two of the chaps with me were killed and one of the pilots has lost his sight. But am I any luckier – to be virtually without legs? They don't think I'll ever walk again. They told me the truth this morning. I demanded to know it. I'm to be one of those chaps in a chair, propelling myself around – a useless lump – oh my God!'

He broke off, and Andra lifting her head was horrified to see the tears running down

162

his cheeks. For some peculiar reason the sight of the man's weakness did not move her as greatly as a show of courage would have done. She could still sympathise deeply, but the fact remained that he had poured out his personal grievances with no mention of *her*. So far as Trevor knew, she was still his future wife. Supposing she *had* been as much in love with him as ever? Wouldn't it have been her tragedy too? Wouldn't this have been a shattering moment for *her?*

She was about to try and utter words of comfort when Trevor opened his lips and fresh grievances poured from him. They hadn't pulled him out of the wreckage in time. It was the fault of some fellow on the ground-staff. He hadn't been quick enough. Trevor's back and legs were irrevocably injured. That meant an end to his life and his work. He'd be a useless lump. He wished he'd died in the crash. *Etc., etc.,* until Andra, feeling slightly sick, rose from her knees and sat down and groped in her bag for a cigarette-case.

He watched her almost resentfully.

'You're damned lucky to be able to move. Nobody knows how lucky they are until they've been done in, like me.'

'Oh, Trevor darling–' she began, but he interrupted.

'Give me a cigarette. And for God's sake

get me out of this hospital. Get me back to *La Poinsetta*. It's a peach of a house – in Newlands. One of the new houses on the Southern Cross Estate. We'll go there, Andra, so that I can get away from all this bloody hospital palaver. I can't take it. They won't even give me a strong drink. I've never needed a brandy more.'

Andra lit the cigarette, gave it to him and put one between her lips, her hands shaking. She wondered when he was going to turn his attention to *her*. But the spate of self-pity rushed on:

'It's one hell of a thing to happen to any chap of my age. What have I got to look forward to now but long years of being a helpless invalid. Just as I'd got my new job and big money, and *you're* here.'

(Now for a mention of her, she thought dully. But his grief was still for himself.)

What sort of an existence would it mean, tied hand and foot to a chair and having to be carried around? Never to dance again. Never to have any fun. Never to have any real married life. Trevor ended up on that note, his voice broken with emotion. He was even snivelling. Sex was out, he said. Everything was gone from him. He still loved *her*. His feelings hadn't changed. But how could he expect her to marry him now?

Andra sat tongue-tied, feeling ghastly. She did not see how she could possibly tell him

164

about Frey and her change of heart, now that he was stricken down so low. He looked at her slyly out of the corners of his eyes and wiped the tears away.

'But you're so sweet. I know you won't desert me,' he whimpered.

The weight that oppressed her became almost insupportable. She felt suddenly that she must scream and rush out of the room. It was a terrible, claustrophobic feeling ... as though the four walls of this little hospital room were closing in and would soon narrow down to a single dimension which would enclose herself and Trevor, locked for ever in an unspeakable embrace.

The sweat gathered on her forehead. She trembled violently. She whispered:

'Let me think. Oh, God... This has been a terrible shock...'

But he caught her hand and began to kiss it feverishly, his lips hot and dry.

'Forgive me ... forgive me, for being so self-centred. I'm not myself. You can imagine what it would be like to be in an accident like that. I saw it coming. For a split second I faced death. Then there was the crash and when I woke up I was here. It is worse than death. You and I were going to be married tomorrow. Everything's been taken from me. Andra, Andra, I can't stand it. Tell them to give you some poison for me. Put me out. I've nothing to live for. I suppose you'll leave me. How can I ask you to marry me now? I have nothing left … nothing.'

His voice broke. Shocked, stupefied, Andra sat there, her cigarette burning away in one hand while Trevor's feverish kisses covered the other. She knew that it was wrong of her but she was seized with a contempt for this drivelling, blubbering man that she would not have thought possible. She could not have believed that he would behave this way – or that any man could be so cowardly in the face of disaster. The very fact that Trevor had once been a big, masterful, physically-strong creature made his total collapse seem all the worse. She knew that deep down inside her she was terribly sorry for him, as anyone would be – but she could not imagine how any man worth his salt could behave in such a fashion.

Then Trevor seemed to sense her contempt. Quickly he controlled himself. He let go her hand and breathing heavily, hid his face against the pillow.

'Good God, what am I saying? Out of my mind. It's the shock. They say I'm still suffering from shock. How disgraceful of me to behave like this. I apologise. It's monstrous of me. Let Mrs Graeme take you off, Andra darling, and look after you. I'll be all right alone, and of course I must offer you your freedom.'

She drew a long breath. She felt as though she suddenly saw that freedom, and felt a little fresh air, but only for an instant, then the nightmare closed in on her again.

'With any luck I'll peg out,' Trevor added under his breath. 'If I haven't got you, I don't want to live.'

These words seemed to seal her doom. She looked at the helpless log of a man who had been reduced so low by shock and misery. Everything that was generous and fine in her nature came to the fore. Ruthlessly she stamped on the memory of Frey and all that she had meant to tell Trevor (that other Trevor who could take care of himself and make a new life). She couldn't be so low, so mean as to abandon him now. On his own admission, he would want to die without her. It was true that this accident meant the end of his career and his health and everything that made a man's life worthwhile. When she had vowed to marry him and love him for ever, and agreed to come out here to marry him, it was a vow that she could have broken only under the old conditions; not under these. She *must* stand by him today. He wanted her to.

'I expect you want to cry off,' he whispered.

She knelt beside him again.

'No, no, of course not. Nothing will induce me to leave you. How could I? You need me now more than ever.'

His eyes lit up. This time she found the relief and joy written in them pathetic.

'Oh, darling, you really mean it? Heavenly Andra. You won't walk out on me just because I'm a wreck now?'

She turned away so that he should not see what was written in her eyes. But she felt both agony and despair. She said:

'Of course, I won't walk out on you.'

'Do you mean you'll still marry me?' he asked eagerly.

'Of course. We won't give up hope. I'll take you to every specialist at home. We won't believe that you'll never walk again.'

'Oh Andra,' he said, 'you angel! You absolute saint! You give me courage again. If I know you are still going to be with me, I can survive. Oh Andra, do you love me enough for that?'

Her fingers twined in his, but she kept her face rigidly hidden against the pillow, away from him, and somehow managed to utter a muffled:

'*Yes.*'

10

The moment Frey saw Andra he knew that something terrible had happened. He was walking up and down the vestibule of the Mount Nelson Hotel waiting for her, as arranged. It was four o'clock. There were few people in the cool vestibule other than a drowsy-eyed clerk behind the reception bureau and two elderly women drinking tea. Frey wore grey flannels. Ashore he was no longer a sailor, just any good-looking Englishman with his tanned face and good figure, and the well-cut coat that spoke of London.

He was in a state of extraordinary excitement, with not the slightest doubt that Andra would keep her promise to break away from Trevor and that she would come to him. He was wholly in love and completely absorbed in the thought of Andra – the desire to build his future life around her. He had been going over in his mind every word that she had said, re-living the moments they had spent in each other's arms. More than once he had asked himself how he had ever thought it possible to exclude love and women from his life, and all the harm the Leonore had done to him in his youth had been melted away in the fire of this passion which had sprung up between Andra and himself.

As soon as she came into the hotel and drew near him his heart sank. She looked ill and drawn, not at all like the feverishly-happy girl he had left earlier.

She came quickly towards him and clung a moment to his arm with both her hands.

'Oh, Frey!'

'What on earth has happened?' he asked.

'Disaster,' she said.

At that word his heart sank still lower. He put an arm around her, caring little who saw him do so. They walked to a table half-concealed by an enormous palm. There they sat down. Abruptly Frey ordered tea and then lit a cigarette and handed it to Andra.

'What sort of disaster?' he demanded.

She told him. While he listened to her story his face seemed to freeze into deep hard lines. He listened without interruption. Then he said:

'This can't be true. *It can't.* I can't let you make such a frightful sacrifice.'

Andra spread out her hands in a gesture of despair.

'I don't see any way out of it, Frey. You can take it from me – speaking from the bottom of my heart – it's the last thing I want to do. I don't *want* to be tied to Trevor for the rest

170

of my life. It's not so easy to be a nurse to a man you don't feel more for than a sort of terrible pity.'

Frey cut the air with his hands as though slicing it away.

'I won't stand for it. I may be a so-and-so but no matter how sorry I am for this poor chap – and by God, I *am* sorry for him – I won't let you marry him and turn yourself into a ruddy sick attendant.'

'Frey, I've just got to go through with it. I've told you what he said. I think he'd try and put himself out if I deserted him now.'

'Then he's a coward and wrong – absolutely wrong – to try and hold on to you. And I say that with no ulterior motive. I'd say it if you told me you were in love with someone else – not me.'

'He did offer to release me.'

'Knowing that you wouldn't agree,' said Frey bitterly.

'I repeat – how *can* I? He needs me much more than he did before. Frey, I swear I'd have left him under any other circumstances and come to you, but I'd never be able to live with myself again if I walked out on him now. How could I ever take my happiness with you, remembering that poor log of a man lying there, feeling himself absolutely alone. What would you have thought of *him* if he'd walked out on me with another girl after I'd had such an accident?'

Frey thrust out his lower lip. He knew that she was right but he did not want to admit it. He saw the whole of his newfound joy slipping away from him in an avalanche. He couldn't stop it. He was filled with despair. And he resented the very idea of Andra heroically sticking to a paralysed man for the rest of her life. Dear God! She was so young. For her it meant a total exclusion of love, passion, laughter, all the years that she should be dancing and enjoying her youth.

He burst out:

'It's not fair on you. It's too much to ask.'

She kept repeating:

'I must stick to him, Frey.'

He kept arguing:

'It's monstrous of him to allow you to.'

Andra stared at the floor. She could only shrug her shoulders helplessly. In her heart she agreed with Frey. She could not control the contempt she had felt for Trevor's weakness. It all seemed like a nightmare in which she was still acting and living.

She had had a bad time with Trevor at the hospital. They had brought her some lunch there, to eat when he had his. She had tried, with a desperate gaiety, to cheer him up. He had clung to her pitifully. When at last she left him, saying that she was deadly tired and must go and rest, he had besought her to go back as soon as she could.

'You make me feel life is worth living

again. For God's sake don't stay away from me too long, darling.'

That was bad enough. And all through their meal he had been making plans for their wedding. A bedside affair to be performed by the Reverend Alistair Graeme in the hospital tomorrow. Then an ambulance would take them to *La Poinsetta,* the home which he had bought and prepared for her.

'I know it won't be much of a wedding for you, my poor girl,' he had said. 'I feel a hound for letting you go ahead with our plans, but if you love me I know you'll want to stay with me.'

Glorious, fantastic egotism. How it oozed from every pore of the man! It was almost unbearable. Yet she could not bring herself to deliver the *coup de grâce.*

Suddenly she put out a hand and caught one of Frey's. Her eyes were full of tears.

'Oh, help me, help me, Frey. It's hard enough *without* you trying to put me off doing what I think to be right.'

He kissed the hand that held his, his body shaking. He had never been so upset in his life.

'But I *don't* think it's the right thing, Andra.'

'You *couldn't* take me away this afternoon, remembering that man lying on his back there, completely helpless.'

'Yes, I could,' said Frey between his teeth.

'You don't mean that. You're much too kind and nice.'

'I'm an ordinary chap and I'm not built on heroic lines. You obviously are.'

'Now you're angry with me,' she said, and the tears began to roll down her cheeks so desolately that the sight of them tore his heart.

'Oh, my God, Andra, don't cry. That I can't stand. I love you madly. That's the trouble. I just can't tolerate the thought of letting you go out of my life and of your sacrificing yourself in this way. I don't want you to be a heroine, I want you to be human – like me.'

'I'm human enough. But I can't go against every bit of my conscience.'

'Can't we compromise? Can't you tell Trevor that you want to wait?'

'Wait for what? You mean just tell him that if he gets better I'll break with him and if he doesn't I won't. No! I've had a long talk with a man in charge of Trevor's case and he assures me he will never recover. I can't go into medical details. I don't understand it myself but he just never will walk again.'

Frey stubbed his cigarette-end on the tray. There was silence for a moment as the waiter brought the tea. After he had gone neither of them made any effort to lift the teapot. They avoided each other's eyes, both sunk in gloom.

After a moment Frey said:

'Well, if this is how you really feel I don't suppose I've any right to try and argue you out of it. I'm not a very fine fellow anyhow. I came in between you and him in the first place.'

Andra drew a long bitter sigh.

'Don't please be sorry about that. It wasn't that you came between us. What happened between us just *happened*. I obviously never really loved Trevor, then I found that I loved you, that's all.'

'I think you must love Trevor quite a lot to be prepared to turn yourself into a sick nurse for the rest of your days,' Frey said with a humourless laugh.

'Oh, darling, do try to understand that it isn't love as much as pity.'

'Didn't somebody write a famous book called *Beware of Pity?* He proved that it can be a dangerous thing. Don't forget that once you are tied to Trevor you'll *never* be able to get out of it. It's the sort of marriage a woman couldn't walk out on. An engagement's different.'

'In one way,' said Andra, 'but not in another. Trevor still believes that I came out here full of love and longing and I suppose in a way I'm still tied to him by all the vows I made. I was prepared to break them while I knew he had his work and his full life and could find another girl. But neither of us is in the same position now.'

Frey suddenly clenched both hands and knocked them against each other.

'It's bloody awful ... *bloody.*'

'I know it is. Oh God, I know it is,' she said and felt frantic with grief and pain. Her thoughts darted in and out, in and out and around this subject as they had been doing ever since she heard about Trevor's accident. *I'm caught,* she thought, *I'm caught like an animal in a cage and the cage is my own conscience. I don't know how I shall bear it and yet I think I'd feel worse if I ran away with Frey.*

They argued and discussed the thing again and again, wretchedly. The tea was never poured out. In the end, they got up and walked out into the sunshine. Frey said that he must get some air. Sweat was pouring down his face. With an arm through hers, tightly pressed to his side, they walked blindly along the long pinewood drive leading down to the city. They walked in silence, and then entered into the final stages of their hopeless discussion. Frey said:

'We seem to have talked this thing out from every angle and you always reach the same conclusion. You feel you've got to go through with the marriage.'

'Yes.'

'It's the most hellish thing that's ever happened to any human beings.'

176

'Yes,' she said woodenly.

'I'll never see you again after this, I suppose.'

'I shouldn't think so. What would be the use? It would only tear us in pieces and start the whole thing again.'

He looked down at her small strained face.

'Not only have I got to lose the wife I thought I'd found but think of her pushing a spinal chair for the rest of her life. That's pretty.'

'Oh, be quiet!' she said on a note of despair. 'You're only making things worse for me.'

'I know,' he said. 'I'm a selfish cynical devil but I love you so much that it's murder to me to be asked to give you up in this way.'

They were still walking. They came to the Gardens, brilliant with flowers. There were few people to be seen except the coloured gardeners. For a few moment they could lose themselves here and get away from the crowds.

They stopped and by mutual consent moved into each other's arms. They clung in a wordless embrace, an agony too deep for tears. Eyes closed, arms straining, they clung and clung. Every bone in Andra's body seemed to ache. She felt light-headed, dizzy with her grief.

'Oh, Frey, I don't want to leave you. You know that I love you. I swear I do. You believe that, don't you? You know, don't you, that I'm only saying goodbye to you because I've got to, or I'll feel cheap and cruel and ashamed of myself until I die.'

He covered her hair with kisses.

'I know that you love me but I think this sacrifice is too much.'

'Forgive me,' she wept bitterly, her face pressed against his shoulder.

'Don't ask that. You're the most wonderful person in the world. A hell of a lot of other women I know would have weakened and done what *they* wanted. I admire you even if I can't agree with what you're doing.'

'Forgive me,' she repeated, sobbing as though her heart would break.

He went on holding her, kissing her, trying to comfort her, finding little comfort himself.

He caressed her tenderly and frantically as though trying to remember every line of her face and form and all the scent and sweetness of her.

'Never to see you again – that's what kills me,' he kept muttering.

The tears dried on her lashes. She looked up at him with reddened eyes.

'Don't you agree that it would only be running us into danger if we go on meeting?'

'Oh, yes, if we've got to be all that holy.'

'Do you suggest we start a sort of clandestine affair once I'm married to Trevor?'

she asked with a bitter sort of laugh.

'Not quite that necessarily but I suppose I'm mean enough to wish I could see you and be with you sometimes. Haven't we got that much right? Can't we ask *that* much of life?'

'You know it wouldn't end with just meeting,' she said under her breath.

'You're damned right, it wouldn't, my darling.'

'And that wouldn't be very pretty, in the circumstances.'

'So you're determined to be very heroic indeed, Andra.'

'Oh Frey,' she said, 'would it bring us any happiness to do the other thing.'

'I can't bear the idea of not seeing you again,' he repeated sullenly.

She gave a sigh and passed a hand over his head.

'Darling, don't let's go on like this – it's killing me.'

'That goes for two of us.'

'Maybe we'll meet again somewhere, somehow.'

'And become beautiful friends?' he said roughly, ironically.

He knew that he was not being helpful – or anything approaching the world's conception of a 'fine fellow' – but he felt utterly unheroic, and he hated Trevor Goodwin. To him, Trevor was a monstrous barrier between himself and the woman he loved and who loved him. Maybe, he told himself with cynicism, this was retribution because he had tried in the first place to induce Andra to break her engagement.

'Perhaps we'd better not meet again, for the moment anyhow,' at length he muttered.

He felt Andra shiver. She looked so white, so ill, that he was suddenly wholly concerned for her suffering. He held her more tightly.

'My poor sweet. What a hell of a day you've had. Are you all right? You look grim.'

She gave a laugh, drew away from him and pulled a powder compact out of her bag, and a comb.

'I should think that's putting it mildly. I'll do something to my face then you'd better find a taxi. I must get back to Mrs Graeme's house. I'm staying there the night.'

'And tomorrow?'

'Don't ask.'

'Tomorrow you'll be marrying Mr Goodwin. What a mockery!'

Her teeth chattered. She had suffered so much mental anguish in these last few hours that she felt unable to accept any more. It was as though she were saturated in pain. Doggedly she powdered her nose and combed her hair. She wondered what Flack and the crowd at the studios at home would have thought if they could see her as she looked now. Years older – awful – she thought.

'Oh God,' said Frey. 'I'd made such lovely plans.'

'I don't want to hear them.'

'Oh my darling, my darling, will you be all right? Can you really go through with this?'

'I must.'

'If you feel you can't, will you let me know?'

'Yes, but I *will* go through with it. Once I'm back in the hospital with Trevor it'll be easier, because he's so absolutely dependent on me now.'

'Pretty ghastly thing for him,' muttered Frey, trying to turn his sympathies towards Trevor.

'Horrible. I just don't know what's going to happen except that I can see we'll probably go back to England together and try to find some specialist who'll do something for him.'

Frey took her arm. They began to walk slowly out of the Gardens back through the pinewoods and to the Mount Nelson where Frey told a porter to find a taxi. He drove with Andra for a short way. She sat back in her corner, exhausted, realising that she had been in Cape Town since early morning and hadn't really seen a thing in it. She had been in a daze. For a moment she held tightly on to Frey's hand.

They must be nearing the Reverend Alistair Graeme's house. It meant a long, long goodbye. Her courage threatened to fail her. When he kissed her again, she kissed him back, her hands locked around his neck.

'Oh, God, I wish I were dead, Frey!'

'If you feel like that – come with me,' he began, then corrected himself. 'No. You want to stick to Trevor. I won't be responsible for altering your decision. I must say I admire your guts. You're a wonderful person – even more wonderful than I imagined. I'll remember you until I die. You can believe me when I say there'll never be anybody else.'

She pulled away from him, silent, despairing, like a white ghost of his golden girl of the ship, he thought.

He took a card out of his wallet and pressed it into her hand.

'That address, the London offices of the Outspan Company, will always find me. *If* at any time you need me, you have only to send me a cable and I'll come to you.'

She shivered, and looked blindly at the card.

'It means a lot to me to know that, Frey,' she said dully, 'Thanks awfully. What will you do now?'

'Get back to the ship – out of this damn city as soon as I can. Thank God we're sailing on to Durban.'

'Don't you come back through Cape Town?'

'Yes, after we leave Port Elizabeth and East London.'

'Oh, God!' she said in a despairing voice. 'I don't want to think you'll be so near me again.'

He squeezed her hand.

'I shan't come ashore again. I shan't come near you. I'll try not to think about *us*.'

She closed her eyes.

He added:

'But I know I will, damn it, *damn it*. I'll think of you every moment and every day of my life. This is it,' he added as the car stopped. 'I've got to leave you here. All I can say is God help you, because you've got a hell of a task in front of you, darling.'

She choked.

'I'm sorry for what I've done to you, darling.'

'Don't worry about me. You made me very happy when we were on board.'

Now it was she who weakened and clung to him, the tears raining down her cheeks.

'Frey, *Frey...*'

'Stick it, if it's what you really want to do, darling,' he said gently, and helped her out of the car. 'But if you alter your decision – let me know.'

Those were his last words. And the last he

saw of Andra she was being welcomed into the house by Mrs Graeme. Then the door closed on her.

Frey told the driver to take him to a club he knew in Wynberg. There remained nothing more for him he thought, than to go and get drunk. Blind to the world. That way he wouldn't, perhaps, remember that Andra was going to make her heroic gesture and marry Trevor Goodwin tomorrow.

11

One morning in September – a cool day which made her think of England – Andra walked into her sitting room and began to arrange some tall lilies in a white jar that stood on a long low table opposite the fireplace. A log fire was burning. Andra sighed as she began to arrange her flowers, and when she stepped back to see them there was no pleasure on her face, only an indescribable fatigue and sadness.

Trevor was in the next room being dressed by a manservant. Soon he would be wheeled in here. He would expect her to try to interest and amuse him, which was now her daily task.

Every morning was the same. Trevor always in the long spinal chair, helpless – and without hope. He had been examined by several well-known South African doctors and any specialists from other countries who happened to be visiting Cape Town. The result was ever the same. No cure for him. Otherwise, his health was good. He was far too vigorous in his mind still, Andra often thought wryly; constantly making plans and unmaking them, perpetually complaining. It was always Andra who was the focus of the grievances. He had become exceedingly difficult, which she tried to accept because she knew what a terrible trial this complete inactivity and ruination of his physical life must be.

Every morning she would sit beside him either in here or on the verandah facing the garden, or play the piano to him, which he liked, or gossip about friends who came to see them. They had many friends. All Trevor's former associates either in the firm or outside it, had been very kind – deeply sorry for the once virile handsome young man and, perhaps, just as sorry for his beautiful famous wife.

Andra entertained for Trevor's sake because the more people who came here, the better he liked it. He could not bear to be alone or bored. Andra was not enough. And for that sometimes she was thankful, because she could leave him with a companion he liked and get away on her own out to the shops or for a walk, or sometimes a drive. Her greatest need was to be alone, as since the day of their marriage he insisted on her being with him day and night. She had to sleep in his room because he would wake and want to talk to her. He would apologise for disturbing her and explain away his selfishness with the plea that the grim hours when he couldn't sleep were unbearable, and that only she could charm and soothe him back to slumber.

He had become her child. She was his mother. They could never live together as husband and wife. There was no comfort for Andra. Trevor was interested only in himself. If he ever troubled to discuss her point of view, he expressed the opinion that she was doing a 'marvellous job', but added that it must make her very happy to do it. Once when one of his men friends had openly told him how lucky he was to have such a beautiful and devoted nurse, Trevor had laughed and answered:

'Oh, sure, but Andra likes looking after me. And she's lucky, too, because I might have been killed in that damned crash. She's still got me. That means a lot to her, doesn't it, darling?'

Andra had answered quietly:

'Of course.'

The head of Trevor's firm, Jack Felders, had been extraordinarily kind. He was a wealthy man. He had done everything that he could for Trevor. Money was no object. Handsome gifts of flowers, fruit, cigars, books and gramophone records were flown out from London to *La Poinsetta*. But yesterday, inevitably, there came the expected business letter from the Company telling Trevor that greatly though the firm regretted his loss, he had not been with them long enough to warrant them giving him a pension, but that they would continue to pay his salary for one year. A new manager had already been drafted into the firm.

How bitter this must be to the man who had worked so zealously to reach the top, Andra appreciated. When that letter had come, Trevor broke down and cried like a baby. Andra was getting used to seeing her big sun-tanned husband in tears. It no longer shocked her. She realised now that Trevor was weak and sentimental but at times even cruel, as so many people of his calibre can be. If he had to be bitter or exacting she was always the target. He had moods in which he flung reproaches at her relentlessly.

'You don't care whether I live or die. You can still get around and do everything you used to do. You're still Miss Andra Lee, the film star. You're not really Mrs Trevor Goodwin... *I'm* the martyr...'

He baited her until her patience broke. Once she turned on him and told him to be quiet.

'I've married you and I'm looking after you. Surely I can't do any more!' she flung at him during that battle of words.

Then he gave her a sly look out of the corners of his eyes and asked:

'Is it so hard for you? Can't your love

stand up to it? If *you'd* been the one to have the accident, I bet I wouldn't have found it hard to nurse you!'

She had wondered … but said nothing; merely shrugged her shoulders. Weeks of scenes with her husband were beginning to affect her nervous system. But she was always trying to harden up and take no notice of him. She kept telling herself that he didn't mean half he said. It was reaction after the shock of his accident. She must make allowances.

She did so until he drove her too far. At times she rushed out of the house. When she returned, she would find him remorseful, meek and ready to weep in her arms again.

'I'm a selfish brute. Don't leave me. Forgive me.'

Such appeals were now his stock-in-trade.

This morning as she finished doing the flowers and waiting for Trevor to join her, Andra allowed herself the rare luxury of thinking about Frey.

Oh God, she thought, how long it seemed since that terrible day when she had said goodbye to *Frey*. Only a couple of months but it was as though she had lived and died twice over since then. She had to smother the memory of him or break. It was too poignant. All that she had lost was too precious, and the burden of self-imposed sacrifice too heavy to be borne.

She had been glad when she heard that the *Outspan Queen* had sailed on to Port Elizabeth. Better to know Frey was miles away rather than here in Cape Town to torment her with his unseen presence. She knew of course, when the ship made the return journey, he would be all too near her again, but prayed that he would not come ashore. He had said that he wouldn't. She could not bear ever to see him again. Yet, having made her terrific gesture towards Trevor, she might even be tempted to run away. Life could be as perverse as that. While she was free she had felt she could not break with Trevor. Now that she was tied to him she longed perversely and bitterly to get away.

She received only one intimation that Frey remembered her, and that was the day after the *Outspan Queen* docked and sailed for England again. A spectacular bunch of red roses arrived from a local florist. With it, a card bearing the initials 'F.R.'. She tore the card in little bits and wept over the roses until her eyes were blind. She arranged them in her bedroom. Long after they had wilted she kept them. She could not bring herself to throw them away. When Trevor had asked who sent the roses she answered: 'Who knows? So many people send us flowers.'

He was content with that.

The memory of her wedding day was best not recalled, although at times, when she did think of it, it had almost a farcical side. It was all so different from the one she had imagined. Almost, she thought, it was like a judgment against her for having fallen in love with Frey.

Mr Graeme performed the wedding ceremony in the hospital. Doctors, nurses and friends gathered round the bed. Andra wore the lovely bridal dress of white lace which she had brought out, because Trevor wanted to see her as a bride 'in full regalia'. It made him feel better, he said. Mrs Graeme turned out to be a rock of refuge. Realising that there was something wrong with the bride, apart from the bridegroom's accident, the good woman had done her best to help the girl through the trying ceremony. At one time she had seen Andra's face go colourless. Mrs Graeme was afraid she was going to faint. She had taken one of Andra's cold trembling hands, pressed it and whispered:

'Courage, my dear. You are doing a fine thing. God will reward you.'

The kind homely words had buoyed Andra up but she had felt unchristian, because she did not believe that there could be a God to reward her. God did not care how much she loved Frey or that she was giving up everything that mattered for the injured man. She saw no use in prayer. She set her heart stubbornly against praying. When Trevor put the ring on her finger she had felt frozen, without emotion. When it was ended he drew her down and kissed her and told her how beautiful she was and what a difference she was making to his life. But her own life seemed to be over.

There had been more torture to follow. After the reception, the champagne, the cutting of the cake and all the kindliness and gaiety of their friends, came the ordeal of the night. She hated now to remember those long hours of lying beside Trevor while he caressed her and told her how much he loved her; how he had apologised because he could never be her real lover. She had been filled suddenly with disgust and with horror because of what she had done.

There had been tears from him even on that wedding night, for he broke down. She stopped hating him and stroked his cheek and kissed him back and whispered to him that she would never leave him. There were other things in the world for them than physical passion, she told him. And all her passion had died – when Frey left her. She knew that.

'But we'll never be able to have children,' Trevor groaned.

'I don't want children,' she had said truthfully.

She didn't. She wanted no child of his. She wanted no close intimacy with Trevor. The whole of her belonged to Frey even though she would never see him again.

Yesterday she had had a long letter from her mother full of the usual gossip about home and father; details of the petty life her mother usually led. It had ended with a paragraph of greater praise than Mrs Lee generally awarded her daughter.

Daddy and I are overcome by the splendid way you have behaved. When I first heard your terrible news I was afraid you might break with that poor boy, but you have done the right thing and I know that God Almighty will reward you...

Another one promising a reward from God. Andra remained bitter and inconsolable. She almost preferred the typically cynical note she had had from Flack Sankey:

By the mother of all living, now you've gone and done it [he had written]. *I thought you were crazy to give up your career and go out to this chap, but to marry him under these circumstances is sheer lunacy. It's a diabolical fate for anyone as young and lovely as you are. Why did you have to do it, Andra? We're all shaken, but I think your action is misplaced virtue. I can only say I admire your nobility, but it kills me, honey. It's murder! Still – che sera sera, and if times get bad and you need money, the old studios would have you back any time. Remember that.*

She did remember those words, frequently. She did not show the letter to Trevor. She had no wish to hurt his feelings, but she told him what Flack had said about the film world wanting her back. Trevor at once declared that he wouldn't leave South Africa and his friends.

'Who the hell wants a dreary wet winter in England and me cooped up in some ghastly London flat!' he had grunted. 'No. We'll stay out here in the sun where we can get servants, as long as the money lasts. I've got some saved up.'

She did not argue for the moment but she knew perfectly well that the time must come when Trevor would have to face up to facts. They couldn't go on living like millionaires in Cape Town. Everything was far too expensive and neither Trevor's savings nor Mr Felders' generosity would cover them much longer. Trevor's half-sister had written to say that her home was open to him at any time that he needed a roof, but she had her school, and her own life, just as Andra's parents had theirs. No, Andra knew that one day she would have to go back to the films and work for the two of them.

She began to feel desperately homesick and longed to go home. Originally she had come out to South Africa believing that she would find great happiness. Instead she had touched bottomless sorrow. She longed on this grey morning in Africa for a grey day in London. She thought wistfully of her penthouse; of Rose Penham coming in to take letters, and of Flack arranging a new contract for her. She needed badly to work and get her mind off Trevor and her marriage.

It *could* have been so perfect out here – with Frey.

(Oh Frey, of the blue, blue eyes, with the tang of the salt sea in your hair and on your cheek and the hardness of your hands pressing me against you. Oh Frey whom I love and will love till I die, where are you now?)

Andra broke her heart during those first two months as Trevor Goodwin's wife. But she steeled herself to be cheerful outwardly and to fit in with Trevor's wishes.

As the white-robed African boy wheeled in the now familiar spinal chair, she went, smiling, to meet Trevor. Without the slightest feeling she looked at him lying there against his cushions, freshly shaven, dark hair smoothly brushed, hands immaculate, and one of his favourite cheroots between his lips. He was still so very handsome. Still the romantic-looking Trevor around whose carriage the Cape Town girls clustered, ready to coo over him and to flirt and flatter him.

'Isn't he marvellous, Mrs Goodwin?'

'Doesn't he look wonderful?'

'Isn't he good and patient and brave?'

'It must be such a joy to you to be able to look after him.'

These were the sort of things they said to her.

Andra busied herself for a moment or two doing the things that he asked. A fresh box of cigars to be opened. The boy to be sent for another box of matches and cursed because there wasn't one in the room. Trevor was always cursing the black boys, which upset Andra because she found them cheerful, willing, amiable creatures and they were obviously terrified of the man who dominated them from his sick couch. He did so at times with the overbearing arrogance of an old-fashioned slave-owner. Sometimes Andra told Trevor dryly that he would not be able to speak to an English domestic in that way or he'd find himself without help. Trevor laughed and said that he didn't intend to return to England anyhow.

He grumbled this morning because there was no sun. He grumbled because the couple who had been dining with them tonight had put them off because their child was ill and the mother didn't want to leave it. He found a loose shirt button and asked Andra to sew it on. She did so, her lips curved in a dry half-amused, half-cynical smile. She wasn't any good at mending. She wasn't, really, a very good housewife, she often admitted it. She was better at the artistic things. And bit by bit there burned deeply into her consciousness the sad conclusion that she would never have made the right wife for Trevor even if he had been as fit as he used to be before his accident.

How could she possibly have made such a mistake? She often asked herself that question but received no answer. Sometimes – all too often – such things happened. Men and women got married believing it to be the real thing and found too late that it wasn't. Trevor's immense conceit kept him from learning the truth about his wife's feelings towards him. Perhaps, being a born actress, she acted too well, she would tell herself with bitter irony, and he really did imagine she enjoyed her rôle of nurse and companion.

This morning, once they were settled, he surprised her by admitting for the first time that they couldn't go on living this way at *La Poinsetta*.

Looking out at the luxurious green of the palm trees, biting on his cheroot, Trevor said that they would 'have to do something drastic or go broke'.

'I was awake half the night thinking over the firm's letter. They're a stingy lot at Felders, I must say.'

'I wouldn't have said so,' was Andra reply. 'I think they've been very good to us.'

'Well the fact remains that I can't work any more and that we're getting through the money.'

'I still have some,' she said. 'I haven't touched that big money I made after my last film.'

'Oh I can't expect my wife to keep me,' said Trevor in a lordly fashion, but she saw him looking at her out of the corner of his eyes in a way she had grown to dislike – it was somehow so mean and sly. She knew that she was expected to tell him that it would be her pride and joy to spend her money on him. She said quietly:

'We're married, Trevor, so whatever I have can be shared. But I'd like you to know that I don't intend to sit here in Cape Town and wait until all my money is spent just on entertaining friends.'

'Well, what do you expect me to do – lie here and moulder?' he grunted.

'I don't think you should moulder, as you call it, as you've got me.'

He turned a critical eye on her now. For once he allowed himself to think in terms of Andra's well-being rather than his own. In his utterly selfish way, he was devoted to her and could not bear her out of his sight – it always gave him a tremendous kick to remember that one of England's famous film stars had given up her career to stay with him. He was even genuine in his gratitude. But it was not in his shallow nature to set his own desires aside and give Andra a chance to live as she should live. He accepted all her sacrifices as voraciously as a starving dog accepts a bone.

'You look a bit washed out,' he said suddenly. 'Feeling all right?'

She shrugged her shoulders. She knew from her mirror that she looked much too thin and hollow-eyed.

'I don't know that this climate really suits me and I don't think I've really recovered from my appendix operation yet. I seem to have no energy.'

Trevor slapped a hand on both his useless legs, twisting his lips bitterly.

'I wish I had as much in *these.*'

'Poor Trevor!'

'Yes, poor Trevor. And aren't I sick of it. Look here, Andra, I've always set my heart against leaving South Africa because it really is my home but I wonder if I wouldn't be wise to let you take me to England.'

A sudden light sprang into her eyes. She felt at once less apathetic.

'Do you mean that, Trevor?'

'You don't really like it here, do you?' he asked rather sulkily.

'Everybody's been very kind and I think the sun and the country – what I've seen of it – is splendid, but despite all the domestic problems and the bad weather at home, I prefer England. Besides, my work is there. I know I said I'd give it up to marry you but I think circumstances have changed so much that I can't afford to stay out of work.'

And now she drew her chair nearer to his spinal carriage and with a flush of excitement on her cheeks began to talk with an enthusiasm which she had not shown or felt for a long time.

'There are two good reasons for going back, Trevor. First and foremost, you could see all the best specialists in London. Secondly, I can get back to films and make big money. I want that, not so much for myself as for you. Life's very hard for you.'

'You bet it is,' he interrupted, grunting.

'You need money, more now than ever. You want things made easy and to have a good valet attendant, and perhaps we can find some sort of treatment that will do you good in spite of all that they say out here.'

Suddenly he put out a hand and took hers and kissed the palms, his restless eyes devouring her.

'Oh, angel, if only we could hit on the right person to cure me. If only there was some hope of my walking again, and of being the sort of husband that I long to be.'

She shivered but her lips smiled.

'There's always a chance. Anyhow, you

agree that I must start earning the bread-and-butter?'

'I've always been dead against it but I suppose I'll have to stand aside now.'

'Why be so against it?'

'It'll take you away from me. I'll be left with some damn'd servant.'

'I'll be home a great deal – I can spend all my spare time with you.'

'You're frightfully good to me,' he said, and for the first time since she married him he added: 'I often think I ought never to have let you go through with our wedding.'

She pulled away from him, moved to the glass doors that opened on to the verandah and opened them, letting the air touch her cheeks for a moment. The shadow of Frey and of the love she had renounced, fell across her and for a moment obliterated everything else. Then she turned and said:

'Please let's go back to England, Trevor. Let me work again.'

He gave her what was meant to be a teasing smile as he looked at the stump end of his cheroot.

'So anxious to get away from me?'

'That's it,' she teased back, lightly.

'Well, if we go, we'll go by boat.'

'Yes, the sea voyage wouldn't do you any harm. We'd get a man to wheel you around and you're a good sailor. You'd hate flying, I know.'

He warmed to her enthusiasm.

'Yes – I'll sell this place and get quite a bit back on it and all the things inside it.'

She looked around her indifferently. There would be little she would miss. Some of the nice china and glass and books that she had brought out with her, she could ship back. Trevor had furnished *La Poinsetta* with the help of a good interior decorator and it was all beautiful but meant nothing to her. Never at any time had she felt it to be *home*.

'We'll find something good in London,' she said eagerly. 'I can write to my old secretary, Rose Penham, who I know would always come back to me. She said so. She could find us a flat on the ground-floor, so that there wouldn't be any stairs for you and you could be wheeled in and out. We'll go to all the big men in Harley Street. I wouldn't start work until I'd been to them all with you – until we'd exhausted every possibility of helping you, Trevor.'

Trevor looked less gloomy and peevish than usual. He spoke on a cheerful note.

'Sounds all right to me, darling. Chuck me that morning paper and let me look at the shipping. I can always get a good cabin through Felders. Jack is particularly friendly with the Outspan Line.'

She handed him the paper and while Trevor examined it, began to walk up and down the lounge, thinking with a growing enthusiasm of the return to London and all her own relatives and personal friends. It would be nice not to have to feel homesick as well as deeply unhappy, and the mad rush of the film studios would certainly leave her less time for thought than she had out here, sitting beside Trevor.

Frey? She wouldn't see Frey. He had told her that he rarely went to London. When he was at home he was more often in Southampton and the New Forest than anywhere.

Suddenly Trevor said:

'Here's the very thing. You said that ship you came out on – the *Outspan Queen* – was a beauty. Well, she's calling at Cape Town on the return voyage to England at the end of this month. I'll book a double cabin in that.'

She swung round, face suddenly paler, her eyes startled.

'No. No, not on the *Outspan Queen*.'

Trevor took his cheroot out of his mouth and stared at her.

'Why ever not? You said you had a marvellous voyage. She doesn't roll and she's newish.'

'All the same, I don't want to go back on the *Outspan Queen*.'

She found difficulty in explaining when Trevor persisted. Her heart beat fast. Her lips felt dry. Under no circumstances would she go back on Frey's ship. She could not bear that. It would be like tearing open a wound that was still a long way from being healed.

She stammered that there was something about the ship that she didn't particularly like. Trevor then shrugged his shoulders, examined the list again and suggested they tried to get on to one of the slightly older ships, *Outspan Star*. That had a good reputation, too, he said. When Jack Felders had had an operation a year ago, he had taken his wife back home on leave and sailed in the *Star*. Trevor had met the Captain. Rather a nice chap.

'Get me on to the office, darling, and I'll have a word with Bill McIlroy who does all the firm's booking. I'll see if he can get us lined up for a really good state cabin on the *Outspan Star*. It sails in a month's time.'

Relief brought the colour back to Andra's cheeks. She drew a long breath. The moment of fear, of danger, had passed. She left Trevor talking to McIlroy and walked out into the garden, hugging her arms across her breast, shivering a little with nerves and the coolness of the wind. It was a really bad day for Cape Town. The air was full of dust and everything was dry. They were wanting rain badly. Mummy had said in her last letter that it was dry in England too – they had had the longest, warmest summer on record and with an astonishingly small rainfall. The leaves were coming off the trees fast. It would be October when they got back, thought Andra. But the mere idea of autumn in Hyde Park, of the sight and sound of London, and the end of her exile out here, filled her with warmth. A warmth in which her thoughts of Frey played no part. She could not see *him*. She was Mrs Trevor Goodwin ... the loneliest woman in the world.

Trevor called her back.

'I think it'll be all right. Bill can pull strings. He'll ring later on tonight and let us know.'

When that long day ended, Andra was told by Trevor that a *cabin-de-luxe* on the top deck had been arranged for them on the *Outspan Star*. It would leave Cape Town on the fourth of October.

She discussed the voyage with Trevor during their evening meal, her eyes full of the old sparkle.

'I'm really thrilled,' she exclaimed.

She sat, as usual, beside him. He had been wheeled next to her at the table, and it always softened her heart towards him to see him eating like this, propped against the pillows, instead of sitting where he should have been, in a chair on the other side of the table. Yet, with a guilty pang at her heart, she had to remind herself that had he been capable of sitting there, *she* wouldn't be here. She would have been somewhere else

– with Frey.

'I hope we aren't making a mistake,' she heard Trevor remark as he ate the curry which the South African cook made so well. 'I shall miss a lot out here.'

'I'll try to make it up to you for it,' she said, and gave him a very appealing smile.

He looked at her through his long, rather girlish lashes.

'Why were you so dead set against going back on the *Queen*? I can't quite fathom that. I only hope the *Star* doesn't roll. These new ones are so much better.'

The light went out of her eyes and the laughter from her lips. She grew suddenly secretive and stubborn.

'I just didn't want to go on the *Queen*,' she said staring at her plate. 'Don't nag me, Trevor.'

'Sorry, I'm sure,' he said in an offended voice.

After dinner they sat in the lounge and played 'Scrabble', a game which neither of them particularly liked but which passed the time for Trevor.

The fact that he had renewed the subject of the *Outspan Queen* had driven the smiles from Andra's face for good and all that night. She felt ill-at-ease and went to bed, her heart aching rather more acutely than usual.

She felt nervous until the house had been

sold and they were all packed up and the last preparations made.

Then came the day of sailing.

A feeling of relief gripped Andra when she was on board leaning over the rails, watching the port of Cape Town fade slowly from view. Goodbye to the fabulous beauty of Table Mountain, the big straggling town where from the very first she had said farewell to all happiness.

Everyone had been kind. She and Trevor had been given a wonderful send-off. Farewell gifts were showered upon the invalid, and Mrs Graeme had almost wept – unemotional though the Scotswoman was – when she took her leave of Andra.

'You're a sweet wee thing and I shall be sorry not to see you any more,' she said when they parted.

'You've been very good to me, Mrs Graeme, and I do hope one day you'll come to England and see us,' Andra had replied.

'Well, you're making a wonderful job of things against heavy odds, my dear,' Mrs Graeme added. 'Stick to it, won't you?'

'Yes,' Andra had answered.

What else was there to do but 'stick to it', she asked herself bitterly.

She went down to her cabin to unpack, leaving Trevor where he wanted to be – in the bar. He had found a special attendant for the voyage, the last of the extravagances to come out of his own money. A medical student capable of acting as his attendant, happened to be travelling home on this particular ship; he was only too willing to pick up a few extra pounds towards his fare.

Inevitably, Andra thought of the day she had landed at Cape Town; of that *other* voyage – that magical heavenly trip out here with Frey. All the excitement and wonder of stolen love. All the breathless thrill of deciding to break with Trevor and marry Frey. Now, reduced to *this*.

She had written to Flack. A cable, typical of the man, had just been handed to her.

Will meet boat stop glory hallelujah we're getting you back stop a star travelling on The Star stop new contract already in hand stop delighted stop
Flack

A new contract already, for Andra Lee. That, at least, meant money and all that could be done with it for poor Trevor.

She went upstairs meaning to join her husband in the bar. He had told her that he wanted to speak to the ship's Commander – by name, James Lyle, if she could contact him. Trevor was quite sure of receiving extra attention and favours because Captain Lyle was a personal friend of Jack Felders. That's how Felders got their state cabin at the last moment.

With a pang in her heart, Andra wondered what the social officer – the Staff Captain on this ship – would be like. Would she sit at his table or the Commander's? It didn't matter. Nothing would be the same in the *Outspan Star* as it had been in that *other*, with Frey.

She came across a deck-steward and signalled to him.

'Could you take this to Captain Lyle for me?' she said, drawing out a letter that Trevor had scribbled. A note from him would work wonders, he was sure, he had told her. The fact that he was no longer manager of Felders and was now of no importance at all had not yet struck home to him.

The steward took the note and smiled at the young woman whom he privately called 'a smasher'. So slim and graceful, such beautiful hair and wonderful eyes. He thought he knew her face but didn't for the moment connect her with the famous *Andra Lee*.

Now he looked at the name written on the envelope, then up at Andra again, awkwardly.

'Miss … madam … I think there's some mistake. This is addressed to Captain Lyle.'

'Isn't he commanding this ship?'

'He did once, Miss, but he died suddenly – a heart-attack – about two or three weeks ago, in East London. He was put ashore there.'

'Oh, dear,' said Andra. 'I'm frightfully sorry. My husband *will* be upset.'

'Yes, madam, we all were. It was very unexpected and he was a very nice gentleman – we all respected him.'

'Then who is in his place? Nobody warned us.'

'I don't think many people knew about the change. It was such a last moment affair, Miss. The new Captain's a youngish chap. It's his first ship, actually. It was all arranged very hasty-like, before we left East London. He was on another ship as a Staff Officer, at the time.'

'What is his name, steward?'

'Rowland. Captain Frey Rowland, madam. Funny name – like, spelt F.R.E.Y.'

For a moment Andra felt as though something had hit her straight between the eyes. She could see stars. She choked. Unbelievingly, she stared at the steward.

'Captain Frey Rowland?'

'Yes, madam,' the steward grinned. 'Bit of a smasher – South African tennis champion last year, madam, and as good as a professional with his camera. We're showing some of his films of wild animals on board. I'd better give you this letter back, hadn't I, madam?'

Andra's fingers clutched at Trevor's note

which the steward held out to her. Her heart beat wildly. She was alive again ... deliriously alive. *Frey was Captain of this ship.* He had been given the command that he had always wanted. He had been out there on the South Africa run just at the right time when they needed to replace a man who had died. They could get another P.R.O. easily enough, but not a Commander. Frey had his Master's Ticket. So Frey was taking this ship home.

(Oh God, thought Andra, does he know that I'm here? Has he seen the passenger list yet?)

She had so firmly set her mind against travelling back on the *Outspan Queen* because she did not want to run into Frey. Her shoulders began to shake with hysterical laughter. What jesting fate had organised such an ironic situation?

She, Andra, had so cheerfully encouraged Trevor to travel with her in the *Outspan Star. And Frey, himself, commanded it.*

12

The steward looked at Andra a trifle curiously. She pulled herself together.

'Don't worry about the note. I ... I'll be seeing the Captain tomorrow, if not tonight,' she said and turned away from the man's inquisitive gaze.

She found Trevor lying in his chair in the bar. Trevor, with a light plaid rug over his legs, smoking the inevitable cigar. He had already found amusement. A couple of teenage Australian girls with very short skirts and sweaters and long, flying hair sat on either side of the handsome invalid. Andra could hear their voices:

'We'll come and talk to you lots, won't we, Carol?'

'I think it's terribly romantic – at least *you* look romantic...' *(Giggles.)*

And Trevor's self-satisfied voice saying:

'I assure you, my sweets, it's damnably *un*romantic for me having to lie here like this but it helps to know that two such lovely girls are aboard to cheer me up. Tell me everything...'

They started to tell him their names and describe their background, and how they were taking their first trip to England. Andra decided that she wasn't needed and gratefully walked away again.

As though drawn by a magnet she walked to the foot of the shining steps that led up to the bridge. Her face was still without colour. Her heart beat at an uncommon speed. She still could not believe that Frey was actually up on that bridge, watching while his ship moved steadily out to sea.

Behind her, life went on...

The sun-deck was crowded. The young and vigorous had already started to play games. The camera-enthusiasts were busy taking final snapshots.

Andra could hear the drift of laughter and conversation – all familiar to her now. The *Outspan Star* was not as new or luxurious, perhaps, as the *Queen,* but built on the same lines. If she wanted, Andra thought, she could no doubt have what other women would call 'a good time' during this voyage, because she was an ex-film star and still young and beautiful; and the very fact that her husband was paralysed would bring her plenty of sympathy. Other men anxious to amuse her. But her whole heart was up *there* on that bridge. She felt half-mad with excitement – and with dread.

She had to drag herself away and try to think of her husband. It wasn't possible for Trevor to be taken down every time to the dining salon, so it was arranged that a steward should take his food on a tray for him into the bar. He could easily be wheeled in there as it was on the same deck as the state cabin which the Goodwins occupied.

Andra had lunch alone. Not, this time, with the *Staff* Captain – a nice, chubby-faced young officer whom she saw gathering his particular passengers around him – but at the Commander's table. Totally fascinated, her eyes rested on his empty chair, which she knew would not be filled while the ship was still so near to land. She would have to wait until tonight before she saw Frey. He must know she was on board, she thought. He must have seen the passenger list. How had *he* taken this rather savage jest on the part of destiny?

She worked herself up into such a state of nerves that her head began to throb violently. After lunch she felt in need of rest. At least life was going to be a little easier for her with Trevor in the hands of young Brian Horne, the medical student now in charge of the invalid. Trevor had already begun to put on a big act for the world – he was smiling, charming, so *very* brave; winning everyone's admiration. It was only when Andra was with him that he dropped the mask and seemed to want to whine and show himself as he really was.

'If I could only walk and get around as you

do! I suppose *you'll* be necking with every Tom, Dick and Harry, and *I'll* not be able to watch you,' was one of his remarks when she joined him for coffee after lunch.

To this she replied with a short laugh:

'I should have thought you knew I have no use for what you call "necking", Trevor. Neither need you take it for granted that Tom, Dick *or* Harry will want to neck with me.'

Then he patted her hand in a lordly way.

'Oh, have a good time by all means. I don't mind, darling. You're so good to me and I'm such a burden.'

This was her cue. She had learned to take it.

'You're no burden, Trevor – I'm glad to be of help.'

'Nuisance about the old Captain – if James Lyle hadn't died it might have made things a bit more attractive for us. Who's the new fellow?'

Andra answered stonily:

'Captain Rowland. He was actually Staff Captain on the *Outspan Queen,* the one I came over in.'

Disinterested, Trevor waved this aside and told her to go and find young Horne to wheel him out on deck where he could lie in the sun for a bit.

'I've got a couple of cuties from Melbourne to amuse me,' he told Andra, with a laugh that set her on edge.

It was such a *self-satisfied* laugh. Even his accident had not taken away Trevor's smug conceit.

Andra was thankful to be alone in their cabin for a while. Rather an elegant, luxury suite had been booked by Trevor's firm. Panelled in smooth mahogany, twin beds with gold satin covers and eiderdowns, writing desk, two good portholes framed by turquoise curtains. Turquoise-tiled bathroom.

The huge bouquet of pink roses on the desk had been sent by Jack Felders. Andra could imagine Jack ordering those flowers and saying to the others in the firm:

'That's *that*. We've seen the last of poor old Goodwin and his wife. Done our stuff!'

Now it was up to her to do *hers,* she supposed, and lay down on one of the beds. Lacing her hands behind her head, she shut her eyes.

'Why, why?' Her overwrought, tired brain kept asking the question. '*Why* didn't I realise what it was going to be like living with Trevor, and how much Frey would continue to mean to me?'

He had become bigger than life-size lately, completely dominating her mind. All her physical self yearned towards him.

She was jittering with nerves by the time that first long day at sea ended. While she changed, Trevor sat surrounded by his new-found admirers and sympathisers in the bar, drinking. Andra was afraid he was going to drink too much on this voyage. The doctor had warned him that it wasn't good for him to over-eat or take too much alcohol. He had to be careful. The effect of the accident had left a strained heart and his blood pressure was high.

Andra changed into a plain white crêpe dress that made her skin look a rich brown. Her eyes were almost too big these days for her thin face. She had lost nearly a stone. That wouldn't please her London doctor. He had wanted her to put on weight. Her arms and legs were much too thin. She wondered if Frey would notice.

Then came the pulsating moment when she walked into the salon and found him already sitting there at his table. She felt sick – even a little faint – as he glanced in her direction. He got up slowly, crushing his table-napkin in his hand.

As though in a dream, she drew closer to the tall, well-remembered figure in the white uniform, unchanged save for those extra broad stripes of his promotion. She summoned all her acting capabilities. She held out her hand and spoke to him gaily.

'How do you do, Captain Rowland? How marvellous to find an old friend command-ing this ship.'

'How are you?' said Frey, and had barely touched her fingers with his before he dropped them, as though they burned. For the fraction of a second their gaze met fully. She looked up into those blue eyes which stared so eagerly down into hers, and her heart seemed to lose a beat.

'How are you, Mrs Goodwin?' he repeated stiffly.' Please do sit down. I see you've been put on my left. Let me introduce you to Lady Comber, on my right...'

Now as they both took their seats, Frey made the other formal introductions between Andra and those whom she had not already met. Most of them had been down to lunch – with the exception of Sir Alan and Lady Cromer, who were 'V.I.P.s' coming from Johannesburg, and a bishop who was travelling back from Natal.

Lady Comber, who was in her fifties and still quite attractive, and had herself been on the stage, showed considerable interest in the lovely film star.

'Thrilling to find *you* on board. I do so admire your work. I hope we are going to see another film from you soon, Miss Lee.'

'Yes,' said Andra quietly. 'I'm going home to do some work.'

Frey, who had been toying with a piece of fish which he didn't seem to want, looked up at Andra quickly now. He said:

'I thought you'd given up your career ...

Mrs Goodwin.'

She controlled her breathing. Her slender hands, holding the menu, shook slightly, showing Frey that Andra was not feeling as cool as she pretended to be outwardly.

'Yes, I thought I'd said good bye to my career, Captain Rowland, but circumstances have altered. Owing to my husband's accident he can't work, so I must.'

The bishop intervened.

'We were all so sorry to hear about your poor young husband, Mrs Goodwin. A very courageous soul – I had a few words with him just now.'

'And *so* attractive,' added Lady Comber.

'Thank you,' said Andra, and lowered her lashes, intensely aware that Frey was watching her.

All through that meal she was aware of him. She was thankful that he talked a great deal to the Combers, but now and again, when he turned to her, she felt as though a tidal wave poured over her defenceless head and swallowed her up, and that she was drowning. She kept having to extricate herself and attempt to breathe normally again.

Once Frey managed to whisper under his breath:

'Why in God's name did you come on this ship?'

'I didn't know,' she whispered back. 'Surely you must realise I didn't know. I deliberately avoided the *Outspan Queen*. So ironic.'

'You can imagine my feelings when I saw your name on the list.'

'I know what *my* feelings have been!'

'I must see you alone for a moment, Andra.'

'Is it wise?'

'No, of course not,' was his answer, followed by a terse laugh, 'but we must meet and talk. Come up on the bridge after coffee. I'll be on the look-out for you. I have my own sitting room attached to my cabin. We can have a drink and a cigarette there.'

She turned now and looked fully at him, a surge of the wildest happiness which she had no right to feel, flowing over her. But it was a glorious sensation. She came to life after long weeks of icy repression and despair.

'All right,' she uttered the words in a fatalistic way, 'I'll be there.'

Immediately afterwards she felt qualms about going. It would be madness – wrong to Trevor. But she was only human. Flesh and blood could not stand *this;* and she was no saint. She didn't pretend to be one, in spite of her quixotic marriage.

After dinner she found it hard to get away from Trevor. His 'Melbourne cuties', as he called them, had met two boys of their own age and were dancing. A bachelor on board, who had met Trevor occasionally in South Africa, volunteered a desultory game of cards with him, but Trevor wanted his wife at his side this evening.

'I haven't seen much of you all day,' he grumbled.

She had finished her coffee. She was mad with impatience to go up on the bridge. She said:

'What do you want me to do, Trevor?'

'Just stick around,' he said.

'Have a brandy, Mrs Goodwin,' said Trevor's acquaintance, who had introduced himself as Erroll Copeland. He worked for an import and export firm in Durban.

'No, thank you,' she said.

Trevor looked at Andra gloomily. He was beginning to notice the fact that she was restless and that her eyes held a feverish expression.

'Aren't you well?' he grumbled.

'I'm quite all right, thank you,' she said, getting up. 'But I need some fresh air, if you don't mind. It's so hot in here.'

Trevor looked resentfully after the beautiful white-clad figure as Andra moved towards the door.

'You might remember I've *got* to stay here, I can't come out with you,' he called after her.

Copeland now looked a trifle embarrassed, and cast a not very admiring glance at the man in the long chair. Sorry though he was for Goodwin, he thought this sort of thing was a bit 'off side'. Mrs Goodwin was a damned lovely girl, and deserved a better fate than being tied to a helpless so-and-so.

Andra, having escaped, put a pale blue cardigan over her shoulders, and walked quickly to the bridge. She had felt stifled in that bar with Trevor. She had felt for the first time since her marriage that she was really and truly imprisoned; as though there were two iron fetters around both her ankles, dragging her back. But now brain and conscience ceased to act. She was all woman, torn with hopeless longing as she walked on to the bridge. She collided with the tall figure of Frey Rowland. He was standing there, waiting for her, his legs slightly apart, his hands doubled behind his back. He moved forward to meet her.

Without speaking, they joined hands and walked together into Frey's quarters. The door shut behind them. Andra took one quick look around the small well-equipped room with its built-in furniture. The shelves were filled with Frey's familiar books, and his hi-fi was there of course, with his records. It was a better cabin than the one the Staff Captain had occupied on the *Queen*. The important-looking desk was covered in papers. There was a portable radio and the intercom from which the Captain could issue his orders throughout the ship. A half-opened door beyond showed the inner cabin, its wood-panelled bed and locker built into the wall.

Frey put his cap on the desk. Breathing fast, he held out his arms.

Andra took a split, scared glance over one shoulder.

Impatiently, Frey said:

'Don't worry. Nobody will come in here. Nobody dares, unless I ring. In any case my steward would think nothing of you being here. The passengers often come up to see me. Surely you remember how the Commander on the *Queen* used to entertain?'

She nodded. The next moment, with a little cry, she was in his arms and he was crushing her against him, his lips hard, urgent against her mouth.

It was a long time before either of them spoke. They stood there with straining arms and lips, giving and receiving endless kisses. At last Frey lifted his head.

'You don't know how badly I needed this.'

'So did I,' she breathed. Her cheeks were red and her eyes enormous with excitement. Just for those few moments she had given herself up entirely to the delirious joy of being in Frey's arms again. He stroked her hair and her cheeks and her slender neck and kissed both her hands from wrists to fingertips. At last he drew her to a little built-in leather-covered seat under a porthole, which opened out to the sea. A dark, violet sea tonight, bejewelled by the light of a full moon.

Now Andra and Frey began to talk rapidly, arms still around each other, fingers feverishly entwining.

'This is stupendous – fate!' said Frey, 'and I don't care whether it's right or wrong. I'm crazy about you and I always shall be.'

'And I am about you. It's been ghastly – the silence between us. I thought I'd lost you.'

'Never for a moment. I found it hard to stop remembering you and every little thing about you.'

'I don't know how I've endured my life.'

He put her away from him and looked long and anxiously down at her.

'You've got some colour now but it doesn't deceive me. You're frightfully thin and there are hollows in your throat. You don't look as well as you were when you sailed out with me to Cape Town in the summer.'

'I was afraid you'd notice. I haven't been very happy,' she admitted.

'I want to know everything. Have you regretted taking the step you took? No, don't look away from me. Look into my eyes and answer me truthfully.'

But she shook her head and turned from him, struggling with the desire to cry.

'I suppose I did wrong and attempted the

impossible. Obviously I'm not very happy, except that my conscience is clear and I did what I felt to be the right thing.'

'But I told you it was wrong at the time. No one has any right to make such a personal sacrifice. Those gestures should be left to religious martyrs – fanatics who want to die for their ideals – or political principles. But you're just a woman – a tender-hearted darling little thing – and you had no right to take on such a load, even for a paralysed man.'

'Oh, Frey–' she began, but he interrupted roughly.

'No, I refuse to be asked to share your heroism. I'm just a man in love with you. I'm sorry for Goodwin and I'll go on being sorry for him but not as sorry as I am now for you – or for myself!'

She gripped both his hard brown hands and held them against her hot cheeks, looking up at him in a despairing way.

'I suppose you're right, but at the time I didn't feel I could walk out on Trevor.'

'Tell me about it. How's it going? Is he good to you? Is he grateful?'

'Yes,' she said with a flicker of the lashes that did not escape Frey's penetrating gaze. He muttered:

'I bet the poor wretched chap is damned irritable and makes your life a hell.'

She sighed.

'That's putting it a bit strongly, but I have to admit Trevor gets irritable, only one can't be surprised, considering all he has to put up with. His life is ruined.'

'I wouldn't think so if I had you beside me, my dear.'

'But, you see, you'd never have allowed me to marry you, in the circumstances,' she said with a brief laugh.

'No, I wouldn't, and that's what I hold against Goodwin.'

She let go of his hands.

'It's too late – it's done. It can't be undone now.'

'Why are you on this ship?'

She explained and counter-questioned him.

'How did you come to get this command?'

'Poor old Lyle's death caught the Company on the hop and I was the only fellow with a Master's Certificate near at hand, so they took me off the strength of the *Queen* and told me to bring this tub home. It was a bit of a thrill – the only thing that made life worth living for me, without you.'

She forced herself to come back to earth and face reality. He knew how unhappy she was. It filled him with impotent anger. He got up and walked to the desk, took two cigarettes out of the box, lit one for her and smoked the other.

'God, what a mess, darling!'

'Yes,' she said, 'but now I've got over the shock of finding you on board it's rather marvellous to be here with you.'

'And you're going to go on coming up here to see me,' he said grimly. 'I'm not going to have you making big heroic gestures and sacrifices during *these* two weeks. They may be the only two weeks we'll ever have together. You say you're going back into films. You'll soon be swallowed up by the studios and your home-life with your husband, and I'm told there's every likelihood of my keeping command of this ship. So I'll be busy, too.'

'You'll like that,' she whispered.

He leaned out of one of the portholes and let the cool air blow in on his cheeks. He felt hot and his throat was dry.

'I don't like anything now that I can't have you. That's a fact.'

'Oh, darling, it's a fact with me, too. I don't enjoy anything any more.'

'Except holding this egotistical invalid's hand.'

'Oh, *darling!* Don't be horrible. I can't bear it.'

He turned back, put his cigarette in an ash-tray, sat beside her again and drew her into his arms.

'It's sheer bloody misery that makes me so horrible. I love you more than I ever thought it possible to love any woman. The thought that you're wearing this' – he tapped her wedding ring – 'just about drives me round the bend.'

'It's no good,' she said, clasping him with both arms and pressing her cheek to his heart. 'What's done can't be undone now. Trevor will be my ... sort of ... child and responsibility until one of us dies. Let you and I just take these days together – yes, let's have them. I won't be heroic. I'll rush up here whenever you tell me I can come.'

'Thank you,' said Frey. His face worked and for a few moments he held and kissed Andra as though his life depended on it.

Time rushed by. She became aware of the fact that it was growing late and that she had been away from Trevor for over an hour. She stood up and straightened her dress and her hair.

'I must go. I don't want Trevor to start being suspicious, or life won't be worth living.'

'I suppose I'll have to meet him,' said Frey darkly.

'Yes, of course. And be as nice to him as you can. Remember how grim his condition is.'

'I'll try to remember it, Andra, but all the time I only feel that he's the barrier between us.'

'I built up that barrier myself, so blame me,' she said, with one of her long, sad sighs.

He held her close.

'Good night, my darling angel. It's been heaven having you here for a while. I don't see why you shouldn't come up every night for an hour, and occasionally during the afternoon. I'll send the Tiger with a message if I'm able to see you – not a written one – I'll just tell him to find you and give it you by word of mouth. He's a discreet little chap and I think he'll know better than to issue the invitation in front of the husband.'

Now her natural sense of humour brought a smile to her lips. Her eyes teased him.

'Is that what all captains of ships are like? Do they always take their lady-friends away from their husbands and inveigle them up to their cabins?'

Frey smiled back.

'I daresay some do, my sweet, but this one had no intention of doing any such thing, I assure you. I meant to throw the usual cocktail party and have some of the V.I.P.s to tea, but no lone women in *my* life.'

'You've changed since you were a Staff Captain, darling.'

'Yes, I've changed out of all recognition. I know it. I don't seem to belong to myself any more, but only to you. And it's been like that since I first met you.'

She listened to this with ecstatic happiness mixed with a sorrow almost too great to be endured. With a last look and a 'good night' she turned and descended the steep staircase and made her way into her own cabin. As expected, she found Trevor had already been put to bed by his attendant. He lay reading a copy of the *Investors' Chronicle* which he flung aside as she came into the room. His handsome face looked sulky and unsmiling.

'You've been the hell of a time, Andra. I thought you'd chucked yourself overboard.'

She avoided looking at him.

'Don't be silly. Why should I?'

'Well, where the hell have you been?'

'Talking to various people, including the Captain…'

She uttered the lie and the truth together, despising herself but knowing that it was necessary. If she was going to snatch these few blissful days in Frey's company, she would have to deceive Trevor, but if he didn't know, how could it hurt him? she argued inwardly. Surely life owed her *that* much happiness, surely she had sacrificed enough for Trevor?

'Well, you might have considered me and remembered that I'd be lying here alone,' began Trevor and enlarged on this theme until he had worked himself into a state of resentment and reproach which, curiously enough, had little effect on her this evening. The colour had left her face. She felt exhausted. She longed only to get to her bed and turn out the light, lie in the darkness and remember Frey. As she vanished into the bathroom carrying her nightgown and wrapper, Trevor called after her:

'Haven't you anything to say to me?'

She called back:

'Not if you're going to be so horrid. I left you in the bar with that Mr Copeland and I thought you were going to play poker.'

'So I did but I started to lose money and I can't afford it now. I can't do anything I like any more. Someone lent me this Stock Exchange literature but it isn't even any good my trying to size up the market and consider my stocks and shares. I can't afford to take risks now I've got so little capital left. You don't suppose I want to live on my wife, do you–?'

'Oh, what does it matter?' Wearily she came back from the bathroom, climbed into her own bed, and punched the pillow.

He turned his dark-fringed eyes upon her. She thought, as she always did, what wonderful eyes they were, in their way. How she had once admired his looks and how utterly wrong she had been about his character, mistaking his dominant personality for fineness and strength when under the façade there lay only the weakness of the bully.

He continued alternately to whine and reproach until at last she snapped:

'Do stop nagging me, Trevor. Let's go to sleep.'

'You don't care whether I live or die–' he began.

Oh God, she thought, I hope he doesn't weep now or I'll really go mad and rush out of the cabin and chuck myself overboard!

But in the end she was where he wanted her to be – seated on the edge of his bed, holding his hand, stroking his hair, comforting, flattering, trying to build up a future in his imagination.

'You know I'll look after you, Trevor. You know I've got Flack's cable here about work and that I'll be able to afford to do all kinds of things for you, and for myself, so that you can play with your own bit of capital and enjoy it. You know...' She broke off. She could not bring herself to utter the ultimate lie and say *'I love you'* (those searing words that she had just said to another man up there on the bridge). She added lamely: 'You know I'm devoted to you and will always look after you, but please don't tie me down to the minute and the hour. Let me have a little freedom if I want it.'

He drew away from her, sulking again.

'By all means. I can't stop you walking off any time you want, but I would have thought you'd prefer to stay beside me.'

On that note she switched off the light over her bed and remained silent. Trevor then switched off his light.

The finale was painfully familiar to her. He apologised.

'Afraid I'm pretty bloody to you, poor little Andra. My smash has upset my whole nature and I don't mind admitting it. But I'm truly grateful to you for looking after me. Thanks a lot.'

That was her cue.

'You know I do it willingly for you, Trevor. Good night, my dear.'

'Good night, darling. And remember I couldn't do without my wonderful little wife.'

She lay there in the darkness holding herself rigid, gritting her teeth, wondering how many nights of her life she'd have to endure this sort of conversation and put up with Trevor's difficult moods. She thought of that man upstairs, her darling Frey, Captain of this ship, lying alone in *his* bunk (remembering her, no doubt). She thought of the whole agonising situation and of her part in bringing it about. Suddenly she prayed, desperately:

'God, don't let me feel too sorry that I married Trevor, and forgive me if I go and see Frey every day, *while I can…*!'

13

It was an unforgettable fortnight for Andra.

By the time the ship reached Las Palmas she had grown almost used to the difficulties of dividing her time between her husband and her lover.

She had even grown accustomed to the moral aspect. Those stolen hours with Frey were always wonderful and thrilling. The ecstasy was so sharp that it resembled sometimes the knife-edge of pain. She went to him, glowing like a young girl. She left him, a woman with heavy heart, under an almost unbearable burden of unhappiness and responsibility. But the moments spent with Frey were worthwhile. Andra's main complaint was that the fourteen days and nights were passing far too rapidly. Before they knew where they were they had reached the last lap of the voyage. The sea grew colder and rougher and as the weather worsened, Trevor grew more fractious and exacting – nagging perpetually at his wife. The magic of moonlight and warm sun was left far behind them now. But the magic for Andra was still to be found up in the Captain's cabin. As she told him, it was like 'coming home' every time she went through his doorway. His room was the only place in which she found happiness or peace.

Sometimes their meetings were not easy … the Commander of any ship was essentially a busy man. When she had to stay away from that bridge which held such fatal attraction for her she had to try to be patient and wait for the next invitation to come from him. It was usually brought to her by his steward, the nice little 'Tiger' who was, as Frey had said, discreet and sympathetic; aware, no doubt, that there was 'something up' between his commander and the beautiful girl who was married to that chap in the spinal chair.

Towards the end of the voyage Trevor was getting less sympathy from the other passengers. It was now directed mainly towards his wife. It was obvious that Mr Goodwin was a bully and that the lovely Andra was both patient and long-suffering.

Of course Frey had had to meet and talk to Trevor. They met on several occasions. Andra had felt singularly embarrassed when the two men first shook hands. She could see that Frey positively bristled … that he didn't take to Trevor. She supposed she could not expect him to, although he was polite enough and sat talking and smoking a cigar with Trevor until he could reasonably make his escape. But when she saw Frey that night he told her frankly that he found Trevor antipathetic.

'I think he takes full advantage of the position between you and he does far too much grousing.'

Andra had to admit that was so. Alternatively, when she next spoke alone to her husband, he criticised Frey.

'I find your pet Captain snooty and stand-offish – too big for his boots.'

'I can't think why. He is far from being "snooty",' protested Andra.

'Well I wouldn't call him good fun.'

Andra said coldly:

'When Frey was Staff Captain on the *Outspan Queen* he was considered *great* fun. He has responsibilities now that he commands a ship.'

'H'm, did you see the way he put his tongue in his cheek when I told him that joke? Barely a laugh out of him.'

'If you mean that beastly joke you keep telling everybody, I'm not surprised Captain Rowland didn't like it. I've told you before, Trevor, that it should be kept for the chaps and not repeated in front of women.'

She could not tolerate Trevor's 'funny stories' which always seemed to her slightly coarse and she knew that Frey had objected to that particular one because she was present.

'He might be old-fashioned, but that's the

way he happens to feel about women,' she told Trevor.

He flung her a sly look.

'I believe you're a bit keen on this Captain fellow. I saw the way you looked at him.'

She could not restrain the colour from flooding her face and throat.

'Oh, don't be so silly!'

'Well, where do you go all the time you're away from me?' he went on. 'Walking alone around the deck or gossiping with Lady Comber or do you nip up and drink gin with the noble Captain?'

If he hit the target she made no sign of it but stared beyond him, her lips mutinous. She was not going to be made ashamed of what she was doing. She was *not*. After a moment Trevor relaxed into a laugh.

'You needn't look so cross, honey. Here I am lying like a log – I suppose I must expect my wife to be unfaithful to me.'

Now she swung round on him, her eyes ablaze.

'*Do* you expect it? Is that what you think of me?'

'Oh don't take me so seriously.'

'I'd like to know,' said Andra, 'what you really feel about fidelity. Should a wife in my position go to her grave never knowing the meaning of physical passion, or should she be forgiven for seeking it outside her home?'

Now Trevor gave Andra an uneasy look.

He frowned.

'You *are* taking me up on this! Am I to understand that you want a lover?'

'I didn't say so but I want to know how *you* would feel about it.'

They were in the bar. It was the evening before they were due to dock at Southampton. Trevor had already finished two drinks and ordered another in spite of Andra telling him repeatedly that it was doctor's orders that he should cut down alcohol and cigars. But he kept saying that they were the only joys he had left in life and insisted on indulging himself.

Now he gave an unpleasant laugh.

'Well if we're being serious, my dear, I *will* tell you. You'll never have *my* permission to be unfaithful to me and I think any woman in your shoes would be a bitch to betray her husband.'

Andra turned away and bit her lips until the blood came. Her hands were trembling. Unwilling to continue this dangerous conversation she walked out of the bar and up on deck. So that was it. Trevor's egotism and selfishness carried him as far as that. He had no understanding and no humanity. He was in his rights, of course. Yes, he had every right to expect fidelity so far as the words of the marriage service went. She had vowed fidelity. Yet one might have thought a bigger man – a kinder one – might have told his wife to consider herself free in the physical sense. He might have felt he was taking enough by accepting her whole life's services, and, as was going to be the case with Andra, her money, as well. He might at least have offered her emotional freedom.

Andra leaned over the rails and hid her burning face in her hands. *Was she a bitch?* She didn't want to be one. Fate had forced her into this position. This voyage had been too strong for her and for Frey. Yet during all the hours she spent in his arms she had never once given herself to him wholly. Her deep innate sense of decency had forbidden that. Frey, himself, had never asked it. That was one of the most wonderful things about him. Better not, he had said, right from the start.

'If you sleep with me I know I shall never be able to let you go again,' he had said.

But when she thought of Trevor, his petty tyranny and lack of consideration, she wondered bitterly why she had not in truth become the 'bitch' of his imagination.

Of course while she dressed for dinner, Trevor apologised for using the word and announced that he knew perfectly well she was faithful and would never walk out on him. He tried once more to be charming – to win the tenderness and approbation from her which he wanted.

With every nerve in her body crying out

against him, she smiled and told him to forget their differences.

'Of course you'll be right on top tomorrow once you get back to your film-fans,' said Trevor gaily. 'Read me that cable that came from Sankey, again.'

She took the cable out of her bag and read it aloud, trying to concentrate on Flack's final message. A long, wordy cable, typical of the verbose extravagant agent.

Rose meeting you Southampton with ambulance for husband stop taken short lease ground-floor flat Queens Gate suitable for invalid stop longing see you
    Flack.

'I've felt better ever since you got that,' announced Trevor, 'it's nice to know we've a home waiting for us. Decent of this fellow to go to so much trouble.'

'The fellow you once spoke of so rudely and said you wouldn't see in Cape Town,' Andra reminded him.

She was rather shocked at her own bitterness. She really mustn't let misfortune turn her into a shrew, she reflected. She never had been one and unless she was going to make a good job of her marriage, nothing would have been worthwhile.

But when she thought of the flat in Queens Gate and her future life with Trevor,

240

her heart sank to its lowest ebb. Oh God, tonight was her last on board! Tomorrow would mean goodbye to Frey again and to all hope of happiness. For the second time she must leave him. This time it would be worse. She had got to know him so much more intimately. They had become so close. She knew now how absolutely 'one' they were in all their likes and dislikes. Frey was not only the perfect lover but, when they forgot their misery for a while, a marvellous companion. They laughed at the same jokes. They seemed to anticipate each other's wishes.

Sometimes in the evenings when she was with him, he played her the records that they both loved. Often he would give her a book to take away and read and the next day she would discuss it with him. When her head ached, he could smooth the pain away. When she needed his passion, his arms and lips were ready and eager, and when she was utterly tired and depressed, he willingly sat quietly with an arm around her, giving her the quiet comfort and reassurance which she needed.

But it was all coming to an end. This would be their last night together.

She had done wrong to see so much of him, perhaps, but, at least she hoped she had behaved with the utmost discretion and Trevor had not suffered.

Tonight there was to be a party. It was the last night on board. A special dinner, and dancing in the ballroom. These were the sort of times when her heart went out to her husband. She took little part in such festivities but sat firmly beside his spinal carriage, knowing how much he had once loved to dance, and how grim it must be for him.

The moment came when the ship's Captain – in the dark-blue uniform which the officers wore at this time of the year – came and asked her to dance. Afterwards, Frey explained that he did this because he supposed that Trevor might think it peculiar if he didn't. He danced with most of the other women.

It was Trevor who persuaded Andra to accept Frey's invitation. But she knew that later that night he would complain about it and taunt her.

The ship's orchestra was playing a waltz. Frey held Andra apart from him, stiffly, formally; all eyes were watching them. His lips moved:

'Oh, my dear darling ... you waltz so beautifully and I love you so much.'

She answered:

'And I love you. It's marvellous dancing with you.'

He looked at her. She wore a dress of midnight-blue satin, cut in the new long sheath-like line. It made her look incredibly slim. Her skin was delicate, and her eyes so beautiful as she looked up at him that his senses swam a little.

'You're a lovely thing,' he said huskily. 'I don't know what in God's name I'm going to do without you.'

'Go on with your work and your life – as I will,' she breathed.

The music stopped. They stood and clapped mechanically. Andra could sense her husband's gaze on her. He was watching them. Heaven alone knew what ugly thoughts were crowding in his distorted mind. She said:

'I must go back to Trevor. Please take me.'

'But you'll come up to me later?'

'Yes.'

'When?'

'How long will you have to stay down here and dance?'

'Oh, I shall get away before eleven.'

'I'm going to do something I've never done before,' she whispered. 'I'm going to wait until Trevor is asleep, then come to you. He generally has a sleeping pill and sleeps pretty soundly for the first couple of hours. I'll put on slacks and a jersey and slip up to you then – if you think it safe.'

'It'll be safe enough for me. I'll let the officer-of-the-watch know I don't want to be disturbed.'

243

'Goodbye for now...'

'Swear you'll come...'

For a moment, under the long sweep of her lashes, her eyes shone up into his.

'I shan't be able to help it.'

He took her to her husband, gave a formal little bow, wished Trevor a good night, and went in search of another partner.

Trevor snorted.

'Not in a very good mood, your Captain.'

'Why call him *mine?*' she said feeling intensely nervous and irritated.

'Oh, I've been watching you carefully tonight, my dear. You two were fairly eating each other up during that waltz.'

Now for it, she thought. Always a price must be paid for any happiness that one snatched illicitly. She supposed this was only fair and tried to be patient while Trevor went on nagging her.

'I'm beginning to believe you had some sort of link-up with that fellow on the other ship. I don't like it. It's damned mean to me ... in my condition...'

On and on, until her nerves stretched like fine wires, threatened to snap at the final twang.

At last she got up, her whole body trembling.

'I'm going to bed, if that's all you want to say. Horne will bring you down later.'

'No, I'll come with you,' began Trevor,

then added: 'No, I won't. I see somebody a little more interested in me than you are, coming over to talk to me. I'll stay and talk to *her.*'

The 'her' was one of the young Australian girls who had fussed round Trevor for the first half of the voyage but who had not seen so much of him lately. She was quite a fetching little thing with long blonde hair. She wore high heels and black silk stockings. She had had rather a lot of champagne and was feeling full of *bonhomie* and well disposed towards the handsome invalid. She sat down beside him, took one of his hands, and looked up at Andra through her heavily-mascara'd lashes.

'Poor lamb! He can't dance. Shall I sit here and cheer him up, Mrs Goodwin?'

'By all means do,' said Andra, with a tight smile.

'Very sweet of you, dear,' said Trevor, 'and just what I need. My wife's been beastly to me.'

Pale and taut, Andra walked away. In her cabin she sat down on the bed. She trembled with cold and nerves. She buried her face against the pillow and thought:

Tomorrow, my real life with Trevor starts and it will always be like this. After tonight I shan't see my beloved Frey any more.

How long would it be before Horne brought Trevor down and she could change and slip up to the Captain's cabin? Supposing Trevor didn't take his sleeping pill, and she couldn't get away? Supposing she couldn't have this last feverish hour or two with Frey?

She beat both fists against her pillow. She felt helpless and desperate. Her tears began to scorch the pillow-case. Her body shook with weeping. For a moment she gave way completely to grief and despair.

She had reached the rock-bottom of misery by the time Horne wheeled Trevor into the cabin. She had realised from the start of this voyage that it would be awkward for them both because there were not two separate cabins left on this ship. She was always disturbed when Trevor came to bed later than herself. Now that she heard him coming, she got up quickly and taking slacks and a jersey, shut herself in the bathroom and changed. By the time Trevor was in bed and Horne had gone, Andra had mastered her feelings. Pale and taut, she faced her husband and asked him if he wanted anything other than his sleeping pill.

He had drunk far too much champagne and was red in the face and noisy.

'Take your damned pills away, it's only one's wife who wants to put one to sleep. My cuties prefer me wide awake...' (He laughed.)

'This wife is quite willing to disappear

altogether if you can't be more co-operative,' said Andra tersely.

He grimaced at her.

'Very shirty tonight, aren't you?'

'It's midnight and I'm tired.'

'Heaven knows why. You don't do anything all day.'

She shut her eyes and dug her hands hard into her pockets.

'Listen, Trevor – if you play me up tonight, I shall just walk out and *stay out,* even if I have to sleep on deck and catch pneumonia.'

He stared at her then laughed again and yawned.

'Oh go to hell, and give me my pill.'

'I opened the gateway to hell the day I married you,' she said, voicing her feelings for the first time. She was bitterly angry and wretched and could not altogether control herself.

Trevor's handsome face was now a study in astonishment. In his vast conceit he had never for an instant imagined that Andra felt this way about him. He was always so sure that his fatal fascination would ensure that no woman would ever leave him.

'I say! I say! You *are* in a temper. Jealous of those blonde babes? You needn't be, duckie. I was only fooling around. Surely you don't begrudge me a little fun.'

She clasped her hands together behind her

back, the nails digging into her palms. The perspiration pearled on her forehead. She had all she could do not to tell him the truth; tell him, too, that she was going to leave him tomorrow and let Grace look after him in Bexhill. She looked so unlike herself that Trevor felt suddenly uneasy. He stretched out a hand.

'Don't be jealous, darling. There's absolutely no need to be. I swear it.'

She gave an unnatural laugh. She was at breaking point. God, *God,* how little he knew her state of mind. Jealous! She didn't care if every woman on the ship monopolised him.

Trevor spoke again, his face assuming its mournful be-sorry-for-me expression.

'Come here, duckie, and say you're not too cross. I know I've stayed up late and had too much fizz. But it's all I can do to keep cheerful. Surely you realise how ghastly it is for me to know that I am such a poor husband to you, darling.'

'You're not sorry for me, only for your-self–' the words were choked from her before she could restrain them.

He looked ludicrously amazed.

'Andra!'

'Well you are – always sorry for yourself, never really for me.'

'Why should I be sorry for you?' he whined. 'When I come to think about it, I

248

know I can never be a one hundred per cent husband to you, unless we find a miracle man in Harley Street; but you've got your two legs and the ability to work and earn money and all the things I've lost. Aren't *I* the one who deserves the pity?'

'Yes, yes,' she said, closing her eyes.

'Of course,' he went on in an offended voice, 'if you're going to start being sorry you married me, I shall quite understand. I'm not the fine chap I was when you were first so madly in love with me.'

That hit her. Sick to death though she was of his ghastly selfishness, she could still feel some kind of loyalty to the man she had once loved. What sense was there now in stirring up mud? She was never going to see Frey again after tomorrow. Why not try to make the best of what was facing her? Poor Trevor … poor devil … he was certainly in a pitiable condition, evocative of sympathy, whatever else she felt towards him.

Her natural generosity and kindness prevailed. She ran forward, dropped on one knee by the bed, took one of his hands, and laid her cheek against it.

'Oh Trevor, Trevor, I don't want to quarrel with you. I don't want us to be unhappy like this.'

The man lay still for a moment. He could feel the wetness of her tears against his palm. He was touched and suddenly ashamed of himself, facing the fact that Andra must indeed have made an enormous sacrifice by going through with their marriage. He had no right to nag or bully or torment her. Now he pulled her against him and began to caress her. Although she did not look at him, she knew that he, too, was crying, those easy unmanly tears which always filled her with contempt.

'There, there, I've been a brute, Andra. Sorry, darling. Forgive me. I owe you everything in the world and I look like having to owe you a lot more. Let's be friends again let's love each other. We can, even if I'm a useless hunk of a man. Kiss me, Andra ... come closer... Say you aren't sorry you married me or I'll put myself out.'

She kept her face hidden. The old suicide threat!... Despicable, but it never failed. And even if she despised this man she could not remain unaware of his wretched fate. She didn't want to kiss him but she let him kiss her. For a moment they stayed close.

'Of course I'll never leave you, Trevor. I'll always look after you.'

'You haven't stopped loving me?' he asked anxiously.

For his sake she forced the lie.

'No.' Then hastily she added, 'Now do take your tablet and try to sleep, Trevor.'

He sniffed.

'Hand me a handkerchief, darling. I'm a

great baby, aren't I? And you're my darling little motherkin.'

She gave him the handkerchief, feeling sick.

He took his sleeping tablet with a glass of Vichy water.

'You are an angel and I do love you,' he said. 'I'll try to be nicer. It's only this miserable accident that's made me so disagreeable.'

'I understand,' she said.

She could see the clock on the table between the beds. Half-past twelve. Frey had been waiting for her for an hour. She thought:

Dear life, surely I won't be discredited in heaven if I take these last few moments with him.

'Come and lie down on the outside of the bed and let me go to sleep holding on to you,' Trevor wheedled her.

She lay down beside him, praying for patience, for the moral strength to go through with this thing.

At long last Trevor slept and his arm dropped away from her.

She switched off the light and slipped out of the cabin feeling guilty and miserable but appalled by the thought of the long future with this husband of hers. Thank heavens dear Rose Penham was going to meet them at Southampton and there would be Flack in London, and all the old theatre friends, and her parents. Some kind of life to help her forget the catastrophic mistake she had made.

When at last she was in Frey's cabin, she sobbed in his arms. He was deeply concerned. She looked so utterly exhausted and ill.

'What's been going on? My poor little love … my poor sweet…!'

His sensitive hands smoothed the hair back from her hot tear-stained face. He switched off the lamp, knowing she would be grateful for the darkness. She could hardly speak. She just clung to him and he felt her slim body trembling violently.

Later he made her drink a few sips of brandy.

'You're all in, darling. This is frightful. What's been going on?'

'Nothing,' she said and pressed her face against his shoulder, 'nothing except that *he* was a little more difficult than usual and that tomorrow you'll be gone.'

Frey's face hardened into granite lines. He set his teeth.

'God, I feel bitter against life for doing this to us,' he said.

'I'm to blame. I know I oughtn't to have married Trevor.'

'Don't let's waste time going into that one all over again. Just let's ask ourselves whether we've got to renounce this love of ours completely. Why shouldn't we meet from time to time?'

'You know we decided that we couldn't. I'd only break my marriage vows completely and our meetings would never be satisfactory. Each time, it would be harder for us to part. I just don't want to be tempted to run out on Trevor, even with you.'

'But I can't stand the idea of what you've got to go through alone for the next umpteen years.'

She drew a long bitter sigh.

'I'll get used to it, no doubt, and my work will help, and perhaps it'll be easier when I *can't* see you. That's why I want the break to be final, Frey.'

'What a damnable prospect!'

'Oh, Frey, *Frey!...*'

A little wildly she flung her arms around his neck and pulling him down to her kissed his lips again and again.

'I love you, Frey, more than anything in the world and I always will.'

'That goes for me too, darling. And what I said to you in Cape Town holds good. You can always get a message to me through the Company. Whenever you want me I'll come to you.'

'That's a very wonderful thought but I shall try not to send for you, Frey.'

'You're too strong-minded for me,' he

said, trying to laugh, pressing one of her hands against his cheek, 'you're a very good little thing really, you know.'

'I wouldn't be up here if I was all that good,' she said with a grimace, 'but I do believe that if you take on a job like marriage you've got to try and stand by it. Particularly in my case.'

'So you won't even let me see you sometimes?'

'Frey, don't tempt me,' she said, agonised. 'Okay, okay...'

He lifted her right up in his arms. She was far too light and fragile. The fact worried him. For the first time, he carried her through into that inner room and laid her on his bed. The tiny light in the headboard lit up her pale, tear-stained face. Her lipstick was smudged. There was nothing glamorous about Andra at this moment but to Frey she remained desirable and beautiful. He felt a deep tenderness that transcended passion. He took a handful of the lovely reddish hair, pulled it down about her neck, kissed it, and ruffled the silken tendrils around her ears. Then he covered her with his eiderdown, bent over her and whispered:

'I want to remember you like this ... on my pillow.'

The tears welled into her eyes.

'You're terribly sweet to me. I'm afraid I've made you very unhappy.'

'We won't go into that. Any unhappiness has been worthwhile, Andra.'

'Lie down beside me,' she whispered.

He did so, and switched off the light. They lay there in the darkness with their arms around each other, cheek to cheek. For Andra it was an hour of exquisite peace and happiness. Somehow, even though she knew that ethically she was doing wrong, she could not feel any sense of sin. It seemed somehow right here with Frey – so much more right than when she lay beside her husband.

Exhausted, she fell asleep in Frey's arms.

The man did not sleep. Through the shadows he watched Andra, ruminating bitterly on the cruelty of the fate that prevented him from marrying this woman. He wanted to remember every detail about her face and form; her perfume, her young touching defencelessness which roused all his chivalry and kept passion under restraint.

The ship ploughed on. The man commanding it heard the clang of bells and knew that it would soon be dawn. He could not let her stay. Reluctantly he woke her up.

'I'm desperately sorry, darling, but I think you should go down while it's still dark.'

She felt stiff and tired but the warmth of his body under the rug and that hour of sleep had given her warmth and strength. She clung to him for a moment wordlessly.

They kissed long and deeply. Then he switched on the light. She stood a moment on tip toe, yawning. She put her arms around his neck, blinking drowsily up into the blueness of his eyes.

'*You* look worn out, my darling...'

'I've got the rest of my life to sleep in,' he said grimly. 'I wasn't going to miss a second of you.'

She was past crying now, almost past feeling. She was conscious only of deadly fatigue.

'Don't let's say good bye. Just let me go,' she whispered.

'God bless you, my darling,' he said.

'God bless *you*,' she said, then turned and walked out of the cabin.

The stars were still shining crystalline, pure, unpitying, she thought – winking up there in the vast canopy of the sky. The sea air blew against her, making her shiver. It was very much colder now. In a few hours time they would be steaming down the English coast.

She had left her captain there alone. He would always be alone, so he had told her, with only the memory of her to sustain him.

When she recalled the gay young Staff Officer who had danced, argued, laughed and made love to her on the *Outspan Queen*, and all their hopes and plans, her heart seemed to break in two.

She let herself noiselessly into her own cabin. Trevor was sound asleep, lying on his back, snoring.

Without undressing, Andra lay down on her own bed and hid her face against the pillow in a fresh agony of grief.

PART III

14

One grey cold afternoon in November when a blustering wind tore through the trees in the park, stripping these of their last dry brown leaves, Andra walked out of the Albert Gate and down the broad road that led to her flat.

She wore a short tweed skirt and a hip-length suède coat with a big fur collar. A scarf was tied around her head. On a lead followed a small golden long-haired *dachshund,* who went by the name of Trigger. Trigger was a sweet and intelligent little animal who had become a great pet and quite an absurd source of consolation to Andra since her return to England. A week after her arrival, he had appeared, wearing a large bow on his blue collar and with a label which said:

I am Trigger. I want to be loved and I will love you.

Nobody seemed to know who had sent him. Rose Penham denied all knowledge. All she knew was that she opened the door one morning to a strange woman who said she was a dog-breeder and had been asked to deliver this dachshund pup to Miss Lee as a present.

Trevor immediately suggested that the animal should be sent away, but Andra had snatched up the silky little body, pressed her cheek against it, looked down into two trustful golden eyes and *known* who had given Trigger to her. She could be certain. For there flashed suddenly through her memory a conversation that she had once had with Frey Rowland on the *Outspan Star*. They had decided that they both adored animals but that neither had ever had the opportunity to make a home for one. Frey had then asked Andra what sort of a dog she liked and she had told him how her mother once owned a long-haired dachshund when she, Andra, was still a little girl. Nobody had really cared for the dog except Andra, who had become passionately attached to it. She had been miserable when it died. She had always wanted another dog of the same kind but her mother did not like animals in the house. They made too much work, she said. So Andra was refused her pet.

'One day *I'll* give you a dog, darling,' Frey had told Andra with sympathy.

He was always wanting to give her something. It was quite obvious to her now that Trigger had been sent by Frey. Henceforth the little dog would be a link with him.

Certainly during these last two months Trigger had done quite a lot to comfort Andra. He was an enchanting little dog with great character and had eyes only for her from the moment she gathered him up in her arms.

The maisonette the Goodwins had rented had a small back garden and this made things easy for Andra. Trigger went with her everywhere, even to the studios when she started work on a new film. At this time of day, on her way home Andra liked to exercise him in the park. Despite himself, Trevor too became attached to the gay, affectionate animal and Trigger sometimes condescended to lie on Trevor's spinal carriage and be caressed by his master.

This afternoon Andra felt cold and tired. She was all too often tired these days. She knew that she needed to put on weight. She did not eat enough, and she smoked too much. She tried to cut down cigarettes and improve her appetite but never seemed to want her meals.

Flack – big business man that he was, and Andra's genuine devotee – had plunged her into hard work as soon as she came back. She was booked for a new film which was to be shot in a studio near London almost at once. The subject was a young girl in love with a married man. Andra took the part of this girl – an innocent, adolescent type attracted by a charming man twice her age.

The latter's part was played by a popular British film star. He was a good actor and in private life a charming person.

Andra got on well with him. She liked her part. There was one scene in which she was torn away from her lover by her father and lawyer. She played it with such desperate urgency and passion that her producer became wildly excited. He kissed her on both cheeks in front of the whole studio and announced that this was going to be the part of her life, and *make* the film.

'You just *lived* that part, darling!' he exclaimed rapturously. 'What a gal!'

She had thought:

'I played it well because I know what it means to be torn away from the one I love. It might have been Frey and me.'

They called the film *The Unlit Fire*. The story of a mature man's effort to light a fire in the heart of an inexperienced girl. Having ignited it, he leaves her. Therein lay the difference, Andra thought, when she compared fact and fiction. *Frey* would never leave *her*. Their fire would burn on until death extinguished it.

She had been filming under hot, trying arclights in airless studios for six solid hours today. She felt worn out and depressed as she drew near the big house in which she and Trevor occupied the ground-floor and basement. She only seemed to find happiness when she was in the studios. Her flat was no home to her, but a place in which she had to play a part utterly repugnant to her. She sometimes felt she didn't even play it well.

The first month back in London had been a nightmare. She went on thinking about Frey night and day. She followed his progress by reading the shipping news. She was curiously relieved when she discovered that the *Outspan Star* had sailed again on its trip to Durban.

A few weeks ago she had telephoned the Shipping Company offices in London and asked if Captain Rowland was still in command. They had given her the answer 'yes'.

Now he would be approaching Cape Town again. With unutterable sadness Andra could imagine all that he must be doing. Walking up and down the bridge. Sitting at his desk writing. Going into that inner cabin – the cabin she remembered with a convulsion of the heart. Time could not heal the wound.

She reached home and let herself into the flat that Rose Penham had found for Trevor and herself. It was well-furnished. It belonged to a Brigadier Jessell and his wife who were stationed in Hong Kong. The Goodwins had signed a lease for a year.

The big sitting room, with its high ceiling,

was papered in dark velvety green. The curtains and covers were pale gold. There were a few pleasant pieces of antique furniture. The whole flat was centrally heated and there was a ground-floor bedroom which Trevor could use. Plenty of space and wide doorways in this converted Victorian mansion, made it easy for Trevor's spinal chair to be wheeled around and Rose, with her usual efficiency, had found a young man to take the place of the medical student who had looked after Trevor on the voyage home.

The first ten days had been spent by the Goodwins in making a positive tour of Harley Street.

So far not one of the specialists had given Trevor hope that he would ever recover the use of his legs, although various kinds of electrical treatment had been suggested and started. No expense was being spared. Andra was thankful that Flack had got her a fantastic sum for her rôle in *The Unlit Fire,* and she was able to pay for Trevor's treatment and buy him all the luxuries he needed.

Sometimes Andra looked back on the old days in her penthouse with regret. Everything then had seemed gay and glamorous. The place used to be filled with her friends. Her new home seemed to be a meeting place for physicians, masseurs and physiotherapists. There was a constant stream of people arriving or going, with short-wave machines, special lamps, and all the clinical paraphernalia connected with the fight against Trevor's paralysis.

He had tried when they first reached London to be less exacting. Except for occasional outbursts, he stopped nagging her quite so persistently. And because she was soft-hearted by nature, Andra was readily touched by any sincere affection or gratitude he offered. But his efforts seemed now to be wearing thin. This last week had been a bad one. He had never stopped complaining.

He missed the sunshine. He loathed the cold dark mists of London in November. He had to stay inside the heated flat because his lungs did not respond well to fog or 'smog'. He was bored.

Andra had a television set fixed up for him both at the foot of his bed and in the sitting room. But he grew tired of that. He missed his own friends from South Africa, he said. He and Flack Sankey had loathed each other on sight and whenever Flack came to see Andra there was an 'atmosphere'. Only when Andra reminded her husband that Flack helped her earn her bread-and-butter, and incidentally Trevor's as well, he had to capitulate and try to be hospitable. He had also got on the wrong side of Rose Penham by being surly and even rude to her. The only friend and admirer he seemed to have made since they arrived in London, was an acquaintance of Andra's, also in the film world; a woman who also had a part (a minor one) in *The Unlit Fire*.

Elissa Parry had already had two marriages both of which had ended in divorce. She was in her forties. Smart, sophisticated, much less intelligent than Andra, and with an ego that could only be rivalled by Trevor's. She was inordinately vain. Beautiful in a hard way; as dark as Andra was fair, with magnificent greenish eyes that she used to full advantage, and a large red sensual mouth. She never stopped talking. Trevor, himself, had little to say about her that was complimentary. She was man-hungry, he told Andra in his rather coarse fashion. But he needed just such a woman to amuse him. Elissa couldn't get anything from *him* beyond holding his hand and listening while he flattered her, drinking in the praise, with which he was always lavish. But she did much to flatter him in return by coming frequently to see him and sit by him. She had a fund of racy stories, and a fondness for drinking gin and stated bluntly that she was 'mad about poor darling Trevor'.

Trevor, of course, used Elissa to try and make Andra jealous, but found that he couldn't do so. But it gave him a perverse and even vicious pleasure to accept Elissa's attentions and invite her frequently to the flat, because he knew that Andra disliked her.

Elissa had first come here, uninvited, with another actor who was a friend of Andra's. She had at once thrown herself at Trevor. He knew that it irritated his wife to come home and find Elissa here drinking with him. He forced her to listen to their flippant, often stupid, conversations which seemed to Andra so pointless. Neither of them had anything instructive or serious to say. It was always malicious gossip about mutual friends, or new 'funny stories' which often offended Andra's taste. But Elissa encouraged Trevor to be coarse and to drink and smoke. Once when Andra rather coolly suggested to Elissa that her husband's medical advisers wished him to be less self-indulgent, Elissa merely opened her large green eyes and murmured:

'Darling, *I* don't encourage him. I only drink or smoke with him when he asks me to because the poor pet has nothing else in life. Don't you think, darling, that it's a mistake to deny him *everything?*'

For Trevor's sake – for Andra knew he did not want her to quarrel with the woman who amused him so vastly – Andra did not tell Elissa that she thought her impertinent. She merely said:

'I am only quoting his doctors.'

But the drinking and the smoking continued, like the shared jokes between the two of them, and after a time Andra stopped trying to be careful of Trevor's health. If Elissa was the sort of companion he craved for, and if he wanted to accept the policy of *'eat, drink and be merry, for tomorrow I die'*, who was she to object?

As time went on and the year dragged to its close, she wondered with great bitterness why she had ever thought she could really help and comfort Trevor after his accident. She was no companion to him. She was only the bread-winner. Her sense of loneliness was complete.

Now it would soon be Christmas. Andra never allowed herself to think of the festive season with pleasure. It could be no sort of Christmas for her, or for the wretched Trevor. All she could do was to buy presents and try to lighten his burden. She knew that he didn't feel well. All his South African tan had gone. He looked flabby and pale, and despite his wonderful features, was not quite as handsome as he used to be.

When she got back this afternoon, Rose opened the door to her – Rose came daily in a secretarial capacity and strove in her devoted way to save Andra (who she still thought of as 'her Miss Lee') from the petty worries and difficulties of life. The rest of the staff was 'staggered' – a morning 'char' to clean the flat, and an Italian woman in the evenings who cooked and served dinner.

Andra rarely went out except to a business meal or on some publicity stunt that Flack made her accept. Usually she stayed at home with the invalid.

'Any messages, Rose?' Andra began as she entered the hall.

'Yes, your mother is here, Miss Lee,' Rose announced.

She refused to use Andra's *other* name. Sometimes when she looked at Andra's thin young face, which bore such an unmistakable stamp of suffering, and she remembered that other radiant Andra who had gone out to South Africa, five months ago, she felt almost murderously inclined towards Trevor. Not even his accident and the tragedy of his paralysis softened Rose towards the man whom privately she looked upon as a self-centred brute.

'My father here, too?' asked Andra, handing Trigger over to the secretary.

Rose took the little dog.

'No, Miss Lee, I'm afraid your father isn't very well. It's about him Mrs Lee has come. She's in the sitting room with Mr Goodwin.'

'Oh, dear,' said Andra.

She never left Trevor alone with his mother-in-law if she could help it. Mrs Lee, in her religious and proper way was always kind and pleasant to the invalid, but Trevor with his customary lack of gratitude, found her a bore and often deliberately tried to shock her, by using the strong language and telling the racy sort of stories that were better appreciated by such woman as Elissa.

Andra had not seen much of her parents since her return home, but on a recent occasion when she had driven down to Godalming, Mrs Lee remarked that she found a great change in Trevor.

'Somehow when you were engaged he seemed so different – such a gentleman,' she had allowed herself to remark.

'Yes,' Andra said, and added with quiet cynicism, 'Men do change after marriage sometimes, and Trevor had that awful accident to sour him, remember?'

'Oh, yes, and I remember how you used to call him your *Roman Emperor,* and I admit he still has that wonderful head of dark curls and his fine eyes and he *can* be charming when he wants. But I don't feel he makes you happy. There isn't any understanding between you, is there?' Dorothy Lee had gone on.

Andra put a speedy end to the conversation, for she had no intention of dissecting her marriage with her mother, and also because she knew it would distress her father if he thought she regretted her marriage. She talked lightly of things.

'Naturally, Trevor's accident has made a difference to both of us. You can't expect us to be as romantic as we were, in the circumstances,' she had laughed, trying to be gay.

Mrs Lee remained silent but her father had given Andra a long enquiring look before which her own gaze had faltered. She imagined that poor darling Daddy, who had suffered so much in his life, guessed the truth. Andra did her best, after that day, not to let the old couple at Godalming see too much of Trevor.

Something must be wrong for Mummy to have come here today, she reflected anxiously. She walked into the sitting room. It was always suffocatingly hot with the central heating full on and a huge fire burning in the fireplace. Trevor liked as much heat as he could get. The air was thick with cigar-smoke. Mrs Lee sat as far away from the spinal chair and that cigar as she could get, trying to find some air near the bay window. She looked her usual thin, melancholy self in an old-fashioned musquash coat, and wearing one of those hideous mushroom shaped hats that she always seemed to favour. She got up and hurried towards her daughter.

'Oh, hullo, dear, such a nuisance – I came *just* after you'd gone to the park with your dog. *What* a long time you've been!'

Trevor, with a malevolent look, first at his

wife and then at his mother-in-law, said:

'Andra enjoys staying away from me, you see.'

'Nonsense, darling,' said Andra, unmoved. She was too used to this sort of jibe.

'Oh, Andra,' said her mother, 'I'm worried to death. Daddy's very ill.'

Andra changed colour.

'What's the matter, Mummy? He wasn't ill when I spoke to him on the phone the day before yesterday.'

Mrs Lee put her handkerchief to her lips.

'He was taken ill suddenly. Our Dr Mackie said he thought Daddy ought to have a second opinion. He came up yesterday to a specialist.'

'A specialist for what?' asked Andra sharply. 'Why wasn't I told?'

'Quite rightly you weren't told,' put in Trevor, throwing a resentful look at his mother-in-law's pale tired face.

He couldn't stand what he called 'dreary women' and he thought Andra's mother one of the dreariest. Couldn't imagine how she'd ever given birth to Andra. And he didn't like all the talk of illness. It scared him. He was scared of death. He had turned his mind against the thought of it ever since the plane crash. He and Elissa thought the same way ... why consider the inevitability of dying when one could still have a damn good time on earth? And a good time for

272

Trevor was no longer connected with Andra. He had begun to find her a bore because she was always so exhausted when she got back from the studio, and was in league with those ruddy doctors who tried to cut down his pleasures. He guessed she didn't really like him any more than he liked her these days. Well – as far as he could be – he was in love with Elissa. He wished he'd married a woman like that. She was immoral but she was damned amusing.

'I don't want to hear about your father – and take your mother into your bedroom, for God's sake, if you're going to discuss the horrid details,' he said rudely.

Mrs Lee gave her son-in-law a horrified glance and opened her mouth to reprove him but Andra took her arm and bundled her out. Trevor shouted after them:

'And don't be too long, Andra. I haven't seen you all day. I want someone to have a drink with.'

In these days Andra no longer slept in her husband's room. She had found it intolerable. There was a small room right at the back of the flat which used to be a nursery for the Brigadier's small children. Andra had cleaned out the nursery furniture, put in a divan bed and some of her own books and pictures and turned it into her retreat. A retreat into which she could escape when life with Trevor become intolerable.

Her mother burst into tears as she sat down on Andra's bed. Andra sat beside her with an arm about her, shocked and troubled. She never remembered before seeing her calm, self-possessed mother in tears. The news Andra was given of her father was far from satisfactory. He had had a prolonged attack of pain, Mrs Lee said, and Mackie came and thought it was something connected with his kidneys. He wanted to take X-rays and make a thorough examination. When the specialist had seen Daddy, he had refused to let him return to Godalming and put him straight into hospital in North-west London.

'You never told me you were up with Daddy yesterday!' exclaimed Andra.

'He asked that you shouldn't be worried, darling. He knew you were busy on your film and that you had quite enough to cope with in your own home.'

'All the same, I've always got time for Daddy – or you.'

'You've been a marvellous daughter to us.'

'I owe a lot to my parents,' said Andra, forgetting in this moment the fact that her childhood and adolescent years had not been so very gay.

'Thank the Lord,' she added, 'I'm not poor and I can help. Daddy must have a private room and every attention. If you'll give me the name of his specialist I'll ring up at once and see what he has to say.'

When Mrs Lee rose and said she ought to get home, Andra refused to let her go.

'There's a spare room downstairs and if you don't mind the basement, Rose will get it ready for you and you're to stay here with me tonight, Mummy.'

'I'd like to dear, but Trevor wouldn't want it.'

'Trevor will have to put up with it,' broke in Andra, a trifle grimly. 'He has plenty of attention and most of my time is spent with him. If my father is very ill, and my mother worried and miserable, I'm jolly well going to look after them.'

There flowed fresh tears from Dorothy Lee.

'What would I do without you. And oh, darling, I had an awful hour with Trevor. He seems to want to be horrid to me. I just can't get over the change in him. I'm sure you can't be happy.'

Andra got up and walked to the door to let Trigger in. She could hear the scratch ... scratch ... at the door. She looked down at the little dachshund. My golden-haired talisman, she thought. Her live, warm gift from Frey – perpetual reminder of his love.

As she picked the little dog up and stroked him, she said:

'Don't worry about Trevor and me, Mummy.'

'I'm afraid you made a mistake,' began her tactless mother, but was not allowed to say any more. Tight-lipped, Andra changed the conversation, went to the telephone and rang up the specialist who had examined her father.

When she put the receiver down, she looked slightly less apprehensive.

'That's good. I don't think you've any need to be quite so worried, Mummy. Mr Symonds – he sounds so charming – says that although Daddy's condition is bad because he should have gone to him years ago, he sees no reason why he should not be operated on with success. Even at his age. So let's look on the bright side and consider that Daddy will recover and be better afterwards than he's ever been.'

'Oh, how *wonderful!*' exclaimed Mrs Lee.

Andra added:

'Mr Symonds said he'd seen me in *Poor Little Rich Girl* and that he's an ardent fan of mine. Wasn't he sweet!'

'I don't think I need stay the night now–' began Mrs Lee.

'Oh yes, you will,' said Andra and called for her secretary.

'I refuse to speak to Trevor again,' put in Mrs Lee who had now recovered herself and was ready and willing to become difficult.

This was where Rose Penham made one

of her gestures towards her beloved Miss Lee and offered to take Mrs Lee back to her own flat for some supper. Then she could come straight back here, Rose said, and go on to the hospital first thing in the morning.

'You've got visitors tonight, haven't you, Miss Lee?' Rose reminded Andra.

Andra nodded. Her lips curled a little. Elissa was coming in for coffee to hear a new Harry Belafonte record that Trevor had bought. She had asked if she could bring her brother with her. Andra had no wish whatsoever to entertain Elissa's brother. She would rather have gone to bed and left Trevor and Elissa alone. But the brother, so Elissa had explained at the studio, was in the Merchant Navy and had just been to Cape Town with his ship and would be interested to talk about it to the Goodwins.

Once Mrs Lee was safely out of the house with the invaluable Rose, Andra walked reluctantly into the sitting room and prepared to face the usual sparring match which she found so exhausting, with Trevor.

Trigger followed her in his busy quick little way and sprang straight up on to Trevor's spinal chair. The invalid had been looking like a thunder-cloud but his brow relaxed a little as he smoothed the dog's long silky ears.

'Hail, friend. The only one I've got, it would seem.'

Andra twisted her lips but without being drawn into answering this jibe, pulled one of the curtains more fully across the window and re-arranged a red carnation that had fallen out of the vase on to the piano. She had hired that piano among many other things, to amuse Trevor but he rarely asked her to play it now.

She heard his resentful voice:

'Well, have you finished discussing the gory details of Papa's probable operation?'

'Yes, thank you,' she answered coldly, 'and although it may not interest you, I am glad to say that the report on my father is better than my mother feared. He is to be operated on tomorrow and the surgeon expects every success.'

'I'm not so lucky, am I?'

She turned to him. She never failed to feel a deep sympathy because of those poor useless legs.

'I'm sorry, my dear. But we have done everything we can.'

'Well, it's not enough. Elissa thinks I ought to go to Vienna. There's a marvellous Austrian specialist she knows of.'

It was on the tip of Andra's tongue to suggest that he should let Elissa take him to Vienna and pay for the journey (which Miss Parry certainly couldn't afford), then she considered this sarcasm unworthy and stayed silent.

'Oh, for heaven's sake, *talk!*' Trevor almost snarled the words.

She faced him, still speechless. He looked her up and down.

'You're thin as a lath and not looking particularly attractive,' he sneered. 'They may like it down on the film set but I don't.'

She did not move a muscle. Then at last she said quietly:

'You don't like me at all nowadays, do you, Trevor?'

The man pushed away the rug that lay across his legs, with an angry restless motion. His face suffused with colour. He flung the butt end of his cigar into the fireplace, aiming it at the grate viciously.

'You don't make yourself very likeable.'

'You mean I'm away all day filming so I can't fuss round you, and that when I am home I'm usually so tired I go to my own room. Also that I don't share your bedroom any more so that you can wake me up all night asking for things. Is that why you don't like me? Or is it because I keep us both? Men never seem to like the women who keep them.'

He ignored this bitter cynicism and laughed.

'You seem to know what makes you undesirable, my dear.'

'Of course,' continued Andra gently, 'I don't compare favourably with Elissa. But

279

you must remember Elissa is not your wife and only has to amuse you occasionally and that when you do spend a little of your own money, you spend it *on her.* She's quite blatant about it. She showed me her new earrings which I believe you gave her for her birthday. Will you remember mine?'

Trevor had the grace to look ashamed.

'If you remind me,' he muttered.

'And Elissa did, of course. How wise of her. But you see, Trevor, things have been bad between us ever since we got to London. Our marriage just isn't a success. You don't realise (and I'm never going to tell you) just what a ghastly bitter disappointment it has been to me. I married you because I believed that you needed me and that you would be utterly bereft if I walked out.'

'Saint Andra,' he sneered, 'don't come that heroic stuff over me. I don't believe it. You went out to Cape Town to marry me because you were just as much in love as I was. I was showing Elissa some of those cables you sent from the ship. She said she could hardly believe you wrote them. She knows how you feel about me now.'

Andra flinched. Her face was without colour and she was trembling. She was so often reduced to trembling by Trevor's black moods. She had begun to wonder whether the smash had not affected his brain. Her mother said he had changed out of all recognition. It was true. And he was getting worse. And his reminder of those cables made her feel the guilty one.

'Why don't I just pack up and walk out of his life and leave him to Elissa?' she asked herself at this moment. But she knew the answer. It was wrapped up in that guilt complex. Because she had fallen in love with somebody else and had been about to break with Trevor before his accident. Who was she to blame *him* if he now turned to a woman like Elissa? *She,* Andra, had changed too. He so often accused her of that. She wasn't the glamorous film-actress; the sweet tender girl of a year ago. She had become hard and cynical. Life had made her so. She had tried not to become this way, but the tragic sequence of events had been too much for her.

She crossed to the fire, leaned her arms on the mantelpiece, rested her head against them, and stared into the flames. The coldness of death seemed to settle in her heart.

'What's the use of us going on like this, Trevor. We are only making each other unhappy,' she said in a low voice.

He narrowed his eyes, staring at the young tired-looking back of this girl who had been so angelically kind and generous to him. What was left of his conscience started to work. He knew that he behaved vilely at times. He was not quite sure, himself, that his whole nature had not been changed by that damnable smash which had ended in paralysis. It was as though a paralysis of the best traits in his character had set in, too – leaving a demon within him. Always he had plenty of excuses for himself, and there was something about Andra which infuriated him these days – something remote, inaccessible, dignified, which did not appeal to him. He had begun to like women less moral more forthcoming (like Elissa). Now that the sex attraction which Andra had had for him was dead, he had little interest in the friendly side of her nature. So the demon in him prompted another ugly remark from him:

'Well, you may want to get away from me, Honeybunch, and slip out of your commitments to the poor paralytic, but I'm afraid you can't expect to divorce me, even for Elissa. I'm scarcely divorceable!' he added with a loud laugh.

Andra turned on him.

'Trevor, I don't know how you can say things like that or act the way you do. You've become an absolute *devil.*'

'And devils don't mix with saints, so there we are,' he laughed again. 'But I've had enough of arguing. Let's have a drink. I'll try to be more friendly if you will.'

'I didn't know I'd ever acted in an unfriendly way towards you.'

'No. You just stay away as long as you can.'

'That isn't true. If I give up my career I give up my income and that would mean disaster for us both.'

'Okay, get on with the drinks, and let's have an early meal – if old Tosca in the kitchen can get the spaghetti ready in time. You know Elissa's bringing her brother in for coffee.'

Andra clenched and unclenched her hands. This was so like Trevor; to be positively beastly, then when he had let off stream, expect her to ignore all he had said and be as nice to him as ever. As a rule she was long-suffering – mindful of his physical disability. But she had been driven too far today. She broke out:

'Incidentally, I *must* ask you, Trevor, not to be so abominable to my mother. She isn't a very smart or clever woman and she can't stand up to your sort of talk. The way you try to shock her is unpardonable.'

Trevor, lighting a fresh cigar, roared with laughter.

'You should have seen her face when I told her that story about–'

'Oh, be quiet!' interrupted Andra. 'Be quiet, you mean, *horrible* man.'

Trevor's jaw dropped. He stared at his wife. This was an Andra he had never before seen. Eyes flashing with anger; face crimson.

'I say, I say! You *are* sitting on your high horse.'

'Well, if you can't be polite to my mother … and I may say she's staying here tonight, although I'll try not to let *you* see her … if you can't be decent to her when you next meet … I swear I'll walk out on you. I won't stand it. You can do ugly things to me but I won't have elderly defenceless people made miserable just because you're such a hideous egotist. Grace says you always were one. I ought to have known it. I can't think how I could have been so blind as to imagine you were my *beau idéal*. But I did and I'm paying for it. And you don't know how much it's cost me!' she added in a low trembling voice.

Trevor passed a finger over his upper lip and frowned.

'Oh well, if you feel like that–'

'I do,' she broke in, 'and I warn you not to drive me too far or I'll leave you to dear Elissa.'

Trevor scowled a little harder. Attracted though he was by Elissa, he knew that she had no money. She wasn't a star in the film world like Andra. He'd be a fool to jeopardise his marriage. He controlled his desire to go on hurting Andra and held out a hand.

'Sorry, sweetie, come and kiss me. I know I'm not very nice these days–'

But he spoke to thin air. This time Andra had not waited to hear the usual apology.

284

She had rushed out of the room and slammed the door.

The dachshund sprang off the couch and went to the door, whining and scratching.

15

The evening was not without its drama.

Elissa arrived looking glamorous, as usual, although Andra always thought she used far too much eye make-up. Away from the studios, Andra disliked looking theatrical.

Andra had reached the terrible conclusion that she was glad Elissa attracted Trevor. At least she kept him amused and in good form. He was at his best when she was there, deliberately sparkling for Elissa or playing the heroic invalid. (Not forgetting to put on his 'neglected little boy' look.) Encouraging Elissa, blatantly, to hold his hand and flirt with him in front of his wife.

It was impossible for Andra to avoid being included in tonight's party although she would rather have spent the time with her poor mother. But once Andra met Elissa's brother, things changed. The atmosphere in the big Queens Gate sitting room was charged with electricity.

The brother appeared to have been christened Reuben Blatt (Andra presumed that Elissa once bore the unglamorous name of Miss Blatt). His name had been shortened to Roo, and Roo he was called.

He turned out to be the exact opposite of his thin sensual sister; as fair as she was dark. He was one of those big boisterous men with coarse blond hair, round eyes and a Van Dyck beard of the same golden colour as his hair. He was in the Merchant Navy.

The very fact that he was a naval officer endeared him from the start to Andra, although she found him rather too loud and too rip-roaring a type to suit her. But he had the geniality of a naval man and was obviously a much nicer person than his sister. He smoked a strong-smelling pipe which his sister told him to put out but Andra politely gave him permission to go on smoking. This endeared her to him. He found the fragile smoky-eyed film star a beguiling, beautiful girl. And he was truly sorry for her fate. It couldn't be much fun, being chained to Trevor Goodwin's side. Roo was sorry for the ill-fated man, of course. But he had heard far too much from his sister about her new 'boy-friend'. He had told her privately that he thought it 'off side' to make up to a newly-married man, even if he gave her, Elissa, the jewellery she coveted. Elissa had given one of her insolent laughs and said: 'But he's paralysed, darling. I can't be involved in a divorce, and I amuse him and his wife doesn't – so what?'

The sea-faring Roo thought this 'off side', also, but Elissa was the only member of the family left to whom he could turn when he was in England, so he was tolerant of her amoral attitude. Andra Lee, however, he found both 'correct' and enchanting.

The cargo boat in which Blatt served as No. 1 had just returned from a South African run. Roo used nautical language and had that way of screwing up his eyes common to sailors who spent much time in the sun looking out to sea. He reminded Andra poignantly of Frey. Frey was not hearty and coarse – on the contrary. But both men had that same clean salt tang of the sea about them and once, when she gave Trevor a tablet which he had to take every three hours and Trevor waved it aside, Roo bellowed at him:

'Come, come, must do as the Skipper says, mate.'

The Skipper!

On board the *Outspan Star,* Frey had sat one day with Andra in his day-cabin. It had been a cold day, when they were nearing England. An electric-fire glowed at them through incombustible logs. Frey, nervy and miserable, had reached out for a bottle of whisky from the wardrobe in which there was a drink cabinet. He had been drinking too much, and Andra said:

'That isn't the way to drown sorrow, my darling. I've tried it. I've had three gins already; a lot for me, and I don't feel one bit better. I don't want to be responsible for my beloved Captain waking up tomorrow with a thick head, either.'

'Okay, Skipper,' he had said, and blown her a kiss. Just one of their light sweet moments of friendly sparring. It all came back to her this evening, and she felt as though her heart would break when she heard Roo Blatt calling her by that name.

Skipper! Sitting by Roo, leaving Elissa to whisper to Trevor whose spinal chair was at right angles to the fire on the other side of the room, Andra felt an almost masochistic longing to speak of Frey.

'Do you people in the Merchant Navy ever come across the crew on the big passenger liners?'

'Not often, ma'am,' said Roo. 'Now and again, of course.'

'Do you know the Outspan Shipping Company?'

'Sure I do, ma'am.'

She drew hard on the cigarette which she was smoking and without looking at him, asked quietly:

'Ever run into any of the chaps on the *Outspan Star?*'

Roo Blatt pulled his beard and reflected, then shook his head and gulped down a mug of beer.

'Nope. Don't think so.'

'I came back to England on the *Star.* I

289

went out on the *Queen*,' she said.

Suddenly Roo set his mug down on the table and smote his fists together.

'Wait. The *Outspan Star*. That rings one of the old eight bells. Sure, I did meet a lot of the chaps at a "do" in Cape Town, just before we left a month ago. She was either going up to Durban or on the return run, I can't remember which, but there was a wedding in Cape Town. The father of the bride who runs the Outspan Company asked every goddam sailor ashore that day to help celebrate. They had a marquee on the lawn rigged up inside like a ship, and all the servants dressed like eighteenth-century brigands. One hell of a nautical affair it was – and everyone got as drunk as all good sailors should. Ha-ha-ha!'

'Roo, do pipe down,' put in Elissa crossly, looking at him with her big green eyes across the smoke-filled room.

'Ha-ha-ha,' repeated Roo, 'I'm telling our hostess about the wedding feast. You know, I've told you already, Liss.'

Trigger sprang off the spinal couch on which he had been sitting with his master, darted at Roo and yapped at him. This made Roo laugh still louder. He picked up the little golden dog and pressed him against his cheek. Trigger wriggled against the indignity.

Elissa resumed her whispered intimacies

with Trevor. Andra's heart was beating a little faster, as she continued to question Roo.

'Were ... were the officers of the *Outspan Star* at this wedding?'

'They sure were, because it was the Captain who was being spliced.'

There followed a frozen silence. Andra's heart now seemed to turn right over. Her hands went to her throat. She felt that she was choking. After a few seconds somehow she managed to speak again.

'You mean *Captain Rowland?*'

'The Captain was a mighty good-looking fellow.'

'Rowland...' Andra heard herself croaking the name although as she said it her whole body felt hot and her feelings were indescribable.

'Sure,' nodded Roo.

Andra's fingers shook so that she could no longer hold her cigarette. She crushed the end into an ash-tray. She was dead white. She thought she had suffered all there was to suffer of pain, but this shock was the worst she had had to endure yet. A jealousy, an envy so bitter and violent shook her that she felt almost mad with it. She was ashamed of the violence.

It couldn't be, *oh, it couldn't be!* Not so soon. It wasn't that she begrudged Frey taking a wife since he couldn't marry *her.*

She was no dog-in-the-manger. But it seemed that he had turned to another woman for consolation so much too swiftly. Her head buzzed with the recollections of all he had said about staying a bachelor for ever. *He could never put another woman in her place.* He had said that.

Andra got up, took Roo's empty mug and poured out some more beer for him, in order to hide her expression and gather time to recover her lost balance.

When she came back to Roo's side her face was still colourless but she spoke quietly.

'Tell me about the wedding,' she said in a flat dead voice.

He wasn't very good at descriptions, he said, scratching his head and laughing, but told her what he could remember. How splendid the Captain looked in his white ceremonials, and the bride – Lord! she was a peach.

'Who ... was she ... what did she look like?' Andra struggled with the questions.

'Blow me down, ma'am, I'm bad at female descriptions,' said Roo chuckling.

But bit by bit the details were dragged from him. It had been a lightning courtship, he recalled that much. The bride's name was Cressida ... by golly, he remembered that name because it was unusual and they all called her Cress.

'A delicious morsel and no doubt, the Captain could supply the mustard,' bellowed Roo.

Trevor and Elissa were listening now, and Trevor echoed the laugh. *Mustard and Cress, ha ha!* Jolly good.

Somehow Andra managed to wreathe her lips into a grimace that could be called a smile but her very heart felt like a stone that had dropped into an abyss of darkness, doubt and misery. She tried to concentrate on Roo's story. Miss Cressida Thomas was the only daughter of the wealthy South African director of the Outspan Shipping Company. The Thomases were 'stinking rich', he said. Nobody had seen such a wedding.

The couple had met at sea. Cress had gone on the run from Cape Town to Port Elizabeth to visit an aunt, but during that short voyage, she and the Captain had fairly fallen into each other's arms. She wasn't even waiting for an engagement. She was a spoiled heiress and her father liked the Captain and let her have her wedding. There it was! Tickety-boo! After a two-day honeymoon, Cress had flown to London and the Captain had sailed back to England. They were to meet in London. There was talk of the Captain quitting the sea and settling in South Africa with his wife. Roo didn't know much about the rest of it. He couldn't be sure of this or that, or the other. He couldn't supply all the information that Andra desperately asked for.

Man-like, however, he enlarged on Cressida's charms. A sailor's dream, he guffawed. *Petite* little thing, and a red-head. A red wavy mane which she wore long; freckles; a turned-up nose and the sauciest pair of blue eyes imaginable. She looked sixteen. But mark you, Roo laughed, all ready for the matrimonial stakes.

Andra shut her eyes, her hands clenching and unclenching in her lap, her nails tearing at a chiffon handkerchief. A red-head. Yes, Frey loved red hair. *She*, Andra, had those reddish lights in her hair which he had admired.

'Oh, God,' she cried to herself, 'this is too much. And I've been imagining him missing me, lonely for me. But he fell for a red-head with saucy eyes and a lot of money.'

Yes, it was a good match for Frey. He wouldn't have to worry about the future. He wouldn't be living in a little cottage by the sea ... on love and bread and cheese and kisses, as he had wanted to do with Andra.

Now suddenly Trevor turned his attention on his wife.

'What's the matter with *you?* You're wearing one of your shocked looks. My poor wife's always in a state of shock,' he said, glancing at Roo. 'Her mother's the same. They don't like rude rough men.'

'Well, I for my part like fastidious women,' said Roo, with a sympathetic glance at his hostess.

'What are you being fastidious about now, ducks?' Trevor demanded of his wife, mischievous as usual, anxious to bait her.

'Nothing. Would you like me to go and cut some sandwiches?' she said and rose to her feet with a gigantic effort at self-control.

'Sounds good,' he nodded. Then as she moved to the door, he called after her. 'Oh, *I* know. You've lost your boy-friend. You've made a *faux-pas*, Roo old man. The noble Captain on the *Outspan Star* was a boy-friend of my wife's and, of course, she's knocked out by the thought that he's got himself married.'

'Well, blow me down...' began Roo.

Here Andra interrupted, the rate of her pulse-beats almost painful, her cheeks burning.

'I ... I have no boy-friends. Trevor's being stupid.'

'Now, now,' said Trevor, 'women are so dishonest. They nag a man about his carrying-on, but don't own up to their own. The Captain was crazy about you, and you know it, Andy. What about that dance the last night on board? You think I didn't see? Oh, I don't mind,' he said and reached for Elissa's hand. 'We've all got to have our fun and games, but don't come this angel-stuff over me, Andra. You and the noble Captain had a reach-me-down and I'll stake my life on it.'

'And why not?' began the amiable Roo who sensed an atmosphere and was sorry for Andra.

But she waited to hear no more. She darted out of the room, shut the door and stumbled downstairs into the kitchen. Thank goodness Mummy had already come home and been helped to bed by Rose. Andra wanted to be alone. For a moment she stood with her back to the kitchen door, breathing spasmodically. Trevor was justified in that last cruel jibe. He might well remember how she and Frey had looked at each other during that waltz. They hadn't been able to help it. But she had given him up for Trevor's sake, and in less than three months' time – on the rebound no doubt – Frey had been caught by a pretty young heiress. He had married her.

'He might have told me. He might have written to me – warned me,' Andra muttered the words aloud. Suddenly the hot resentful tears began to drip down her cheeks. She couldn't check them.

Somebody turned the door handle and almost knocked her over. Elissa's brother had followed her downstairs. Speechlessly she stood staring at him. The big bearded man saw to his dismay that she was crying.

'Blow me down, did I really put my foot in it? Were you and the Captain really–' he began.

'No, no,' she broke in in a suffocated voice. '*No*. Go upstairs again, please.'

'But you're upset, ma'am.'

'Please leave me alone,' she broke in again and snatched a clean tea-towel and dabbed miserably at her face.

He looked down at her with kind eyes.

'Never could bear to see a female cry. I really am sorry, ma'am, if I said anything hurtful. Wouldn't have mentioned the wedding if I'd known.'

She could not find words but shook her head dumbly. He thought he'd never seen anything more pathetic than the beautiful young film star (who must surely be one of the great successes in this country), standing there with the tears raining down her cheeks, smudging her mascara, while she dabbed at her cheeks with the coloured tea-towel. He said:

'I *have* hurt you. Your husband was right. That chap from the *Outspan Star* meant something to you.'

She turned away.

'If he did, it's over, and please, please don't tell them upstairs that you found me like this.'

'What do you take me for? I wouldn't dream of it.'

She drew a long sigh. She turned to the long mirror that hung on the wall which was papered gaily like most of the rooms in this flat, and tried to straighten her hair. She felt broken-hearted, but she stopped crying. She wished she were dead. She wished she had died before she ever met Frey. If only she had had a weak heart, the shock of this man's news might have stopped her heart beating. She felt she had suffered and borne enough. The thought of Frey spending his honeymoon in this country – perhaps even in London tonight with his Cressida, killed her. *Mustard and Cress*. Oh, *God!* How that coarse joke stung!

'Look,' said Roo, 'can I get you a strong drink or a cigarette?'

'No thanks. I'll be all right.'

'I've kinda taken a fancy to you and I'm not all that stuck on my sister's behaviour. She's a devil with the chaps and I told her she had no right to start anything with a man like your husband.'

Andra gave a hollow laugh.

'Now that you know how I feel about ... about someone else ... surely you can't blame your sister, or my husband.'

'Maybe not,' said Roo doubtfully, 'but from what I can see, you're a hell of a good wife and it isn't every girl who would have married a chap like that after his crash. He'll never walk again, Elissa tells me.'

'No, never.'

'So a pretty little thing like you for the rest of your natural, is chained to his invalid chair.'

'Yes.'

'Well, I call that heroism.'

Andra shook her head. She kept her face turned away from Roo. He meant to be kind but she wished he'd go away. She was at breaking point. What did it matter now that she had made her supreme sacrifice for Trevor? And why all that heart-break over Frey ... why all that intolerable pain and loving and renouncing? He hadn't even kept faith with her for three months.

Suddenly she swung round and faced Roo, looking up at him with anguish.

'Tell me ... if you can remember ... did he seem very happy ... very much in love with his bride?'

'Why sure, he did, ma'am,' said Roo awkwardly, in that soft drawling Middle-west voice that he appeared to have cultivated on his travels.

Andra tried to harden up. Well, if that was so, why waste any more tears? Why be so unhappy? She must tear the thought of Frey out of her heart by the roots.

She gave a defiant laugh.

'Let's change the subject. *Finita*, as they say in Italy. Help me cut these sandwiches, Roo, and we'll go up and I'll get a bottle of champagne and we'll open it and drink to your next voyage. Will it be back to Cape Town? Maybe you'll run into the newly-married couple. If you do, give the noble Captain, as my husband calls him, my love and my good wishes.'

Roo shook his head at her sadly.

'You poor little thing!' he said.

It wasn't altogether the best thing he could have said. He might have done better to accept the idea of the champagne party, and remain cheerful and impersonal. For now, Andra broke down and the next moment was sobbing her heart out in the big bearded man's arms. He stroked her hair and kept muttering:

'There, there, you poor kid!'

When Elissa's voice was heard calling down the stairs that Trevor wanted to know what the heck was going on, and where his sandwiches were, Andra pulled herself together. She left Roo, who was quite a handy man, to cut the sandwiches and darted into her bathroom to sluice her face with cold water, make it up again, and brush her hair.

Afterwards she never quite knew how she got through the rest of that evening, but she was aware that Trevor watched her with some astonishment, and perhaps, a touch of irony because she insisted on opening the champagne and drank a little too much, smoked too much and laughed a little too loudly.

Elissa whispered to Trevor.

'I think your wife must have taken a fancy to my brother. She's quite lit up tonight.'

Trevor grunted.

'Not she. I know my Andra. It's because she's upset. It's my belief she's taken a knock because of that Captain fellow getting married. I'll have a few words with her when you've gone.'

But he didn't have a chance to do this, because at midnight, immediately after the guests had gone, Andra telephoned to the mews at the back of the house where Trevor's valet-attendant had a room. (He was handsomely paid by Andra to come in at any time the patient desired to go to bed.)

Trevor then started on the unfortunate Andra.

'Pray what got into *you* tonight? Grieving for the noble Captain, or cooking something up with the brother of my girl-friend?'

To his surprise, Andra turned on him like a tigress.

'Leave me alone. If you start picking on me tonight, Trevor, I ... I'll walk out and stay out, so I warn you.'

'Well, I like that–' he began.

'I mean it,' she interrupted, in no mood to put up with an hour of jibing from Trevor. But she had scarcely reached the door before a call from him made her turn back and this time, in alarm, to him. He was trying to struggle up from his pillows. His face had gone almost purple and his eyes protruded.

'Andra ... help me!...'

She rushed to him.

'Trevor, *what is it?*'

He did not answer. His hands clutched at his heart. He choked and moaned. Suddenly she realised that he was having some kind of seizure. It was what his doctors had warned him might happen. Too much drinking, too much smoking, and too much excitement, had brought on this attack. He was unable to take any kind of exercise these days. Since the shock of the accident and the injury to the base of the spine, his heart had weakened. Andra had struggled so hard to diet him and keep him quiet, but in vain.

Tonight's over-indulgence had been too much.

Trevor's head fell back on the pillow. Andra wondered for a moment if he were dead; he looked so ghastly.

She rushed out into the hall, screaming for her mother. Mrs Lee, wrapped in her coat, rushed up the stairs, with her grey pigtails flapping.

'My dear, what is it? Is it a burglar?'

'No, it's Trevor. He's had a heart attack. I think he's dead or dying. Go and stay by

302

him, Mummy. Get some brandy out of the drink cupboard. Give it to him. I'll phone the doctor.'

'Mercy on us!' exclaimed the startled Mrs Lee who had been wakened out of her sleep.

Andra disappeared into the bedroom and picked up the telephone-receiver.

16

Roo Blatt rang the bell of the Goodwins' flat in Queens Gate and waited outside the door rather self-consciously, carrying an enormous bunch of chrysanthemums. The stiff cellophane paper in which they were wrapped was wet with sleet. The overcoat of the robust looking naval officer was also wet. He had had to find a parking place for the car which he had hired for his leave, but even on the short walk here he had managed to get wet from the driving ice-cold rain on this bleak December evening.

Only two weeks to Christmas. Roo should have been back at sea a fortnight ago but his ship had developed propeller trouble and was still in dock; which didn't displease Roo because he had far more to keep him in England – particularly in London – than usual. Every day for the last three weeks he had brought flowers and left some kind of message for Andra Lee. Never before had a woman so occupied his thoughts. From the first night he had met her with his sister at the party on that night in November, her memory had haunted him. But he had not seen her. According to her secretary she would see nobody.

Trevor Goodwin was dead.

Roo had been thoroughly shocked when his sister rushed into his room the morning after the party, her usually hard face broken into lines of genuine grief, and with the tears pouring down her face.

'My God,' she had said, 'my God, Roo, *Trevor's gone!*'

Roo, roused from his sleep, had blinked at her stupidly.

'Gone where?'

'Passed out of this world. He had a heart attack soon after we left last night. Andra's secretary has just phoned me. Andra thought I ought to know.'

Roo felt quite sorry for his sister. She seemed really cut up. She sat on the edge of his bed sobbing and saying she would never get over it. She had been furious when Roo reminded her cynically that other men in her life had died or departed and that she had 'got over it'. Then, her tears drying, she turned the heat on Andra.

'*She* killed him. *She* was so rotten to him.'

'Don't be ridiculous, Elissa,' Roo had said coldly, withdrawing his sympathy.

'She didn't deserve that wonderful man. So courageous, so sweet, and all she thought about was her career.'

When Roo had reminded Elissa that the career had meant bread and butter for Trevor

Goodwin, Elissa ignored this and accused Andra of having had a love affair and so broken Trevor's heart.

'That, my dear, I most devoutly believe to be untrue,' was Roo's comment.

'Oh, she's got you, with her big eyes and all that glamour she can pour out when she wants to,' Elissa had sneered.

But Roo continued to defend Andra.

'I think she *is* a sweet girl and must have had a hell of a lot to put up with. *De mortuis nil nisi bonum,* and all that, but I don't fancy poor old Goodwin made life easy for Andra. Don't you forget, my dear Lissa, *you* were the girl-friend and the girl-friend always comes off better than the wife.'

After this cynicism, Elissa had departed, vowing that when Andra next turned up at the studios she would tell her exactly what she thought of her and waste no pity. Roo then fell to thinking hard about the young widow.

That Andra was intrinsically good, he was confident. All that stuff his self-centred, unscrupulous sister had poured out about Andra's cruelty to Trevor, cut no ice with Roo. He fancied he could tell a good woman when he met one.

That poor little Andra had cared for somebody else was true enough. He could not forget how she had sobbed in his arms that night, after he had dealt her *her* death blow, breaking the news to her of Rowland's wedding in Cape Town. Roo felt uneasy about that. He wished he had kept his big mouth shut. In a queer way, he felt responsible for hurting that poor little soul. He was a kindly, impulsive man. He had started his campaign of flowers and messages, begging Andra to see him when she could. So far there had come in return only neat little typed messages from Miss Penham, telling him that Miss Lee thanked him enormously for all his kindness but could not see him – or anyone – just for the moment.

Roo understood. Whether Andra was in love with Goodwin or not, she had been his wife. His sudden death must have shocked her. He knew pretty well what was going on, because the papers told him. It was front-page news that the husband of Miss Andra Lee, the film star, had died of a heart attack, following a party. There were numerous photographs of Andra, and sensational accounts of her marriage to Trevor after his plane-crash in South Africa. The writers of gossip columns gorged themselves on the romance and drama of it all, telling the world of the big sacrifices Andra Lee had made in marrying her injured fiancé. There were shadowy, scarcely recognisable pictures of her standing between her mother and Grace Goodwin at Trevor's funeral, which took place in Putney Vale. There were reports that she was carrying on with her work, saying 'the show must go on'.

Of course, Elissa sneered about the whole thing and vowed that *she* was the real widow and ought to get the sympathy. But she admitted that she had thought twice about being openly unpleasant to Miss Lee on the set. Elissa had her own career to think of and couldn't afford to quarrel too finally with Miss Lee. She told Roo spitefully that Andra looked *frightful* and that her producer wasn't very pleased about it.

The last time Roo had phoned the flat in Queens Gate, Miss Penham who appeared to respond sympathetically to his enquiries, informed him that Miss Lee's mother was now living with her in Queens Gate. Also that Mr Lee had come successfully through his operation, and that Miss Lee was arranging shortly for him to be flown with her mother to the South of France for a month's convalescence.

Roo was determined to visit Andra once more before he went back to sea. At last he had succeeded. Miss Penham had phoned him this morning to say that Andra would see him for drinks at six o'clock today.

When he saw her his heart seemed to turn over in a way it had never turned before. The big burly practical sailor who had always 'had a girl in every port' realised that he was quite a long way towards being in love with Andra. She had wrapped herself around his heart in an unaccountable fashion. He was glad to note that she was not in black. She wore a plain grey wool dress with a gold necklace. She looked thinner and paler than on that night of the party but gave him one of her wide sweet smiles.

'Do come in. I am delighted to see you. You've been so very, very kind. Not more flowers!...' She laughed as she took the chrysanthemums he held out. 'You really have been turning my room into a garden, Mr Blatt.'

'I thought that it was "Roo",' he said gruffly as he took off his damp coat, and ran his hand over his rough hair and beard.

She led him to the fireplace. The room was warm and he found it delightful after the ice-cold and wind outside. Even the little dachshund gave him a welcome, and as he stroked Trigger's silky-gold head, Roo hid a certain amount of embarrassment that he was feeling.

'Afraid you've been having a grim session,' he murmured.

'Very grim,' said Andra.

'Can I smoke my pipe?'

'Smoke away.'

While he lit it, Andra walked to the door, called for Rose and asked her to put the chrysanthemums in water. She avoided looking at that other door opposite the sitting room; the door of the room in which Trevor had spent so much of his time. After his death it had been shut up and was not used until her father and mother came to stay. Then she turned it into a double spare room. But the sight of it depressed her, and even to remember the spinal chair in which Trevor's attendant used to wheel him around was melancholy.

As Roo had imagined, Trevor's death had been a considerable shock to Andra. She had expected him to decline but not so soon, or, somehow, so rapidly.

After meeting Frey Rowland, she had realised that she could never love Trevor but only look after him and give him tenderness and friendship. Once they had got back home and Elissa had come into it, the gulf between Andra and Trevor had widened beyond repair. She would have been a hypocrite if she had pretended to be a grief-stricken widow. Her sorrow was for him, not for herself. Once she had loved him and she thought it tragic that he should have been involved in that terrible smash, then virtually drunk himself into the grave.

She had never been very close to her mother but Mrs Lee had done her best since the death of her son-in-law, and it certainly helped Andra to know that her cherished father had been so successfully operated on and was now convalescent. Grateful that she had the money to spend, she had sent them off to the South of France only yesterday, and felt the better after it. What she needed now was to be quite alone for a bit.

Rose Penham had, of course, been a tower of strength, helping to deal with the mountain of correspondence. Letters had reached Andra from near and far. Roo Blatt's flowers had, in fact, been lost in a welter of bouquets which were sent from friends she knew or fans who wanted to show their sympathy.

Flack had proved his friendship by cutting short the sympathy and impressing it upon Andra that it was her job that mattered now, and that whatever happened, she must bring all the inspiration and vigour that she could to her rôle in *The Unlit Fire*.

She had, in a way, been able to lose herself and forget Trevor's unhappy life and death when she was working at the studios. She saw and spoke to Elissa daily but knew that the smiles they exchanged were forced. They did not waste much time in each other's company – apart from the filming.

As far as money went, Andra was all right. She had all that she needed, including the life insurance that Trevor had taken out long before his accident. But Andra wanted nothing, really, from him. All she needed was forgetfulness. Memories were too painful now. After Christmas she intended to put this flat up for re-letting. She longed to get away now, and Flack considered it would be better publicity for her to go back to the type of glamorous modern flat she had occupied before she left England.

If *The Unlit Fire* was as big a success as they all expected, she would not need to worry; so Flack assured her.

Roo was asking her now:

'Got any plans? Or are you just staying on here?'

She shook her head and told him what she had in mind, while she poured out a cocktail for him and one for herself.

He thought how graceful and exceedingly lovely she was in her clinging grey dress with the firelight turning that burnished head to a coppery red. What a little 'so-and-so' Elissa was to malign her! What hussies jealous envious females could be. Roo was all the more sure as he looked at Andra now that she was a darned nice girl and had done her best for Trevor.

He felt that under no circumstances should he mention the name of the captain who had got married in Cape Town although he wanted to talk about the chap. And as if Andra sensed this, she suddenly lifted her head and said:

'Have you any idea whether ... whether the ... whether Captain Rowland is in London at the moment?'

'I don't really know,' said Roo. 'Don't even know if he's in England.'

'Yes,' she said quietly. 'The *Outspan Star* docked at Southampton yesterday. I only wondered if you had happened to run across him. Still – I don't see why you should, unless you go to the sort of club he goes to, and anyhow if he's married now, I expect he and his wife will be staying in a hotel so you wouldn't be likely to see him.'

She rambled on. Roo felt that she was nervous and on edge. He broke out:

'I'm damned sorry, Andra. I feel so guilty. The way I came out with that news must have shaken you to pieces and I'm sure it's all been on your mind lately. It seems tough, now you're free.'

She winced. It was typical of this man to be blunt, yet she knew that he was kind of heart and admired her. She liked Roo, notwithstanding the fact that he was Elissa's brother.

She liked him if only because he had seen Frey so recently. Yet, *oh God, if only he hadn't seen Frey at his wedding!*

'Tough' was the word Roo had just used. It was more than that, thought Andra bitterly. Since Trevor died she had faced the fact that she was once more alone in the world and free. She had felt it a monstrous cruelty on the part of the fate that Frey should have gone out of her life so quickly. If only he had waited! That was what hurt ... that he had replaced her with such speed. What would *he* think when he heard her news? Possibly he had seen no English papers since Trevor died or missed the reports in the Cape Town papers. If he had known, she imagined that he would have written to her.

'Maybe one day I'll run into him,' began Roo, but she cut in:

'I did not mean to talk about Frey. Forget it. Tell me about your next trip.'

'Look here, would you come out and have a spot of food with me?' asked Roo suddenly.

She gave a little half smile and shook her head.

'Forgive me if I say "no".'

He looked disappointed.

'Don't want to be seen out in public yet, is that it?'

'No, that's not it. I don't think people feel like that nowadays. Life has to go on and Trevor would be the last person to like the idea of a mourning widow. It's just that I don't particularly want to go out. After filming I get so terribly tired these days. My doctor says that at the moment I have no energy at all.'

'I wish you'd come out with me even to a quiet little spot in Kensington, somewhere,' he persisted.

'I can't tonight, Roo, even if I wanted to. I've got my producer dropping in for a conference.'

'I may be back on board ship tomorrow – I'm expecting a call any time,' Roo grumbled.

'Surely you won't mind leaving this grim weather and sailing to the sun,' she smiled.

'Somehow I mind leaving *you*–' he began.

'You're very kind,' she broke in colouring, afraid, suddenly, that he was going to become sentimental.

Roo forged ahead.

'I've thought a lot about you. You just don't know.'

'Just be my friend, Roo, and let's leave it at that?' she said on a warning note.

The big bearded man took the rebuff on the chin. He swallowed his feelings.

'Well, I still feel that I brought you bad news and I wish I could do something for you, Beautiful.'

Her lips quivered.

'You're a *dear*. I shan't forget your kindness. As for hurting me – I – had to know sometime, hadn't I?'

'I just wish it hadn't been through me, and my God, I don't understand that fellow. I'd have waited for you a lifetime.'

Now she turned from him because tears stung her eyelids and the hand that held her glass trembled. Her face looked wan and wretched in the firelight. She could not bear to look into Roo's bright blue eyes – remembering those other eyes that had been so very blue; so very much the eyes of a sailor. She felt an anguish more acute than any she had suffered since she and Frey said goodbye. Suddenly she put down her glass and said:

'Please forgive me. I just don't want to talk about Frey – or myself. You must stop it.'

'Oh, hell,' said Roo miserably. 'I've put my foot in it. I'm a clumsy brute.'

Before she could answer, the front door bell rang. Andra darted to the sitting room door and called to Rose.

'I'm not in to anybody. Not *anybody*. Mr Blatt is just going and I don't want to see anyone else.'

Roo set down his glass and rose.

'Reckon I'd better move on and leave you in peace,' he said gloomily.

'Just wait a moment and let this visitor get away,' muttered Andra.

She had not really recovered from the ill-effects of the last two weeks. Her nerves were in a shocking state, she reflected. She had been mad to bring up Frey's name. What could the thought of him do now but make her more tragically unhappy?

She had got to learn to live without Frey or the hope of ever belonging to him. She must learn to exist, without the mysterious bond that had once existed between them … even when they separated. He belonged now to that girl he had married in Cape Town. And Trevor was dead. *She*, Andra, had got to carry on without either of them.

Rose Penham peered round the door.

'A very persistent caller – a gentleman, Miss Lee, but I told him you didn't want to see anybody, but he said he *knew* you'd want to see him, so he is coming back.'

'Did he leave a name?' asked Andra wearily.

'He scribbled something on a sheet of your notepaper and told me to hand it to you. Another of your Fans! My, *my!*' said Rose cheerfully and gave her adored employer an envelope.

Andra opened it and glanced at the note.

Roo had just begun to mutter once again that he had better go, when he saw her flush crimson, and then sway where she stood. He rushed to her side and supported her by the arm.

'I say – you all right?'

Andra choked.

'It just can't be. *It can't.*'

'What can't?' asked Roo.

'You told me…'

'I told you what?'

'That … that Frey Rowland had got married.'

Roo scratched his head and pulled at his

beard which he always did when he felt nervous.

'That's right. Captain on the *Outspan Star.*'

Now Andra had recovered herself, although her cheeks were burning red again and her eyes enormous.

'This note,' she said in a strange voice, 'is from Frey. *It was Frey Rowland* who rang the bell. Listen – he says in this note:

I have only just heard about Trevor. Deeply distressed you are ill. I will come back in an hour's time when you may be alone and hope you will see me. I love you as much as I did – if not more. Still yours and yours alone.

Frey.

Andra, in her agitation, actually read this intimate message aloud.

'You see! He can't be married. He *can't* write such words, unless he's mad. Or are *you* mad? Have you made some frightful mistake?'

'Now really – this is awful – how can I have made a mistake?' began Roo.

Andra darted to the door and called Rose back.

'I know I told you I wouldn't see anybody, but I wanted to see *that* man above all others. When did he say he'd come back? *Will* he come back?'

Rose, the inevitable pad and pen suspended in mid-air, glanced at her employer over her glasses in an astonished way.

'Why, Miss Lee, dear, he said he'd be back in an hour's time. I told him one of my whoppers, I'm afraid. I said the doctor was with you.'

Andra's heart thudded. Sweat had broken out on her forehead. She drew the back of her hand across it.

'Wait a minute,' she said over her shoulder to the stupefied Roo, and fled into her bedroom. She unlocked a small drawer and drew from it a box of photographs through which she searched feverishly. She pulled out one of a man in white uniform standing on the bridge of a ship. Frey, with his cap in one hand, smiling at her in the old devastating fashion through half-closed eyes. She tore back into the sitting room and held this snapshot up in front of Roo who was sucking at an empty pipe, looking glum.

'Is this the man who was married to that girl in Cape Town? *Is it?*'

Roo took the photograph to a lamp, put it under the light, regarded it for a moment in silence, then, feeling extraordinarily unhappy, answered:

'No. Definitely not. The Captain *I* saw married was tall like this one, but much plumper and with a square face. Who is this?'

'This,' said Andra hysterically, 'is Frey Rowland, Captain of the *Outspan Star.*'

'Now see here,' said Roo, gulping, 'look, we've got to sort this one out or go balmy.'

'You're dead right, we've got to sort it out!' said Andra breathing fast. 'I think you've made a ghastly mistake, Roo. I ought to have asked you more questions at the time, and shown you this snapshot and so on. But it never entered my head there might have been a mistake. But there *must* have been. Frey came here alone and says in this note that he is *mine* only. He can't be married!'

Unhappily, Roo stared at the snapshot again.

'Don't understand. But I may not be wrong. You've got me all worked up and muddled.'

'And you've got me in such a state that I can't breathe,' exclaimed Andra, and sat down suddenly because her legs were trembling. She felt weak. She kept reading and re-reading the note that Frey had scribbled. He had only just heard about Trevor and he still loved her. He *couldn't* be the man this idiot, Roo Blatt, had seen married to a Cape Town heiress. The whole thing seemed preposterous and inexplicable, yet there must be an explanation. She realised now that when Roo first told her the story she had accepted what he said as *verbatim* and not attempted to confirm it. It had never entered her head for instance, to telephone the Shipping Company and say *'Is it true Captain Rowland is married?'* Why should anyone do such a thing? Besides, Trevor had died immediately after she had learned about Frey's marriage. She had felt too upset and confused and tied up with legal affairs – the aftermath of the sudden decease – plus her film work, to probe into Frey's personal affairs. She had just thought … well – he is married and he hadn't got in touch with me so that seems conclusive.

Now she motioned Roo to a chair.

'I want a lot more details from you and you're going to answer a lot of questions,' she said breathlessly.

He stared at her, inwardly nettled and afraid that he had made a howling blunder. Nevertheless the beauty of those big eyes, stormy and passionate, caught him by the throat. Andra was like a little frozen statue that had thawed and come to glorious life. She must, he thought, be a hell of a lot in love with this fellow.

Her questions poured out. He tried to answer them coolly.

How had he first been invited to this wedding? As he had originally told her – everybody in Cape Town who wore a naval uniform had been asked to it by the parents of the bride. Did he get a written invitation?

No – he didn't. None of the chaps off his boat got one. They were just told by their own Captain that all the officers had been invited, not to the Church, but to the reception.

Who had told him that it was Captain Frey Rowland of the *Outspan Star?* Well, he didn't actually remember the name *Frey,* but that it was Captain Rowland, he was sure. But now Andra, to whom this thing meant so much, stopped accepting casual answers. She wanted *proof,* and she was fast coming to the conclusion that Roo Blatt was a nice big *stupid* man. Her whole being was singing wildly with a hope that had not been with her for weeks, yet she had to make *sure* this time.

'Were you sober, Roo Blatt?' she asked severely. 'At that reception, were you sober?'

He did not take offence. He suddenly bellowed with laughter.

'Dashed if I was, ma'am. I'm never sober at weddings. It wouldn't be right and proper if a seafaring chap like me attended a marriage in his right mind.'

'You idiot!' exclaimed Andra, agitatedly tearing at the handkerchief that she held. 'How unsober were you, then?'

'Nicely bottled with the rest of the chaps, I suppose.'

'So bottled that you didn't really know who the bridegroom *was.*'

The big sailor pulled at his beard and dug into his memory and found that his reminiscences of that wedding in Cape Town were very hazy indeed. He knew what sort of dress the bride had worn. Somehow he knew that because his gaze had feasted on Cressida's *petite* loveliness as she stood there on a kind of dais, receiving the guests. And he remembered that the bridegroom had a square jaw and was plumpish but not like the tall chap in *this* picture Andra had just shown him.

Andra seized his wrist and shook it.

'Didn't you hear the bridegroom's Christian name mentioned?'

'No. Roland, they called him. *Roland.*'

'Spelt how?'

'R.O.L.A.N.D, I suppose.'

'You suppose! You don't even know. Oh, my God, you've been weaving a story out of a haze of drink and you can't really testify to anything. And you broke my heart. You just broke it, like that...' she snapped her fingers.

Roo looked into the blazing lovely eyes and felt ashamed of himself and yet amused. To think that the soft sad little thing could turn into such a stick of dynamite. Made her all the more fascinating, of course. No wonder she had a reputation as a 'star', and a string of men after her, he thought.

'Look,' he said, 'I have admitted that I was

bottled at that party, but to the very best of my knowledge, I believed that the Captain's name was Roland, however it's spelt.'

'But that might have been his *Christian* name. It mightn't have been the Commander of the *Outspan Star* at all,' she said, trembling. 'Supposing it was the *Staff* Captain? Supposing you got the whole thing mixed up, you – you – clot!'

'Oh, I say,' Roo protested, and pulled mournfully at his beard.

'Well, *do* something!' exclaimed Andra.

'Anything, anything. If I've made a mistake and hurt you unnecessarily, I'll shoot myself.'

'That'll be a fat lot of use,' gasped Andra.

'Well, what shall I do?'

'Go to the telephone in the hall and find the number of the Outspan Shipping Office. There's always somebody there on night duty, and they'll have records. Ask them the name of the Captain on board the *Outspan Star* who recently got married in Cape Town. If it was in fact, my Frey, the actual Commander of the ship, then come back and tell me and I'll tear this note into pieces and ask Frey how he dare write such words – a newly-married man!'

Roo took his pipe out of his mouth and went docile as a lamb, to that telephone. Andra didn't dare go with him. She sat in a chair with her face buried in her hands,

324

trying not to think, not to count on anything, although she knew that her whole world was centred on what Roo had to say to her when he came back.

When he did return – it seemed after a considerable delay – he came on tip-toe as though he was afraid to disturb her. He looked more sheepish than ever. He glanced at her out of the corners of his eyes. White-faced, she looked back at him.

'Well – what did they say?'

'I'll never touch a drop of drink again, I swear I won't,' he mumbled. 'I really have been a muddle-headed blundering lunatic.'

She sprang up.

'What did they say?' she repeated.

She had to drag it out of him because he was in such a state. The number had been engaged and he had had to wait and he felt all kinds of a fool but he was really pleased, he said, to tell her that it was not Captain Frey Rowland, the Commander, who had been married at all. It was just one of those shocking mistakes due to a coincidence of names. *Rolland* it was. *Captain Rolland* – he'd thought it was pronounced Rowland, but the Shipping Company had called it 'oll' like 'moll'. Like *Molland* would be.

'Oh, stop saying all those silly names,' Andra broke in and now her eyes were dancing like stars and her cheeks were carmine and she kept moving around the room as though she was skating on ice.

'It's like this,' said poor Roo. 'I just heard the name Captain Rowland. I never met the actual *Commander* or knew *he* was called Rowland. I was too bottled, I admit it, but it looks as if it was the Staff Captain, Dick Rolland, who married that girl Cress, and not your ... your boy-friend.'

Silence. Andra was standing still now, looking into the fire as though she saw all her dreams about to burst into flames in that grate and send out a million sparks of rapturous happiness.

'Can you ever forgive me?' went on Roo. 'I mean I never will forgive myself but I am glad if it's going to mean something good for you now. I swear I am.'

She thought:

He isn't married. He didn't break faith with me. It's all been a nightmare but now I'm awake. Oh, Trevor, Trevor, surely if you're anywhere around you'll be glad for me, because I did try to do my best for you.

'Won't you speak to me?' she heard Roo ask plaintively.

To his astonishment she sprang across the room and put her arms around his neck, and hugged him, her cheek against his bearded face. She said:

'Oh, Roo, Roo, you *did* break my heart, but tonight you've mended it again. Don't think badly of me for being so happy. Tell

326

me I am justified if I take my own happiness now.'

Never in his life had Roo Blatt known a greater relief than when he hugged that beautiful fragrant figure back and felt himself forgiven.

'You take what you can get, Baby,' he said huskily. 'You're as sweet as sugar, and as I told Elissa, you're good, and I can't tell you how glad I am that chap is coming back to you tonight.'

17

Only once before in her life could Andra remember such a feeling of wild excitement as permeated her body and brain while she waited for Frey.

That was when she had been a little girl; perhaps about six years old. She had awakened on Christmas Eve to see the shadowy figure of Santa Claus creeping to the foot of her bed. She had pretended to herself that it wasn't Daddy, that it was really Santa Claus. Keeping her eyes half open, not daring to stir in case the magic vanished, she watched him stuff her stocking full, and lay some boxes on the foot of her bed. After the bearded figure vanished again, she had reached down and touched all the parcels – her little heart throbbing like the heart of a bird when it is caught between two hands. She was still afraid that it wasn't true. Ecstatic because she found it *was*. And the knowledge that she must wait till daylight because Mummy had made her promise to do so, was both dreadful and sweet.

Oh, blessed, wonderful Christmas Eve, and all the mad thrill that only a child can feel! That blissful anticipation, punctuated by the delicious terror that when she woke nothing would be there, and that it was all a dream.

The exciting memory of that night had stayed with Andra through her adolescence and her adult years. She had thought several times that nothing so wonderful would ever happen to her again. But it *had* happened ... now, seventeen year later, on this wet cold gusty night two weeks before another Christmas. A Christmas that might have been so desperately sad; in fact Andra hadn't wanted to think about December 25th before Roo Blatt confirmed that message brought by Frey. But now she felt the same childish ecstasy as she walked up and down her sitting room, one eye on the clock, both ears straining for the sound of a knock, or the front door bell; for the beloved footsteps.

The mad delight of the child – grown to womanhood – was hers again.

Would he come? Or would he decide not to after all? Would she wake and find the whole revelation had been a figment of imagination? Was it true that Frey still lived only for her? Was it, indeed, true that she, herself, was free, and that in the course of time she could break all links with Trevor. Take off his ring and replace it with the one that Frey had wanted to give her.

Rose Penham had gone. The flat was empty except for Andra.

She had taken off the grey wool dress because she had felt it to be dreary. She had put on one that she hadn't worn very often, but in which, dear old Flack Sankey said 'she looked like a dream'. It was in the new mink colour – velvet – with long tight sleeves and a short wide skirt; a wide belt clasping her waist, making it look very small. The dress was a little off the shoulder and edged with mink. Andra wore no jewellery, only her black pearl earrings. She had made up her face with care – not too much – and for the first time for months she had needed to add no colour. Her cheeks burned. The reddish mane of hair was brushed back and pulled round into a single shining curve at one side of her neck.

She glowed. She was the star of stars. She was one hundred per cent Woman. Soft, seductive, vibrating, waiting for her lover. She wore a light flower-fresh perfume. She was incarnate youth and every man's desire.

When the hour had passed – Frey had said he would return in an hour, and he had not come – she began to *will* him to come.

'You must, Frey, you must. Oh, my dear, my dear, *you must come*, or it'll kill me.'

Frantically she closed down on the hovering memories of poor Trevor, yet she prayed to him.

'Forgive me for not loving you always. You know now, don't you, all about Frey, and how I fought myself and stayed away from him and married you. Wherever you are, please do smile on me and wish me luck, poor, poor Trevor!'

Up and down this room, up and down, into her bedroom to look in the mirror and pat a lock of hair or dab a little more perfume behind her ears; back to the sitting room to put more coal on the fire. Switching on the radiogram, switching it off. No music. Just silence, like the silence of that other Christmas Eve, when she, a happy child, had huddled under the bedclothes. Heart beating fast, full of the same frantic glorious hopes.

'Oh, come soon, Frey. Don't change your mind,' she kept crying the words aloud, agonised.

She thought of *The Unlit Fire* and her part in it. How at the studios, yesterday, Robert Carey, her producer, had stopped her in the middle of one of the love scenes when she was supposed to be on fire at last – the little girl who had never before been awakened. And how she had suddenly burst into tears and run off the set. When he had followed her into her dressing room, deeply concerned, she had gone on weeping and said: 'I'll never play it properly, Bob – there's no fire left in me. It's all burnt out...' She had refused to let them shoot that scene again, but Robert had tried to comfort her. 'You'll get it some time without knowing it, Baby. Don't lose your grip. You're doing fine.'

But all the way home in her car she had gone on crying desolately, remembering Frey and her lost love which had left her so empty and anguished.

'Now,' she thought, standing in the middle of the room with her arms uplifted. 'Now, I could play my part and Bob Carey would throw his hat up in the air.'

She walked to the window and drew aside the curtains. Sleet still beat against the window panes and blurred the lamplight. She watched one or two people struggling with their umbrellas against the wind. Her heart gave a great convulsive beat as she saw a taxi come down her side of the road, but it passed on. Sick with disappointment she turned back and let the curtains fall.

'Oh, God,' she whispered, 'if he doesn't come … if he's changed his mind, I won't be able to bear it.'

The radiance and the joy seeped out of her slowly as though remorseless fingers squeezed her. Her fingers felt ice-cold. She couldn't even bear to light a cigarette. She stood for a moment in front of the fire, rigid, eyes shut, trying not to think at all.

The sound of yet another taxi. She clenched her hands. Then the slam of a car door just outside the house. This time Andra unwound and rushed to the window and looked out again.

She saw him.

Her heart beat in a mad uncontrolled way. She peered out and looked at that tall familiar figure. Frey, in civilian clothes, wearing a Jaeger coloured coat with the collar turned up, hat under his arm. How dear and well-known to her, that short-cropped dark hair with its grey threads. He was paying the taxi driver. She couldn't really see his face. She pulled the curtains again and ran into the hall and opened the main door. After that she fled back into her room, leaving both doors wide open, letting the cold and the rain beat in from the raw winter's night.

She heard his step, then a knock at her door, then his voice:

'Anybody in?'

She called out, breathlessly, hands pressed to her hot cheeks.

'Yes, me. Come in!'

He came into the room. Holding hat and gloves in one hand he looked at Andra for a moment as though the sight of her dazzled him. Which indeed it did. For Frey, it was like gazing upon a glorious vision which he had never expected to have the privilege of seeing again.

Afterwards, Andra remembered that little

Trigger had not barked when Frey walked in. It was as though in the dog's subconscious mind, he knew that this was the friend who had given him to Andra, but as Frey stood there, Trigger walked up to him, sniffed at his ankles and then wagged his tail.

The silence and the waiting became an agony, yet neither Andra nor Frey could move or speak. Then the man suddenly tore off his rain-wet overcoat and flung it on the floor. He walked straight up to that beautiful figure in the mink velvet dress, and pulled her into his arms. He took one ravished look at the beauty of her face and her shining eyes. He had no need to ask Andra if she still loved him. The love was there for him to see. Neither did it seem the moment for casual greetings or conversation. And Andra knew that all the explanations could follow, knew also that it didn't matter what lay in the future, or how soon she would throw up her career for Frey, or whether he would leave the sea or not. For her this was the beginning of the world. There had never been another world or another life. She gave a deep gasping sigh. She closed her eyes, and he held her in silence, closely, closely, as though he could never let her go again.

The publishers hope that this book has given you enjoyable reading. Large Print Books are especially designed to be as easy to see and hold as possible. If you wish a complete list of our books please ask at your local library or write directly to:

Magna Large Print Books
Magna House, Long Preston,
Skipton, North Yorkshire.
BD23 4ND

This Large Print Book, for people
who cannot read normal print,
is published under the auspices of

THE ULVERSCROFT FOUNDATION